stay
with
me

Books by Jody Hedlund

Waters of Time Series
Come Back to Me
Never Leave Me
Stay With Me

Knights of Brethren Series
Enamored
Entwined
Ensnared
Enriched
Enflamed
Entrusted

The Fairest Maidens Series
Beholden
Beguiled
Besotted

The Lost Princesses Series
Always: Prequel Novella
Evermore
Foremost
Hereafter

Noble Knights Series
The Vow: Prequel Novella
An Uncertain Choice
A Daring Sacrifice
For Love & Honor
A Loyal Heart
A Worthy Rebel

The Colorado Cowboys
A Cowboy for Keeps
The Heart of a Cowboy

To Tame a Cowboy
Falling for the Cowgirl
The Last Chance Cowboy

The Bride Ships Series
A Reluctant Bride
The Runaway Bride
A Bride of Convenience
Almost a Bride

The Orphan Train Series
An Awakened Heart: A Novella
With You Always
Together Forever
Searching for You

The Beacons of Hope Series
Out of the Storm: A Novella
Love Unexpected
Hearts Made Whole
Undaunted Hope
Forever Safe
Never Forget

The Hearts of Faith Collection
The Preacher's Bride
The Doctor's Lady
Rebellious Heart

The Michigan Brides Collection
Unending Devotion
A Noble Groom
Captured by Love

Historical
Luther and Katharina
Newton & Polly

WATERS OF TIME #3

stay with me

JODY HEDLUND

 NORTHERN LIGHTS PRESS

~ 1 ~

May 28

SOMEONE OR SOMETHING WAS WATCHING HER.

Sybil Huxham traced her fingers over a crack in the damp wall of the underground passageway, the chill in the stone just like the chill pulsing through her blood.

Normally it took loads to creep her out. Very few things could throw her off and genuinely stagger her.

But over the past three days, every time she came to Reider Castle to investigate, she hadn't been able to shake the peculiar sense that she wasn't alone. Especially now, in the dark bowels of the ancient dungeon. A strange presence seemed to hover nearby, one she couldn't define.

She slowed her steps, the echo of her combat boots tapering until she paused altogether. Steeling her shoulders, she cast another glance behind her, hoping to glimpse whatever was trailing her.

The passageway was empty. No one was there. No one had been anywhere she'd searched. Not today and not during her other meticulous investigations of the various rooms of the abandoned castle.

Regardless, she held her mobile up higher, letting the

torchlight illuminate the splotches of mildew growing in the cracks, as though to gag the walls from telling their secrets. If the stones could speak, what would they say?

"Go on," she whispered. "Spit it out."

She waited, her muscles tensing. A raspy rustling seemed to swirl in the dank air. Almost as if someone really was trying to talk to her.

A shudder worked its way up her spine, and she drew her black leather jacket closer around her body. She'd experienced moments over the past few years where she'd felt as if she were being watched, even followed. But this was different.

Was the fortress haunted? Like many other castles around Kent, this one had been built in the Middle Ages, making it seven or eight hundred years old. Maybe spirits of residents from long ago wandered the hallways.

She'd never been the superstitious type, but with all that had happened lately, she wasn't sure what to believe anymore.

"If you need something, then just tell me." She spoke a little louder, as if that could convince the ghost—if that's what it was—to answer.

Good thing the lab door ahead was closed, and Isaac couldn't witness her loss of sanity.

After their breakup two years ago, she'd switched jobs to ABI, the Association of British Investigators, a private investigative company, needing some distance from him at Kent Police. They still worked together occasionally, like now. Thankfully, being around him had gotten easier with the passing of time, especially after he finally got over her and started dating someone else.

Regardless, she didn't want him to hear her attempting to converse with ghosts. She wasn't sure she wanted to hear it herself.

"Get a grip, Sybil." She swung around and continued toward the lab, her long ponytail swishing out her frustration. She had to stop getting caught up in the particulars of the case she was working—the oddest and most perplexing of any she'd ever investigated. Instead, she had to focus on catching the criminal—Dr. Lionel—who'd gotten away when they'd raided his lab.

As she reached the heavy oak door, a garbled whisper passed by her, louder and more distinct than the last.

Prickles formed on her neck.

The sound didn't mean anything. She was simply tired from lack of sleep from pouring all her energy into the search for Ellen Creighton—now Lady Burlington—who'd been kidnapped and held prisoner in Lionel's lab. Now that Ellen was safe, Sybil needed to take a couple of days off to sleep. And hit the gym.

Yes, she'd have a rest and CrossFit workout, then she'd be getting on just fine. She'd sacrificed too many of her early morning classes lately. She had to be more consistent if she hoped to be ready for the Run, Swim, Run competition next month.

Regardless, she fumbled against the handle, unable to get the door open fast enough. As she pushed into the room, the modernized fluorescent lights and whitewashed bricks formed a stark contrast to the drabness of the remainder of the castle.

Isaac sat at the wall desk in front of one of Lionel's

computers that had been left behind, in the same hunched position as the last time she'd been down. He had a pen tucked behind an ear and held in place by his blond hair and glasses. Even with his receding hairline, he was a handsome man—stocky and muscular—the bodybuilding type she'd always been attracted to.

"Any luck?" She stopped behind his chair.

"Getting closer." He was staring intently at the monitor at a long list of commands his fingers were rapidly punching on the keyboard.

As one of the best computer forensic investigators in the department, Isaac had already spent hours hacking the system. Now that he was in, he was attempting to recover any of Dr. Lionel's data he could. She was hoping he'd unearth clues about other hidden laboratories, addresses, anything that could give her a lead to his whereabouts.

If only her team had been able to infiltrate the lab without alerting Dr. Lionel and the others of their presence. But despite their best efforts, the security cameras around the premises had picked up their movement, giving Dr. Lionel and his staff sufficient time to escape and flick a button to protect their data. Ever since, she'd done nothing but go over every detail she'd missed.

Stop beating yourself up for failing to apprehend the criminal. The past was in the past, and she had to move on and do her best now to hunt him down. And hunt him she would, even if she had to leave the country to do so. Her tracking skills had earned her a reputation as one of the best private investigators in the Canterbury area. That was why Harrison Burlington had hired her last year. And why he'd hired her again when Dr. Lionel had kidnapped Ellen.

A yawn pushed up and escaped before she could smother it. The digital clock on the wall read 1108 hours. Only an hour until kickboxing during her lunch hour. She'd missed too many of her kickboxing classes lately too. But not today. Hopefully, the rigorous training would wake her up.

"Coffee's fresh." Isaac cocked his head toward a simple coffee maker on the counter, the carafe filled halfway.

She crossed to it and poured the thick sludge into a ceramic mug that said: *Don't talk to me until this cup is empty.* Isaac had always made brew strong enough to wake the dead. She lifted the cup and blew on it while inhaling the aroma. In the mirrorlike glass partition in front of her, her reflection stared back. Straight brown hair smoothed into a perfect ponytail, a heart-shaped face with high cheekbones, wide green eyes framed by naturally long lashes, and her mouth set into a serious line.

Her form-fitting white shirt under her jacket and her black jeans revealed the muscles she'd worked hard to gain. She might be petite in size, but she could deadlift 120 kilograms and squat 80.

She'd honed her body just as she had her reputation. If only she could motivate Dawson to do even a fraction of her workout. But her brother refused to budge from the flat he shared with one of his war buddies.

Stifling a sigh, she took a sip of coffee. As she swallowed, a glint in the reflective glass caught her eye. Shelves of medical supplies lined the opposite wall—with syringes, needles, beakers, flasks, and tubes filled with chemicals she couldn't begin to name. All of it stuff Dr. Lionel had left behind when he'd fled.

She'd been through it all already. Another investigator had cataloged each piece. But the refraction wasn't coming from the shelves. It was coming from a niche in the wall someone had bricked in to transform the old dungeon into a useable room.

She spun and located the spot again—a place where the caulking between bricks had fallen away. Without taking her gaze from her discovery, she set down her coffee and crossed the room. She probed her fingers into the hole and extracted a slender glass tube.

As she turned it over and examined it, she saw nothing out of the ordinary. From what she could tell, it was another test tube like the others already on the shelf. Same shape. Same size. And empty.

She started to place it into a holder but halted.

Something had to be different about this test tube. Otherwise, why would someone tuck it into the wall?

She twisted it around, studying it more carefully. Unlike the others, the plastic stopper was shoved down tighter. What other reason would anyone have for pushing it in unless they were trying to contain a substance and prevent leakage?

Did that mean something was still inside?

She held it up toward the light. Was there a droplet? Or was the spot just another glint of light?

Her heart landed a sidekick against her ribs. Was this the remains of holy water? The coveted medicine that could cure any disease?

Such water had been bottled and sold in medieval times, particularly to pilgrims who visited shrines, like those at Canterbury Cathedral. Some believed the water was mixed with the blood of saints, which brought about healings. Others attributed the water's healing to God's supernatural intervention. Most recently she'd learned of a theory that traced the water back to the Garden of Eden.

Of course, the majority of people considered the stories of healings to be nothing but fables. But not her. If she'd ever doubted the age-old tales about holy water causing miracles, she no longer did. She'd witnessed firsthand the healing properties. And she'd also witnessed the strife, greed, and violence associated with pursuing it.

The powerful drug was exactly what Dr. Lionel had been attempting to get his hands on in order to learn how to replicate and sell it. No doubt if he could figure out how to create it, he'd become one of the wealthiest and most powerful people in the world. And no doubt he intended to keep searching for it, doing whatever he had to—including committing more crimes—until he located it. Which was why she needed to find him . . . before he hurt someone else.

She plucked at the stopper.

If it had remnants of holy water inside, maybe one of Lionel's workers was hoping to save it for someone who was sick. Perhaps adding to it until they had enough.

Dr. Lionel wouldn't have any motivation to hide a stray tube. But maybe his assistant, Jasper, had done so in an effort to collect enough to save his dad suffering from a debilitating disease. Jasper was already in prison. He hadn't made it too far from the castle before a pair of constables had caught up to him in the woods nearby. She could visit him soon and ask him about the test tube.

Or she could test it herself.

With a final tug, the stopper came loose. She peered inside. The amount was less than a teardrop. It wouldn't go far. But would it be enough to heal someone? Someone like Dawson?

Her heart gave another kick, this time a powerful roundhouse. Could it heal his partial blindness?

Ever since the accident in Afghanistan, he hadn't been the same. It was almost as if when he lost his sight, he'd also lost his will to live. Getting back his vision would be the miracle he needed. Maybe it would motivate him to do something with his life.

She cast a glance toward Isaac, still focused on the monitor and his complex programming.

No one would have to know she found it. She could sneak it out to Dawson.

But as she studied the miniscule droplet at the bottom again, her mind spun with the implications. And the truth. The droplet wasn't sufficient to work healing. If so, Jasper—or whoever had hidden it—would have taken it.

She'd learned enough about the holy water to know that approximately a tablespoon was required to initiate a miracle. She also knew there wasn't a tablespoon of holy water to be found anywhere in the castle. She'd searched every millimeter of the estate for herself and had only discovered one bottle in an ancient cabinet in the great hall. She'd given it to Harrison right away, hadn't contemplated keeping it.

But this?

No one would have to know she'd found this, would they? No one would care since it was such an insignificant amount. It might not even be holy water.

Even as her conscience played a tug-of-war, already her integrity was winning. She had to do the decent thing and put the test tube into the collection of important items in the investigation. She had no right to it.

She twisted the stopper and a slight dampness brushed against her thumb. Had some of the contents been on the stopper? Was it now on her skin?

It wouldn't hurt to test it.

The trouble was, if it really was holy water, there was no telling what might happen to her. Every time she'd watched someone drink it, they'd fallen unconscious or into a coma. She wasn't sure what such a slight amount would do—probably nothing—but she needed to be careful, just in case it made her woozy.

Harrison had proposed that holy water could not only heal diseases, but that somehow it also allowed people to cross the space-time barrier after putting them into a coma.

It had most certainly put Harrison into a coma, and he claimed he'd traveled to the year 1382 during his unconscious spell. He'd never lied to her before and had no motivation to fabricate a story about going to the past. At the same time, she wasn't ruling out the possibility he'd had nothing more than a realistic dream while he'd lain comatose.

She bent and sniffed her thumb. It was odorless. Would it also be tasteless? She wouldn't be a good investigator if she didn't find out, would she?

She crossed to the hospital bed where Dr. Lionel had kept Ellen as his prisoner. She perched on the end. Then before she could talk herself out of it, she lifted her thumb and licked the damp layer.

A wisp of wind and warmth whispered around her, sending goosebumps over her arms. In the next instant the blowing turned into a roar that swept through her body. The electricity went out, and all turned dark.

Except for a faint glow behind her.

In the space of a few seconds, her senses went on overload. Mustiness, soil, maybe even the stench of urine assaulted her nostrils. Cold, damp air crept around her. And a strange silence set her on edge.

A door with iron bars stood several paces away. She blinked, trying to adjust her eyes to the darkness, but with each blink the door only came more into focus and took more shape. Where had it come from?

No, it wasn't real. She was hallucinating.

She closed her eyes.

Before she could open them, a man's hand snaked around her mouth and clamped down hard.

- 2 -

"WHO ARE YOU? And from whence do you come?" The harsh question rumbled near Sybil's ear.

In a maneuver she'd practiced more times than she could count, she grabbed the man's arm and jerked him forward. In the same motion she squatted so that he landed on her hip. From there she rolled and flipped him over her back high enough that he flopped on the ground in front of her with a thud and an *oomph*.

Before he could react or catch his breath, she bent and squeezed his windpipe and at the same time pressed her knife to his jugular.

His face contorted with obvious pain. His eyes pinched closed. And his mouth clamped shut, as though to hold in a moan.

Even with the tautness of his features, she could see that he was in his mid to late twenties, close to her twenty-seven years. His jaw and chin had a layer of scruff that matched his dark hair. Most of it was tied at the back of his neck, but some strands hung loose. His features were sharp, strong, and almost regal. But it was obvious he was injured.

And not because of her defensive move. It wasn't intended

to harm, just disable an attacker. Her pressure against his neck was meant to do the same.

She loosened her grip but waited warily. It was possible he was acting weak so she'd lower her guard. But she was too smart for that. She'd seen the tactic used all too often during her years working as a police constable.

The real question was, how had this man entered the lab without her being aware of his approach? Had he disabled the power lines? And why wasn't Isaac coming to her aid?

"Did Simon send you?" he asked through clenched teeth.

"Did Dr. Lionel send you?" She didn't move her knife. But as she finally glanced at the source of the light, her hand faltered.

A candle rested on a bare patch of floor.

An earthen floor. Dirty straw scattered about. A few plain blankets. A wooden bowl, empty except for a scattering of bones picked clean. And a large pot in the corner.

Sweet holy mother. This wasn't the lab.

Her chest tightened, and she released her prisoner, stumbling backward until she bumped into the door. Had the taste of the holy water done this to her? Was she really seeing into the past, or was she hallucinating?

As she grasped the iron bars, their solidness told her this was all too real and not a dream. Was she in a time overlap the way Harrison had described? He'd mentioned that a person traveled back to the era they last thought about and to the location where they were in the present.

Had she gone to 1382? And if so, was she in the dungeon? After all, that's what had existed in the lower levels of Reider

Castle long ago.

Harrison had insisted he'd experienced a few time overlaps into the past after ingesting only a miniscule amount of holy water. He claimed the crossings were brief, lasting only a minute or two.

Was that what was happening?

The man pushed himself up from the ground, his movements slow and stilted. He wore loose-fitting wool leggings with boots laced up over stockings. But his chest was bare. And as he stood, the candlelight fell across his back, revealing numerous bloody welts.

He'd been savagely beaten. By a belt. Maybe a whip. Or whatever instrument was used in the Middle Ages for punishment. No one deserved to be hurt so badly, not even a criminal.

With a grimace, he straightened and faced her, the shadows falling across his features. As he pulled himself to his full height, he squared broad shoulders that only seemed to highlight his rounded pecs and bulging biceps. At least a head taller, he exuded a powerful presence, as if he was an important person.

If he was trying to intimidate her, it wasn't working. She wasn't afraid of him. He was injured and unarmed. Even if he hadn't been at a disadvantage, she could fend for herself. With her police training as well as her blackbelt in kickboxing, she'd learned to fight better than most.

His gaze stumbled over her tight shirt and jeans, and his sights jumped back to her face. "Who are you?"

"Sybil Huxham."

"Did my brother send you to seduce me?" He seemed to be using great care not to let his attention drop below her chin. She supposed her modern clothing would appear odd to someone accustomed to women wearing dresses.

This wasn't the time or place to worry about modesty, not when he was in trouble and not when she needed to find out more information about him before the holy water wore off. "Who are you and why are you in the dungeon?"

He crossed his arms, which served to emphasize each taut and well-defined muscle in his chest and arms. "If you do not know the answer to those questions, then you are clearly not from here."

His stilted, formal way of speaking revealed more than anything else that he was likely of the aristocracy, maybe even a nobleman of Reider Castle itself. Had his brother done this to him? The man he'd called Simon?

Ultimately one thing truly mattered. "What crime earned you the beating and lockup?"

"I serve my king and country, but my brother is not so honorable." The clipped words were loaded with gravity, almost desperation. "He has twisted his own crimes and blamed me for his treachery, condemning me to die as a French spy."

Although a dozen questions immediately surfaced, she squelched them. She was losing time, could almost feel the lab and Isaac's presence behind her, pulling her back. Besides, she'd learned to read people well over the years, and the earnestness in this man's bearing and expression told her he was telling the truth. That was all she needed to know.

She rattled the door. "I'll help free you." She didn't know how yet. But she'd work out something.

In the passageway outside the cell, the wall had gaping holes in some places and was crumbled in others with large piles of rubble. The low ceiling, too, was a patchwork of beams that appeared to have been hastily secured in place.

Was this due to the earthquake aftershock in 1382, the one that supposedly Ellen had experienced in the dungeon? The conditions certainly attested to a recent catastrophe.

Bright lights flashed on the wall, numbers that read 11:11. Was that the digital clock in the lab?

Sybil rubbed a hand over her eyes, and when she removed it, fluorescent lights blinded her.

The dungeon was gone along with its musty scent. Instead, the waft of strong coffee hung in the air, mingling with the faint aroma of antiseptics. Warmth and brightness dispersed the coldness and darkness. And there wasn't a trace of the man anywhere. Just Isaac in his rolling desk chair in front of the computer, and she was still on the hospital bed.

She hadn't been gone long. Maybe a minute. Two at most.

Gone? That wasn't the right word for what had happened to her, since her body had remained in the present. But how else could she describe the strange experience?

Her vision blurred again, this time with an overwhelming exhaustion. She lowered herself against the partially raised bed, closed her eyes, and let sleep claim her.

• ● •

Sybil shivered. As her lashes fluttered up, she glimpsed dark walls and an earthen floor. Confusion sifted through her.

At the sight of a man lying on his side, his head resting on his arm, her mind cleared. She was seeing the dungeon and its prisoner again.

His eyes were shut. But the light of the candle revealed his face more clearly than the last time. Handsome features, a well-proportioned chin and forehead with dark brows puckered together. The thick layer of stubble around his mouth accentuated his lips.

He was still shirtless, had likely had the garment torn from his back during his whipping. Or perhaps clothing aggravated his open wounds. Whatever the case, his body was undeniably beautiful, more so than most bodybuilders and athletes she trained with.

As though sensing her presence, his eyes flew open. She hadn't noticed the color last time she'd seen him, but the rich brown was deep and intense.

"You're awake at last," came Isaac's voice.

She shifted and the vision of the man disappeared. In its place was the shelving unit filled with supplies. Isaac stood at the end of the hospital bed. Behind him, the digital wall clock read 5:33. It was after 1700 hours. That meant she'd been asleep for six hours. When was the last time she'd slept for that long, even at night?

Such tiredness had happened to Harrison each time he'd ingested the holy water residue. He'd claimed that the vibration and expenditure of energy and heat during the time crossing depleted the body, causing an exhaustion. The same fatigue had come during the awakening from the coma.

It was also possible she'd slept longer because she was already languishing from the stress of the past two weeks of work.

She sat up to find that someone—probably Isaac—had covered her with a blanket.

"Was just about to order takeaway. But now, maybe we can go to the pub and grab a bite?" His arms were stiff and straight, his hands stuffed into his pockets. He glanced at the floor, avoiding making eye contact. But the hopeful note in his tone was too telling. He wanted to spend more time with her.

"What about Liana?" The moment the question was out, she wished she could retract it. Even if Isaac hadn't still been dating Liana, she didn't want to go out with him. They weren't right for each other, and there was no sense pretending otherwise.

"Liana's working." As he darted a look at her, his eyes radiated with attraction, desire.

She thought they'd put their past behind them and both moved on. Was it possible that working in such proximity was stirring up his old feelings for her? She couldn't let that happen. Had to just stay friends.

"Can't." She pushed up and swung her feet over the bed. She'd missed her kickboxing class again, but she could try to make it to an evening CrossFit workout. She also had to drop groceries off at Dawson's. "I've got a busy evening."

Isaac shrugged. "Right. Okay."

She stood but then wavered, dizziness sending her off-balance. For a second, the man in prison came into focus again.

He'd pushed himself up to his elbows, and his dark gaze seemed to beckon her toward him. But in the next instant, he was gone, and Isaac was at her side grasping her arm and steadying her.

"Maybe you should head on back to your flat, Sybs, and look after yourself."

"I'll be fine." She hated his nickname for her. It held too much familiarity, as if he was still a part of her life. And it was the nickname her mum had always called her—before she'd gone missing. Letting anyone else use it seemed sacrilegious.

Sybil stepped away from him, then stumbled toward the door. "You won't mind shutting down and locking up when you leave?"

She was already out the door and nearly had it closed before Isaac responded. "Sure thing. See you tomorrow." The forced cheer said that he'd taken a gamble at resurrecting their relationship, and it hadn't turned out the way he'd hoped.

As the heavy door closed behind her, she held up the torchlight on her mobile again, ignoring the prickles forming on her skin, the same as earlier when she'd been in the passageway. Was it possible the voices she'd heard had been people from the past, maybe even the man in the dungeon speaking to someone?

Harrison had called the phenomenon entanglement—when the past, present, and future coexisted and were intertwined. Of course, his explanation had been more complicated than that, something about how different quantum particles shared an existence even though physically separated, that the wave systems didn't collapse but split into alternate versions that were equally real.

At the time Harrison had shared his theories, she'd listened as carefully as always, stowing away the details and information he presented, yet she hadn't known what to make of it all.

But now? After the instances of seeing the dungeon and the same man, she had to conclude his theories had merit, didn't she?

With each step she took toward the stairwell, she waited for the whispering voices. She half hoped she'd see the man in the dungeon again. But the echo of her footsteps was the only sound in the corridor. Too soon she reached the steep stone stairway.

She paused at the bottom and glanced quickly back over her shoulder. If she thought she'd catch a glimpse of the past, only dark stone walls filled her vision.

In some other far away time, a man was suffering and would die for crimes he didn't commit. Or had the holy water caused her to have such vivid hallucinations that she couldn't distinguish what was real and what was a figment of her imagination?

She started up the stairs, her steps sluggish. Most likely she'd had nothing more than a realistic vision. For her sanity's sake, she'd be better off putting all thoughts of the prisoner in the dungeon far from her mind and never thinking on him again.

~ 3 ~

AT THE JANGLE OF KEYS in the dungeon lock, Nicholas Worth snuffed out the candle wick between two wet fingers and shoved it behind him along with the other items his mother had sneaked to him underneath her cloak when she'd visited him earlier.

She'd taken a risk in giving him anything, especially the food and the salve for his wounds. But he was grateful she'd dared it.

As the door of the dungeon creaked open, his pulse spurted faster, and he fervently prayed that the angel who'd visited him was materializing and coming to save him. She'd told him she'd help free him. While he hadn't exactly been a man of prayer in recent years, he didn't doubt that God Almighty had sent the angel and message to encourage him to remain strong.

When she'd first appeared in his cell, he'd been surprised— believed Simon had his guards deliver her while Nicholas had been sleeping, that perhaps he'd been overcome by his pain so much that he hadn't noticed their coming and going.

The angel had been exquisite, her womanly form on exhibition, nothing concealed by the strange-looking undergarments. At first, he'd assumed Simon had instructed her to seduce him into revealing more information regarding the English strongholds against the French, especially since he hadn't been able to flog the classified details out of him.

But it had only taken the woman flipping him to the floor for Nicholas to realize she was no ordinary maiden. She not only had unusual strength and fighting capabilities, but her beauty was unearthly, her body perfect, her skin smooth, and her hair the color of new dark leather.

She hadn't given him much of an opportunity to explain all that had happened between Simon and him, yet she'd rapidly seen to the heart of the matter and believed him. She'd confirmed her angelic status when she'd disappeared before his very eyes, not once but twice.

The last time had been only seconds, but it let him know he hadn't only imagined the first visit. Maybe she'd known he would need a second revelation. He was, after all, too oft a skeptic.

The dungeon door banged against the stone wall, causing a cascade of dust and small stones in the walls that had yet to be repaired. Simon strode through, two guards on his heels, their bootsteps clanking, their torches casting ominous light.

Had his brother come to usher him outside to the whipping post for another public punishment? Simon relished such displays of his power, liked causing people to cower in fear, thrived on making them grovel before him.

Nicholas sat up straighter, having no intention of showing weakness any more now than he had during the whipping. The slight movement sent tremors along the gashes, but he held back the twitches of pain.

Simon approached the door but stood out of reach. His brother was smart, well aware of Nicholas's reputation as a fierce warrior and his ability to fight proficiently under almost any circumstance. Indeed, the moment Simon or one of his guards drew close enough, Nicholas could snake a hand through the bars and disable him before he had the chance to react.

"What say you for yourself, Brother?" Simon's brows angled sharply above his eyes. Though they shared the same dark hair and eyes they'd inherited from their father, Simon was two decades older than Nicholas's twenty-nine years, and they had scant else in common.

"I have no more to say this time than the last, my lord."

"I know you have information." Simon was a big man, although more from his overindulgence in drink than from his strength. His long black tunic strained at the waist against his leather belt, and his leggings were too tight, emphasizing each of his fleshly rolls.

He stared through the darkness of the dungeon at Nicholas, contempt in every aged line of his face, and his mouth pinched behind his forked beard.

"I have already told you the king sent me to spread the word of the plague throughout Kent and the Weald. That is my mission. Naught more."

It was much, much more. But Nicholas remained steadfast in the tale he'd told everyone from the start, especially because he suspected Simon was the spy they'd been looking for, the person funneling vital information to the French regarding their fortifications along England's southern coast. That's why

Nicholas had come back to Reider Castle a fortnight ago, to discover more.

During his initial searching, he'd only come across a couple of receipts of deliveries from Paris. It wasn't enough to convict Simon. That's why he'd used the excuse several days ago to sneak back into Reider Castle with Ellen when she'd been intent on freeing her father from Simon's clutches. Nicholas had managed to liberate Ellen's father, but she'd become trapped down in the dungeon after an earthquake.

With Ellen's status unknown behind the rubble, Nicholas had offered to go in again and attempt another rescue. He'd used the opportunity to memorize a set of numbers—likely a code—within a French missive he'd located on Simon's writing table before heading down to the dungeon.

In the middle of his digging to find Ellen, Simon had shown up with a dozen guards, arrested Nicholas, and had him severely whipped. Along with accusing Nicholas of being a spy, Simon had also accused him of setting witches free and spreading the plague.

Of course, Simon needed to deflect any suspicions away from himself, wanted Nicholas to take the blame for spying even as Simon gleaned information he could pass along to the French. For what? What were the French giving Simon in return for betraying England? Gold? Land? The promise of power?

Nicholas was tempted to ask his brother why he'd done it. But at this point, Simon still didn't realize Nicholas had discovered he was a spy. Once Simon knew his espionage wasn't clandestine anymore, he'd have one of his guards slice

Nicholas's throat to silence him sooner rather than later.

Now he had an angel on his side. He just had to make sure he survived until the angel returned to help him.

"If you are not colluding with the French," Simon said after a moment, "then tell me what you are really doing as you ride throughout the countryside and forest. Perhaps then you can convince me of your innocence."

"The plague is truly a threat, Simon. The people need to know about it so they can take precautions."

Simon's lip curled up into a smirk. "What a convenient way to gather the information you need from other spies."

"You know me better than that." Nicholas spoke calmly, unwilling to let Simon goad him to anger. "There is no one more loyal to the king than I."

"Perhaps the beautiful witch turned your loyalty away from the king. Perhaps she was also a spy, sent to England by our enemy."

Simon was referring to Ellen. Although at one point Nicholas had considered the possibility she was a spy, he'd then gotten to know her sufficiently and realized that while her stories were fanciful and far-fetched at times, she wasn't working for the French.

As with every other time he'd thought about her death, the guilt slipped around his neck like a noose and choked him. If only he'd gone in for her father alone and hadn't given in to her pressure to accompany him. If only he'd taken more care to make sure she hastened out at the first signs of the earthquake. If only he'd stayed and dug through the rubble right away. Maybe he would have been able to save her.

As it was, Simon claimed that when his men cleared out the dungeon after the earthquake, they'd found her lifeless body amongst the rubble. He'd had enough decency to allow her kin to come claim her and give her a proper burial.

Nicholas shifted, his back still on fire. "Lady Ellen was not a spy, my lord, and you and I both know it."

Simon nodded at the guards. One of them stepped forward hesitantly, holding chains and shackles.

"Since you persist in your treason, you leave me no choice but to force you to confess."

Nicholas wasn't surprised Simon intended to whip him publicly again today.

His brother would do it again on the morrow, and the next day, until Nicholas finally died or revealed information to benefit the French.

Nicholas pushed up from the ground and approached the bars. As soon as the first guard opened the door, Nicholas would attack and overcome him.

"Do not think about resisting me, Brother." Simon peered down the passageway and out the dungeon doorway.

Nicholas followed Simon's gaze. On the opposite side of the door stood Mother flanked by guards. Her eyes brimmed with fear and an apology.

Saint's blood. He should have known Simon would figure out another way to torment him.

As the other guard approached, a ring of keys in his hand, Nicholas fisted his hands at his sides and squelched the rapidly rising anger. He was helpless to do anything to save himself, not without putting Mother at risk.

If only he'd found a way to provide a home for her so she no longer had to live at Reider Castle. He'd hoped eventually to gain the king's favor for loyal service and be rewarded with a parcel of land in the Weald, the forestland to the south of Reider Castle. But so far, Nicholas had earned nothing other than his usual pay.

Simon was watching him again, obviously waiting for him to react. "We can prevent this messy business altogether, Brother. If you freely own your crimes, I promise a swift death instead of the hanging, drawing, and quartering you deserve for treason."

Yes, a swift death was preferable to the method reserved for highest crimes of treason. "You may as well slay me today." Nicholas said the words gravely. "For no matter how much you torture me, I will never betray my king or country." *The way you have.*

Those final words begged to be spoken, but he held them back. Instead, as the guards unlocked the cell door, he prayed his angel would come to rescue him ere it was too late.

- 4 -

EVERYTHING SHE'D EVER DONE to help Dawson had failed.

Stifling a frustrated sigh, Sybil placed both bags of groceries on the table, shoving aside dirty dishes, takeaway containers, and pizza boxes.

The blare of the TV from his bedroom wasn't a good sign. It meant he was lying in bed and sulking. Like usual.

"Hey, Sybil." Acey limped into the kitchen with his cane, his pant leg empty, his prosthesis missing. A massive man with curly red hair and a full red beard, Acey had enough energy for a whole platoon.

Sybil nodded at Dawson's closed door. "Bad day?"

"Got that right." The tap of Acey's cane against the vinyl floor was heavy as he made his way to the fridge. The ground-level flat was spacious, but the place was sparsely furnished without a single decoration. A light above the sink dispelled the darkness that had fallen in the May evening.

She'd hoped after eight years home from the war, Dawson would have his life sorted out. But with every passing day, he fell farther from the vibrant and caring man he'd once been.

She yanked items out of the bags—apples, bananas, lettuce, a cucumber, milk, organic wholegrain bread, nuts, and other healthy foods. The kind of food Dawson needed to eat instead of the junk littering the kitchen.

"Tried to set him up on a date last night." Acey swung open the fridge door and pulled out a carton of OJ. Without bothering to close the door, he popped off the cover and guzzled the juice.

Sybil folded her recyclable bags, then started tossing the past few days' worth of leftovers into the rubbish bin. "I take it he wasn't keen on it?"

Wiping his tattooed arm across his mouth, Acey shook his head. "Shame too. She was a right pretty little thing." He shoved the OJ back on the top shelf before rummaging around.

Not for the first time, Sybil wished Dawson had taken up Acey's outlook on life. Acey had lost half his leg and hadn't let the disability stop him from living. Why did Dawson let his lack of sight hold him back?

"She got here, and he wouldn't even open his door to meet her." Acey slapped the fridge closed with a force that told Sybil he was more flabbergasted than usual with Dawson's attitude. "Shouted at me to shove it—well, you can guess where."

Sybil nodded curtly, appreciative that Acey always made a point of controlling his swearing around her.

"Last time I try to help him." Acey tugged open the freezer and grabbed a gallon of ice cream. The lid was gone, and a spoon stuck out. Acey shoveled the spoon deeper, his arm muscles straining. "I don't think I can keep doing this, Sybil."

She paused in crumpling a piece of greasy aluminum and gave Acey her full attention. This wasn't the first time Dawson and Acey had a row. But she'd never heard Acey mention quitting. Was he serious?

He peered back at her, his eyes brimming with sadness.

A knot looped tightly in her middle, adding to the tangle already there. What would Dawson do if Acey left? His emotional state was already precarious. Any more instability would tip him over the edge.

"Don't give up yet."

"Yet?" Acey released a bitter laugh. "We've been trying to help him for years. And you can't help someone who won't help himself."

"We'll work out something." But even as the words fell out, deep in her heart she knew the truth, had just told herself the same thing when she'd walked into the flat: Everything she'd ever done to help Dawson had failed.

Acey stuffed a huge chunk of ice cream into his mouth.

She waited for him to respond, to offer a suggestion like he normally did. But he chomped on the first bite while he mined for another spoonful.

"I'll have a word with him," she offered.

"We've already said it all."

He was right about that. But they had to keep working to save Dawson, didn't they?

Acey crammed in another obscene amount of ice cream. "We've already done it all too." Acey's tone contained finality, as though he'd read her mind.

Protest pushed for release, but she bit it back. Between Acey and her—and Mum before she'd disappeared—they'd labored tirelessly to resurrect Dawson, to give him a reason for living. Was it finally time to admit they hadn't made any progress? That Dawson was no better now than the day he'd come home from the hospital? That maybe he was worse?

Acey stabbed the spoon back into the container and returned it to the freezer. When he turned to face her, something in his expression made her brace herself for what he was about to say.

"I've put off proposing, and Chloe has been patient—never met a woman more patient. But I need to get on with my own life now."

"Right. I understand." Honestly she did. Chloe was a nice girl, a professor of architectural conservation at the University of Kent. The two had been dating for ages and were good together. Acey couldn't keep placing his life on hold for Dawson. They were nearing thirty, and it was past time for them both to settle down and start families.

She volleyed the crumpled aluminum into the bin but overshot. The piece hit the wall and pinged back forcefully. Wasn't that the story of her life? Trying her best but never hitting the mark?

"I'm sorry, Sybil." Acey white-knuckled the handle of his cane. "This isn't what I'd hoped for either."

"You've done more than any friend should have to."

"If our situations were reversed, he would've helped me the same way."

"He was a good guy."

"And he still is . . . somewhere underneath all his pain."

"I hope so." She wanted to believe it, but at times she couldn't put aside the feeling that a large part of Dawson had died in the war.

"I'm planning to propose this weekend." Acey didn't look at her.

"When will you move out?"

"How long do you need in order to make other arrangements for him?"

Would any length be sufficient, short of a miraculous healing?

The racing in her mind came to an abrupt halt. A miracle. She needed a miracle for Dawson. And she knew of only one way. Through holy water.

But other than the miniscule amount in the test tube she'd found in the lab of Reider Castle, there was no holy water anywhere to be found. The scarcity was why Dr. Lionel had sent Ellen into the past. He'd tasked her with finding the holy water and acting as his courier, delivering a steady supply to him in a special alcove under the dungeon stairs. At least that's what Ellen had secretly told her about the reason for the kidnapping. Ellen and Harrison had given other more plausible reasons to the police, deciding it was for the best not to share their theories about the holy water and time traveling.

Sybil had agreed that it was wiser to leave such speculations unspoken to protect Harrison's upstanding reputation in the community. Most people would ridicule Harrison and Ellen if they claimed they'd crossed to a different time. Others, who were like Dr. Lionel, might threaten them.

Even though Ellen hadn't delivered a supply of holy water to Dr. Lionel, she'd insisted it was possible for people in the past to place holy water in locations that still existed in the present—like that dungeon stairway alcove at Reider Castle—

and transfer it to the current day.

Harrison had tried explaining the phenomenon to Sybil once. He alleged that something in the molecular makeup of the holy water—particles that moved at the smallest wavelengths—allowed it to defy the constraints of time and travel from one era to another.

As with everything else Harrison had revealed, the time-traveling of holy water was far-fetched. But she'd had no reason not to trust his word, hadn't known how else to account for the mysterious appearances of holy water in places she'd already checked.

Even so, she'd remained skeptical . . . until today. After her experience with the time overlaps, she had to put any remaining doubts aside and embrace the possibility that someone in the past had supplied the holy water to them in the present. If it'd been done before, could she find a way to have holy water deposited again—this time in Reider Castle for Dawson? Or in the crypt of Canterbury Cathedral where other flasks of holy water had shown up?

Was it feasible she could taste another drop of the holy water from the test tube, set the man in the dungeon free, and ask him to do this favor for her?

Her heart raced forward at even the hint that she could orchestrate a miracle for Dawson.

"Don't want to push you, Sybil." Acey was studying her.

"I'll work it out."

"You sure?"

Was she sure? "No. But I'll give it a go anyway." Sybil crossed her arms and stared at Dawson's bedroom door. Then, squaring her shoulders, she marched toward battle.

She didn't bother knocking. She'd learned that when he was in a terrible state he wouldn't answer. She'd end up talking to his rigid back. But for what it was worth, she owed it to both of them to have one last attempt at a conversation.

As she threw open his door, the blare of the TV and the stench of unwashed clothing greeted her. Except for the light from the fast-moving images on the screen, the room was dark.

She picked her way through piles of clothing and rubbish to the bed where he was sprawled out, his back facing her, his head buried in a pillow.

He'd always been a handsome man, with the same green eyes and brown hair a shade darker than hers. Tall and lanky, with beautifully proportioned features, he'd once been approached by a modeling agent. But Dawson had been too eager to run off and join in the war efforts to pay heed to anything else.

If only he'd never gone . . .

When she reached the edge of the bed, she lifted her boot and gave him a swift kick in his hindquarters.

He grunted but otherwise didn't budge.

She flipped on the bedside table lamp. The glow brought to life even more of the chaos that surrounded Dawson—musty towels, crumpled mail, crushed beer cans. And a plastic bottle, tipped over, pills scattered around it.

She didn't have to read the prescription to know what it was. His OxyContin.

He was only supposed to take the pain reliever as needed on the rare occasions his injuries became unbearable. Even after a dozen surgeries, four of them on his eyes, his body still bore painful scars from the blast that had killed three soldiers and injured both Acey and him.

She let her shoulders slump. She'd tried over the past few years to control his pain meds, had wanted to keep him from becoming another statistic among the growing number of opioid addicts. But it looked like he was headed down that path.

Dawson had always been a sensitive soul. As children, he'd taken their dad's desertion hard. As they'd gotten older, he'd hated the danger of their mum's job in counterterrorism and the toll the long hours had taken on her as a single working mother. When Mum had disappeared four years ago, he'd lost his lifeline and had slid into depression.

"For pity's sake, Dawson." She brushed a hand over his tousled hair the way their mother always had. "What have you done now?"

With heaviness settling deep inside, she expelled a sorrowful and unsettled breath. Maybe he wasn't an addict yet, but he was probably close to it.

If that wasn't fear enough, she lived with the dread that one day she'd come to his flat and discover he'd ended his life once and for all.

She couldn't let that happen. She was the strong one and had to make sure he survived—any way she could. Even if that meant she had to resort to unusual methods, like getting her hands on the rare and coveted holy water.

It was worth a try for Dawson's sake.

- 5 -

HAD SHE LEFT HERSELF ENOUGH TIME to accomplish her mission before Isaac arrived to begin another day of investigating the computer system?

Sybil glanced at the wall clock again. 2:00 a.m. or 0200 hours. If she slept for six hours after the overlap to the past similar to the last time, then she'd wake up at about 0800 hours. Most likely Isaac wouldn't arrive until 0900 hours. She'd be awake by then and already working.

She settled herself more comfortably on the hospital bed, careful not to disturb the spot on her finger that contained the dampness of the holy water. She'd considered dripping the liquid directly onto her tongue. But in doing so, she risked dropping and shattering the test tube when she fell asleep or became unconscious or whatever happened during the overlap. Even though she'd nearly drained the liquid, she had to protect the tube and try for one more overlap after this one.

Her mission on this second visit was to ascertain how to release the man from the prison cell. On the third visit, she'd orchestrate the overlap so she could free him. She'd ask him to help her in return by finding a way to deposit a bottle of holy water in the crypt of the cathedral since once he was free, he wouldn't be able to return to the castle.

Surely he would do this little thing for her, for Dawson.

After her visit to Dawson's, she'd gone to her CrossFit class. The intense workout had helped her burn off some of her frustration, but it hadn't taken away the growing sense of panic that she had to do something for her brother before he gave up on life altogether. She'd already lost too many people and couldn't bear to lose anyone else.

Freshly showered, she was wearing a clean outfit—her staple of black jeans, tight shirt, and jacket—and had left her hair down to dry. She considered braiding it or wrapping it up into a knot. But she usually left it loose when she slept.

The overhead fluorescent lights were off, and the lab was lit only by one of the desk lamps. As tired as she was, a strange anticipation coursed through her.

Squeezing her eyes closed, she lifted her damp finger. The liquid was odorless and tasteless. If not for the wet spot, she wouldn't know where it was.

"1382," she whispered. "And the man in the prison."

With the time and destination secured in her mind, she stuck her finger in her mouth and clamped down around it. Air poured into her body, rushing to each limb. In the next instant, the earthy mildew scent was back along with the chill of the unheated cell.

But this time, there was no light. As she stood and stretched out her hand, she couldn't see even an outline. Maybe he was already gone.

"Hello?" she whispered.

"My angel," came a weak reply from a short distance away.

Angel? No one had ever called her an angel before. A fierce terror. A hard woman. A tough fighter. But never anything feminine.

She could hear him shift just slightly, followed by a hiss.

"You've been beaten again?"

He didn't reply.

"How bad?"

"I shall not survive another."

She fumbled for her mobile and attempted to turn on the torchlight. But it didn't blink on no matter how many rapid pushes she made.

"I've come to plan out your escape." She crawled in his direction, an arm outstretched, not wanting to bump into him and cause him even more pain.

"I cannot move."

Her hand skimmed flesh. His arm.

His fingers clamped around her wrist, and he pressed two small items into her palm. "Fire-steel. For lighting the candle."

The smaller rectangular piece she recognized as flint. But the oddly shaped piece of metal wasn't familiar. Even so, she struck the flint against it, awkwardly at first, until she realized the loop was there to provide her a better grip.

She'd learned to start fire from flint in one of the survival classes she'd taken. She'd gotten quite proficient at it but had never done it in the dark or without flammable tinder.

While working, she had to put the escape plan into place. "Listen . . . ?"

"Nicholas."

Nicholas was the nobleman who had helped Ellen and her

father. Was he now being punished for the assistance? If so, all the more reason to help him.

"Listen, Nicholas. I don't have much time during my visits. So next time I come, you'll need to be ready to act." Sparks lit up the darkness. She lowered the flint, drawing the straw together into a pile. As she struck the flint and fire-steel again, the sparks landed in the straw. She bent and blew gently on them and was rewarded a moment later with a flame.

Nicholas thrust a stubby candle at her, and she dipped the wick into the flickering fire, igniting it just as the flame in the straw fizzled out to smoke.

Holding the candle by its wide pewter base, she took in Nicholas lying on his side, eyes closed. His face was pale and his breathing shallow. She leaned across him and peeked at his back. It had been bloody and bruised the last time, but this was worse. The flesh was mangled to shreds, some places deeply.

"Sweet holy mother." No wonder he'd said he couldn't move. She was surprised he was conscious at all.

He pushed another item at her. A tin. "Salve. I need you to put it on."

She opened the container, dipped her fingers in, and leaned across him again. As she lowered her hand against one of the long gashes, she hesitated, breathing in the pungent herbs she couldn't name.

"Do it." His voice was hoarse. "Without the medicine, my wounds will surely fester."

She began dabbing on the ointment in a thick layer across the worst gash. "Where are the keys to unlock the door?"

"The guards hold them."

"How many guards are there?"

"Two."

She lathered more onto the next wound, tending him as swiftly as possible, fearing that at any second she would be pulled back to the lab and not be able to finish helping this man. He didn't move except for his face to tighten in pain.

The outside of Reider Castle in the present time was dilapidated and overgrown. She knew it wasn't that way during 1382. In fact, once he was out of the dungeon, no doubt he would need to overcome many other guards. "After I release you from the dungeon, will you be able to make your way to freedom?"

"'Tis possible."

"Then once you are free, will you repay my kindness by putting a bottle of holy water in the crypt of Canterbury Cathedral? The column with the human head has a hiding place in the mouth."

His fingers closed around her upper arm with more force than she'd believed he was capable of having in his weakened condition. Although his grip was tight, it wasn't menacing.

Kneeling beside him and arched over him, she paused to find his eyes open and fixed on her, his brows arched. "What need have you for the holy water?"

"It's not for me. It's for my brother."

"What ails him?" Nicholas's grip remained unswerving, as did his gaze.

She sensed he wouldn't be satisfied unless he had the truth, but how could she explain that Dawson's section had been in charge of disposing of munitions and one of them blew up?

This man from the Middle Ages would think she was a lunatic if she mentioned land mines and shrapnel. But the longer she hesitated, she was drawing his suspicion. "He lost a portion of his eyesight during a war." She spoke as much of the truth as she could. "As a result, he also lost the will to live."

Nicholas was silent. And this time she could feel him studying her as she slathered more of the salve over his back.

"I've tried everything to bring him back to life, and now I'm desperate."

She leaned down farther to reach his lower back. The welts disappeared into his woolen trousers or whatever they were called. The material stuck to his flesh, dark spots of blood seeping through. It was clear some of the wounds streaked his buttocks. She tugged at the waistband to pull it down.

"No." The one word was quiet but loaded with a tension she didn't understand. Was he concerned about his modesty? She'd seen plenty of trauma victims, and modesty was the last thing anyone worried about in a dire situation.

She glanced at him again, and this time, his lids were lowered halfway, and he was staring at the place where her body pressed against him, her chest brushing his arm. She'd only been attempting to tend his back and hadn't meant anything by the contact. But she'd clearly overstepped the bounds of 1382, and maybe he assumed she was hinting at a sexual hookup.

She wasn't easily embarrassed, but in this case, a strange flush settled inside. She sat back on her heels and handed him the tin. "I'll let you finish."

He didn't take it. "There are two bottles of holy water in a hiding spot under the dungeon stairwell."

She knew exactly where that hiding place was. She'd searched there already several times. "You're sure?"

He nodded. "I put them there just in case . . ."

Just in case he'd located Ellen and needed to revive her?

Sybil pushed down her question. It was better not to say anything about what she already knew of the past. It would only make him wary. "We'll use one for you, to heal your wounds—"

"With the salve, my wounds will heal on their own."

"But you're weak—" The candle flickered out, and in the next instant the supply shelves materialized.

"Nicholas?" she whispered, staring at the place he'd been just seconds ago, almost feeling his presence still there.

Though weariness fell over her, she fought against the pull to sleep. Instead, she tried to visualize him. For a second, she thought maybe she heard his voice, heard him say her name.

Then the sensation went away, as if the connection to the past was lost, like a phone line gone dead.

According to the digital clock, she'd stayed in the past about four minutes. That was more than previously. Maybe the extra minute or two had to do with taking in a slightly large blot of the holy water. Was it possible that the more one ingested, the longer one crossed time, until reaching the point of a coma and complete transfer to the past?

Whatever the case, she had enough left for a final overlap. She could only pray it would provide sufficient time to get the dungeon keys and set Nicholas free.

Unable to hold her eyes open a second longer, she let the

blackness of slumber claim her, all the while thinking of Nicholas, that his body wouldn't survive the trauma of being beaten again and that she didn't want him to die before she had the chance to set him free.

~ 6 ~

"SYBIL, WAKE UP."

A gentle shake roused her out of a heavy exhaustion.

"Are you ill?" The concern in the question prodded her again.

Isaac. Work. She was supposed to be awake before he arrived.

With a start, her eyes flew open and she sat up. "What time is it?"

Isaac stood beside the hospital bed, a coat slung over his arm and a coffee travel mug in the other hand. "A little after nine. Don't tell me you worked all night."

"Something like that." She wrangled a hair tie from her pocket and began to comb her hair with her fingers into a ponytail.

His brows were arched high above concerned eyes. "You're going at this too hard, Sybs."

"I always go at everything hard." She wrapped the elastic around her hair, her mind already scrambling with plans for the day ahead. First on the list, she had to check the alcove under the stairway and find out if Nicholas had placed holy water there as he'd claimed.

She also had to sort out the best time to make her last overlap into the past. Probably after night fell so Nicholas could make his getaway from the castle under the cover of darkness. But if she waited all day, what if he received another beating? What if she showed up and found him dead—or too incapacitated to escape in his own strength?

Isaac released an exasperated sigh. "You can't keep going like this."

"I'm fine." She hopped from the bed and fought off a wave of dizziness.

"No, you're not." He reached out to steady her.

She dodged him, a sense of déjà vu hitting her. This interaction was just like their arguments when they'd been together—Isaac complaining she worked too much and her insisting she didn't.

As if realizing the same, he dropped his hand and took a slurp from his coffee.

With a tug at her leather jacket to straighten it, she froze. There, across the lower part of her T-shirt, was a long rusty stain that looked like dried blood. Her shirt had been spotless when she'd put it on after showering last night.

She gave herself a once-over, searching for any injuries she might have sustained over the past hours of deep sleep. But she saw and felt nothing that could have caused the blood. It had to be Nicholas's. From when she'd leaned against him.

A tiny shiver raced up her spine.

She hadn't just imagined him, hadn't simply hallucinated. The sights, sounds, smells—everything had been so vivid. And now, this trace of his blood proved she'd gone to the past and that he'd been real.

She crossed to the door, hoping she could escape before Isaac said anything they'd both regret, something that would make working together impossible. She didn't want that to happen, since he was the best at his job.

"I think I finally figured you out." His statement was laced with sadness.

She paused, her hand on the door latch. "Don't say it—"

"You and Dawson are more alike than you realize. After losing your mum, you're both running scared. He's hiding behind his blindness, and you're losing yourself in your work."

She didn't want to think about the truth of Isaac's observation. It was easier to ignore. Especially today with so much at stake. Regardless, she knew Isaac genuinely cared about her, maybe was still a little bit in love with her. And she couldn't fault him for his kindness and concern.

"You're a good man, Isaac." She opened the door. "Which is the sum of why we didn't work out. You deserve someone better than me, someone like Liana."

She hated to throw his girlfriend in his face again, but Liana needed him to be all in and not hanging his hope on a past relationship. Without waiting for his reply, she exited the lab and closed the door behind her.

The darkness of the passageway enveloped her, and she flicked on her mobile's torchlight, sending a beam ahead. As she started toward the closet, she tried to mute her bootsteps, hoping for the whispering and voices that only yesterday had creeped her out. She knew now that those were voices from the past. She wasn't sure how she was able to hear them. Maybe the presence of the holy water in the castle had something to do with it. Or maybe now that Harrison and Ellen had made a connection to 1382, it was easier to slip between the eras.

Whatever the case, today she understood so much more than she had previously.

When she came to the base of the stairway, she stopped in front of a square door. She lifted the latch and crawled into the tight closet that had been carved out under the stairwell long ago. She lifted her mobile, shining the light on a gap where a stone had been removed, revealing a hiding place that was big enough to hide money or jewels. Or small bottles of holy water.

She couldn't see into the secret nook from her angle. But the unknown hadn't stopped her before. She reached up and slipped her hand inside, feeling around.

Her fingers bumped against a bulbous glass bottle, measuring approximately eight or nine centimeters. She brushed against another. There were two. Just like Nicholas had said. Which meant he'd placed them there after she'd searched the spot earlier in the week.

A thrill pulsed through her, and she couldn't contain a grin.

Carefully, she lifted one out, the opaque glass a faded green, similar to the other bottles of holy water she'd seen. She swirled the container and could feel the liquid at the bottom move.

A tremor worked its way through her chest and made her tremble. This was the miracle for Dawson that she'd been praying and waiting for. A miracle that would bring back his eyesight. With the renewal of his vision, he could finally return to living and working and dating. He wouldn't have to rely upon her or Acey. He'd have his independence again . . . and his dignity.

She wanted to phone Harrison and Ellen and tell them about this find along with everything she'd experienced with Nicholas. They'd be able to relate. And since Ellen had been in Reider Castle, maybe she'd be able to pass along tips to streamline Nicholas's escape.

No. She couldn't. Harrison and Ellen were leaving on a honeymoon. They didn't need to get involved in her drama. More than that, something inside cautioned against involving anyone else. She could keep this her secret and wouldn't have to explain what she intended to do with the holy water.

But did she really have a right to this secret? The coveted holy water wasn't hers to use for Dawson.

Yet if she left the bottles, there was no telling what someone else might do with them if they searched the castle again. They might empty the water and throw away the opportunity for a miracle. Or maybe someone else who knew their value would hear of the discovery and find a way to steal them, especially because Dr. Lionel had black-market ties to several terrorist groups.

She didn't think his research was sponsored by any terrorists. His pharmaceutical company brought in millions of pounds in yearly profits, and he didn't need the outside support. But if a terrorist group had a vested interest in seeing Dr. Lionel succeed, they would probably help him hide. If Isaac could discover a trail of information about any of the terrorist groups Dr. Lionel had intended to sell to, then maybe they could narrow down where he'd gone.

Whatever the case, for now, she had to keep the information about the new bottles of holy water to herself.

Quickly, before she changed her mind, she tucked one bottle into the inner pocket of her leather jacket. She pushed the other back in the stone alcove as far as it would go so no one would be able to easily see it. Only someone who climbed into the closet and crawled over and felt around for it would find it.

She sat back and dusted off her hands. For now, the second one was safest if she left it undisturbed right where it was at.

Backing out of the closet, her legs and arms trembled again. Even when she stood and latched the closet door, she was shaking. This discovery was tremendous. Life-changing, really. She could do nothing more at that moment than rush over to Dawson's flat, give it to him, and watch the miracle unfold before her very eyes.

~ 7 ~

SYBIL SWUNG OPEN DAWSON'S DOOR and made her way through the obstacle course on his floor.

He was sitting up in his bed, curtains drawn against the morning light. The TV was still blaring at the same volume as the previous night—a chat show—and he was staring at it and didn't so much as blink at her entrance.

His right eye was completely blind, but he could see blurry images out of his left. And nothing was wrong with his hearing—thank their Father in heaven for that. She guessed he kept the noise loud to drown out the sounds of real life that came from the busy street outside their flat, noises that reminded him of all he'd lost.

He held a beer can in one hand and a vape in the other.

As she stopped at the edge of the bed, she waited for him to turn his head toward her to acknowledge her presence or at the very least snap at her and ask what she wanted. But he didn't move except to raise his vape and take a drag.

She couldn't summon the usual frustration today, not with the bulge in her coat pocket and the anticipation that tapped an increasingly louder beat in her chest.

"Dawson." She withdrew the green bottle. "I've got

something for you."

"Don't want it." His face was in terrible need of a shave. The overgrowth of his beard hid his handsomeness as did his overlong stringy hair.

"This is good news."

He released a scoffing laugh. "What? You and Acey work out what to do with me?"

Isaac's words about Dawson from a short while ago pushed to the front of her mind: *"After losing your mum, you're both running scared. He's hiding behind his blindness."*

Was Dawson running scared? And if he was healed of his blindness, would he only find something else to hide behind?

She couldn't think about that right now. Maybe a healing wouldn't make all his problems go away. But a miracle as powerful as regaining his sight would change him. How could it not?

She peered through the door into the kitchen. Acey was gone for the day at the secondary school where he taught British history. She and Dawson were completely alone. Even so, she was by nature a cautious person. And with her connection to Dr. Lionel and possible terrorist organizations, she had to be careful not to draw any undue attention to Dawson or herself.

In fact, while driving to his flat in the old part of Canterbury, she'd contemplated how they would explain his healing to doctors, friends, and acquaintances, especially after countless specialists had determined there was nothing more they could do. She still hadn't come up with an answer.

It wouldn't take long for people to wonder about the

source of the miracles and make connections to the ancient holy water. After all, most people who were familiar with Canterbury's history understood the rich heritage of pilgrimage to the shrine of St. Thomas Becket and the healings pilgrims had once experienced after drinking the holy water sold at the cathedral. The stained-glass windows in Canterbury Cathedral's Trinity Chapel testified to the miracles.

First Ellen and Harrison. Then Dawson. Would the ill and diseased from all over the world descend upon Canterbury, hoping to drink holy water and experience a miracle too? Would more criminals like Dr. Lionel show up and make demands?

"Listen, Dawson." She cradled the bottle in her hands, afraid she'd drop and break it. The ancient glass was as fragile as the decision. Would it bring the happiness she hoped for, or would it shatter their lives into more broken pieces?

"I want you to drink some medicine I found." She lowered her voice and again glanced toward the kitchen.

"I've already got all the medicine I need." He tipped up his beer and took a long swig.

"This is different."

"What is it?"

"You have to promise you won't say a word about this to anyone."

Something in her tone must have caught his attention. He shifted his head slightly, the closest he ever came to giving her his full attention. "Is it illegal?"

"No." She couldn't keep the irritation from her tone. "You know me better than that."

He shrugged and turned away, already losing interest.

"Promise you'll stay silent on this?" She had to make him understand the danger and strife that could come as a result of the holy water, but she also didn't want to scare him away from drinking it.

The heated discussion on the TV distracted him even more.

She grabbed the remote on his bed, pointed it at the screen, and hit the power button.

Silence fell over the room.

"Turn it back on." Dawson's command came out a menacing growl.

"Listen to me first."

"That's all I can do." He spat out the words bitterly. "Listen to you rant about one thing or another every day."

The words stabbed into her, just the way they always did. She tried to remind herself that he didn't mean what he was saying. His accusations weren't even true. First, she didn't see him every day. And secondly, she never ranted. She was, instead, a woman of few words.

Even so, she took a step back, as if that could ease the impact of his harshness.

It never did.

All she wanted to do was help him. Why couldn't he see that?

She brushed her thumb over the rounded body of the glass. This momentous occasion wasn't going the way she'd planned. She should have known it wouldn't. Nothing with Dawson ever went according to plan.

"Give me back my remote." He waggled his fingers at her.

Time to stop being the nice sister and get tough. She threw the remote through the door and into the kitchen. It landed on the floor with a clatter and slid into a chair leg. "Drink the medicine, then you can get the remote for yourself."

He sat forward with a roar and pitched the beer can in her direction.

She easily dodged the flying missile. It exploded against the wall, spraying liquid everywhere.

"Are you insane?" he yelled.

"The medicine is ancient holy water and will heal you."

This time he threw one of his pillows. "Go away!"

"Drink it first."

"No."

"If you do, you'll be able to see again."

Dawson released a slew of swearing and then grabbed the lamp off the bedside table. He chucked it at her, and she easily stepped out of its path. As it crashed against the floor, he fumbled for something else to throw. Sightlessly he skimmed, his cursing growing louder and echoing with deep helplessness.

"Drink it, Dawson!" she shouted above his angry words. "Please, I'm begging you!"

This time he tossed one of his vaping pens.

It hit her chin, and the force of it left a stinging mark. She pressed her fingers to the spot to find them sticky with blood.

Dawson grew suddenly silent. Although he couldn't see her and what he'd done, no doubt he realized he'd hurt her.

"It's the miracle cure—"

"I mean it, Sybil." His voice was monotone, dead, as

though he'd lost the will to fight and live all in one throw. "Leave and don't come back."

Her breath snagged sharply in her chest. They'd had plenty of rows over the years—none quite like this—but he'd never told her not to come back.

"I'd be better off without you coming in here and nagging me all the time and making me crazy with your ideas of what I should and could be doing better."

"This is different." She held up the bottle, wishing he could see for himself what she'd brought and understand its significance.

"No, it's never different. It's always the same—you trying to fix me instead of accepting me the way I am."

Again, his words pierced her, this time with guilt. Was that what she'd been doing all this time? Making him feel like she didn't love him for who he was because he was blind? If so, she hadn't meant to. "I'm sorry, Dawson . . ."

"This is who I am now." He held up his arms, giving her a good look. "I won't get better."

"But that's why I'm here, because I found a cure."

"I don't need you or your cures." His expression turned to steel, and he pointed at the door. "Now go."

She hesitated.

"I loathe your visits. I wish you'd gone missing instead of Mum."

This time his words hit their mark, right in the most sensitive spot in her heart. She remained frozen for several long seconds, unable to move or breathe. Anguish rippled out from her chest and brought the swift sting of tears to her eyes.

He was silent, too, and stared unseeingly at the dark TV screen.

She fought to keep the tears at bay. But despair battered her chest, and she wasn't sure she could keep her defenses up.

She crossed to his dresser, placed the bottle of holy water at the center, and then left his room and his flat without speaking to him again. She got in her Ford Focus and forced herself to drive. During the twenty or so minutes to Reider Castle, her thoughts swirled fast, reviewing every second of her interaction with Dawson, the last cruel declaration echoing louder with each replay.

As she headed down the driveway over a bridge that spanned a meandering river, a single sob escaped. The sound was too loud in the silence, and she cupped her hand over her mouth to keep the rest at bay.

She rarely allowed herself to display emotion, especially cry. And she couldn't now either.

As she rolled under a crumbling arched gateway, the bailey came into view with its broken walls. The grass was long and green with wildflowers growing in clusters. Except for a butterfly, the place was deserted with no signs of life. Only Isaac's car remained parked to the side of the castle among the weeds.

She brought her car to a halt next to Isaac's and killed the ignition. With her hand still cupped over her mouth, she stared ahead at the barren yard. Loneliness and despair rose swiftly within her, and she could no longer contain her sobs.

Dawson didn't want her in his life. He loathed her and told her not to visit him anymore. And worst of all . . . he wished she'd gone missing instead of Mum.

Hot tears trickled down her cheeks.

"Why?" She choked out the word. "I've given you everything I have. I've loved you unconditionally, even when you treated me like rubbish. After all that, *you* loathe *me*?"

She slapped her hands against the steering wheel. "How dare you!" Her anguished cry echoed against the closed windows. "You selfish narcissist! You're not the only one who was hurt when Mum disappeared! I lost my anchor too!"

More tears spilled over, but she rapidly wiped them away. She wouldn't grieve over Dawson, not when he'd so callously cast her aside.

Brushing at her cheeks again, she checked her reflection in the rearview mirror. Her eyes were red, her face flushed, and the gash on her chin was the glaring reminder that Dawson didn't love her anymore.

As the pressure of more sobs welled up, she pushed open the car door and climbed out. She took a deep breath of the damp air, the clouds hinting at rain. Then she slammed the door shut and started toward the side entrance that led to the ground floor.

Maybe before doing anything else, she needed to head to the gym and release her pent-up emotion on a punching bag. She wasn't in the right frame of mind to focus on the investigation.

She halted. In the same instant, a raspy whispering swirled near her ear and the faint words "whip him."

~ 8 ~

SYBIL STILLED HER BREATHING and strained to hear more. But this time the only rasp was the wind blowing through the tall grass.

Had she just heard someone speak about whipping Nicholas again? Maybe the person was at this moment—in the past—heading down to the dungeon.

Her nerves tensed. Did she have enough time to free Nicholas before anyone reached him?

Pushing herself to a jog, she headed to the side door. She had to extract the last residue in the test tube and create another overlap with Nicholas. But before she did so, she had to make sure she positioned herself correctly for the crossover. She didn't want to end up in his locked cell. She needed to be outside of it to find the keys.

If she situated herself near the dungeon stairs, then when she time traveled, she'd have to face the two guards Nicholas mentioned, and they would be armed. Since objects she carried seemed to travel with her during the overlaps, she would have her knife, but she'd have an easier time if she had two.

She'd seen several on the wall in a ground-floor room that had been converted into a study. The current owner of the castle didn't live on the premises, and most of the furniture was covered with sheets. However, the wall hangings were still visible, including old knives and swords that had been artfully arranged as decorations above a mantel. Upon seeing them for the first time, she'd been impressed by their quality and sharpness.

The guards of 1382 would have swords, but she'd never wielded a sword and would only put herself at a disadvantage by carrying a weapon she didn't know how to use expertly. She'd be better off having two knives that she could brandish with deadly precision. Besides, she had her kickboxing skills. Hopefully, she'd be prepared enough to disable two guards and wrest the keys from them.

She made short work of taking one of the knives from its mount on the study wall. The pommel was encrusted with a blue jewel, the grip was engraved with a rose, and the double-edged blade of about twenty centimeters tapered to a deadly pointed tip.

She wished she had a sheath for the weapon but guessed any leather casings had disintegrated long ago. She laid it at the base of the stairwell instead of carrying it with her and frightening Isaac and garnering his questions.

As she entered the lab, she crossed to the spot in the wall that contained the test tube, trying to act as normal as possible. The last thing she needed was for him to suspect she was up to something. He was used to her comings and goings, but he also saw more than he let on—a trait of a good investigator, but one that didn't allow for much secrecy.

She was counting on him being miffed from her rejection

earlier and not talking to her for a few hours, but as she extricated the tube, he spoke. "You've been crying. What's amiss?"

Making sure her body was still blocking the spot in the wall, she slipped the tube into her coat pocket. Then she turned as casually as she could.

His attention hadn't wavered from the screen, and his fingers hadn't slowed in their tapping of the keyboard. How was it possible that even when Isaac—her ex-boyfriend—was busy and focused on work, he still cared about her? But Dawson—who was her flesh and blood—never asked about her life, never showed any concern, never reached out about anything, not even to wish her well on her birthday last month.

Anger sparked inside, hard and abrasive like the flint she'd struck against the fire-steel. Dawson was a horrible brother. The worst. And she'd be better off separating from him and his negativity instead of always letting him drag her down.

Isaac paused and swiveled his chair so that he was facing her. "How are you getting on?"

Her first reaction was to tell him this was none of his business. But his eyes were kind and filled with genuine concern. She owed him the courtesy of kindness in return. "Dawson's got to me."

"He's being a prick again?"

She nodded, a lump pushing up into her throat. She'd offered her brother holy water, for pity's sake. It was the best gift she could give him. But he'd been absolutely terrible to her in return.

"I say you need a good long break from him."

"You're right—"

"This time a holiday someplace far away where you can't go running back the first time he texts you that he needs groceries or money for an overdue bill."

She bristled at Isaac's underhanded way of bringing up her previous failed attempts at taking breaks from Dawson. Before, she'd always gotten fed up with her brother for his demands and his lack of gratefulness. But this time, he'd told her not to come back. This time, the parting felt final.

Yet, what if he texted her in a few days? Would she be able to stick to her resolve to give him exactly what he'd asked for?

"I vow I'll cut the ties with him." She started back through the lab.

"You need to, Sybs. He's draining the life from you. Pretty soon, he's bound to suck you dry."

Isaac was right about that too. With every passing day, she'd felt as if she was losing more of herself so that now she didn't really know who she was anymore.

When she reached the door, she paused. "I'll be gone most of the day, but I'm leaving my car here."

He didn't respond, which meant he was waiting for her to offer more explanation. But what could she say, that she planned to hide in the closet under the stairs, overlap into the past, and then sleep for six hours afterward? He'd have her committed to the nearest asylum.

"Just lock up when you're done, and I'll be back later."

There was another beat of silence.

Was he suspicious of her? The last thing she needed was for him to investigate what she was up to.

At last, he heaved a sigh, one laden with disappointment. "Right, then. Will do."

Had he hoped for a deeper conversation? That she'd bare her soul? That they'd finally talk about how Dawson had come between them and been the main reason for their breakup? She wasn't ready for that discussion, doubted she ever would be.

She opened the door, then glanced at him over her shoulder. His attention was riveted to her, the longing in his eyes undisguised. "Many thanks, Isaac. You're a good friend."

"I'm always here for you."

With a nod his way, she exited. As she started toward the closet under the stairs, her heart bowed under the weight of disappointing him. Maybe rather than a holiday, she simply needed to move someplace new where Dawson couldn't use her, where Isaac wasn't pining after her, and where memories of her mum didn't haunt her every day.

She picked up the dagger, opened the closet door, then climbed inside. She turned on her mobile torchlight to aid in closing the door and making sure it was secure. She wouldn't be able to fasten the latch on the outside, but from what she could tell, the door would stay closed, and she'd be able to sleep without Isaac noticing she was inside. The confines were tight, only one meter high and one meter wide, about the size of the door.

Nevertheless, she situated herself as comfortably as possible. Then she dug the test tube from her coat pocket. She struggled to get any of the remaining residue to drip onto her finger. After futile efforts, she slid her pinky inside the tube and wiped it around, stretching it as far to the bottom as it would reach to absorb every last molecule.

She set the test tube aside, picked up the dagger, then darkened her mobile. "Time to get on with it." Taking a deep breath, she stuck her finger in her mouth and washed it clean.

She waited for the blowing and rushing to move through her. But this time, there was nothing. Not the musty scent, not the coldness, and not the strange lighting.

Maybe everything was different because the closet under the stairs was different. She shifted, intending to put her ear against the door and ascertain what she could about the guards, but her hand bumped her mobile where she'd discarded it on the ground. How had it traveled to the past if she hadn't been holding it?

She picked it up and the screen flared to life.

That was strange.

She cracked open the door to the sight of the very same passageway she'd walked down moments ago.

Disappointment needled her. She hadn't crossed time. She was still in the present.

Why hadn't the holy water taken her to the past?

She picked up the test tube again, and this time she wet her finger first before rubbing it around the empty bottle. She swiped it thoroughly, went through the same steps as before, then popped her finger into her mouth.

Closing her eyes, she held her breath and waited for all the signs that she'd crossed the space-time barrier.

Nothing happened.

"Whip him" resounded in her head and made her muscles tense. She had to get to Nicholas. Now. Before it was too late

to help him.

But what if she couldn't go again? What if she'd used up the holy water?

She shook her head, trying to clear her frustration and think calmly and rationally. When she'd been working with Harrison to find Ellen, he'd talked about his overlaps and about reaching a point where he could no longer fabricate them. He'd eventually concluded that the body built up a tolerance to the holy water like other drugs, requiring higher doses to have the same effect.

She pushed to her knees and crawled to the nook on the opposite wall where she'd left the second bottle of holy water. As much as she resisted the idea of disturbing it, she'd have to open it and use a little. She had no choice.

She found the bottle where she'd left it. As she pulled it out, she gave it a shake. It felt like it had the same amount of holy water as the one she'd given to Dawson. She wouldn't need all of it. But how much would be sufficient?

Lowering herself back to a comfortable position, she used the tip of her knife to ply away the stopper. It crumbled easily, and she had to work to keep pieces from falling inside the bottle. After it was open, she once again made sure she had her knife and the dagger.

As a memory popped up on her mobile screen from five years ago, she tapped it, bringing up a snap of her, Dawson, and Mum. From their holiday at the White Cliffs of Dover. The three of them were standing at the edge of a precipice, the bright blue of the strait behind them. And they'd all been smiling. Even Dawson.

Sybil touched her finger to her mum's face, the features so much like her own. Then she traced Dawson's smile. Even though he'd been smiling, that last year before Mum disappeared had been hard for him. He hadn't liked that Mum had moved up to Fakenham in Norfolk for work. Sometimes Sybil wondered if Mum had really moved for her job or if she'd done it to force Dawson to be more independent and stop relying upon her so much.

The smiling face of the beautiful woman looked back at her. "I'm sorry, Mum."

As much as she'd tried to keep pushing Dawson toward recovery the way Mum would have wanted, Sybil had obviously failed at it. In fact, she'd only made things worse.

"I loathe your visits. I wish you'd gone missing instead of Mum."

Dawson's words tore at Sybil, and she pressed a hand against her chest to ease the ache. If she could trade places with her mum, she would.

Should she go missing? Why not give her brother exactly what he wished for?

"Fine, Dawson." Frustration rushed in again to lay siege to her heart alongside the pain. "I'll go missing if that's what you want."

She'd stop visiting him and barging into his life. She'd give him the chance to figure out his own way forward without interfering. Isaac had told her to take a break from Dawson someplace far away where she wouldn't be tempted to rush to aid him the next time he needed her.

What was farther away than 1382? She could take a trip to

the past, help Nicholas escape from Reider Castle, and bring an end to the danger plaguing him. After all, in his weakened condition there was no guarantee he'd make it out without assistance.

Her pulse gave an extra hard thud. Did she dare do something like this? She was well aware of the risks such a trip would entail. She'd watched Harrison drink the water and put himself in a coma. She'd anxiously waited for the holy water to show up in an old vault in his home. Even when she finally had the holy water and revived him, Harrison had still almost died, had needed a second dose to keep him alive. They'd been lucky enough to locate a final vial for him to drink.

She might not be as fortunate. Of course, when Harrison learned she was in a coma, he'd immediately recognize what she'd done and would try everything in his power to keep her alive. At some point, she'd have to find holy water to leave in a hiding place for him. While that sounded easy enough, from Harrison's stories about his efforts to retrieve the water, the task was incredibly difficult.

But if she died doing this, who would miss her? Certainly not Dawson—not after everything he'd said. Not her dad—she hadn't spoken to him in years. Not anyone at the agency—she was out on cases so often, she rarely saw her coworkers.

Isaac might miss her at first. But he needed to get over her and move on with Liana. Her friends from kickboxing and the CrossFit gym would miss her, but they had busy lives of their own.

She lifted the bottle and fingered the rounded middle. Basically, she was alone in life.

Usually she didn't mind being by herself. Why, then, did her future suddenly loom so lonely and bleak? Was it because, for as selfish as Dawson was, she'd had someone in her life who needed her? Had purpose in taking care of him? Had clung to the hope he'd change? Now with all that ripped away, she had no idea what she truly wanted out of life.

She brought the bottle closer to her mouth. If she was going to execute this mission, then she needed to do so soon. From everything she'd learned from Harrison about time crossing, it could take hours to revive in the past, depending upon the body's depletion of energy used during the entanglement exchange. It was possible for the exhaustion to last anywhere from a few hours to a dozen.

If she slept for twelve hours, she wouldn't wake up until after dark, which would work to her advantage in assisting Nicholas to freedom. But after so many hours, he'd be even weaker from another whipping, maybe even dead.

She shook her head. She couldn't take the chance and wait twelve hours. Nicholas needed her now. She'd have to create a more immediate but less permanent crossing like the previous two she'd experienced.

Without further debate, she tipped the bottle and drank about half the liquid—at least from what she could gauge from the weight of the bottle.

She leaned her head back, closed her eyes, and waited.

Silence surrounded her. And the ping of a text.

Sighing, she peeked at her mobile. It was lit up on the ground with a message from Isaac. The few words in the banner said: *Here to talk more if you need a listening ear.*

"Stop, Isaac. Just stop." With a curt shake of her head, she took another miniscule sip from the bottle and held herself motionless, her muscles taut with the desire to return to 1382.

Maybe the liquid wasn't genuine holy water after all. Nicholas could have been mistaken. What if the two overlaps with him were all she'd get?

"No." She wanted to go back. He needed help, and she might be the only one who could give it to him.

"No," she protested again, this time louder. "I have to do this."

With a defiant tilt of the bottle, she emptied the last of the contents into her mouth. As she swallowed, the closet faded away, and the world turned black.

~ 9 ~

AT A COMMOTION OUTSIDE THE DUNGEON DOOR, Nicholas closed his eyes and forced himself to relax. If he pretended to be half dead from yesterday's beating, Simon might spare him a whipping today.

Simon intended to kill him. Of that Nicholas had no doubt. But he was counting upon the fact that Simon needed to wrest information from him first. He had likely been paid by the French and now was desperate to give them something useful.

Nicholas had long since extinguished the candle. The wick and wax were nearly used up, and he was saving the remainder for when his angel visited him again. Not to view her beauty. No, he wanted to have the light so she could see while she aided him in opening the dungeon door.

He didn't know exactly how she intended to get the keys from the guards, but she'd indicated she would do so. As an angel, she could probably accomplish much more than mere mortals, and he'd hoped she would work her miracle ere Simon and the guards came after him again.

But apparently, that was not to be.

The key clicked, the door squealed open, and footsteps

slapped down the corridor toward him. As the torchlight fell over the cell, he remained motionless.

"Sir Nicholas looks dead, my lord," said one of the guards.

"Nicholas is not dead," came Simon's testy reply. "Sit up, Nicholas, or I shall make Lady Theresa take your place at the whipping post this day."

At the threat to his mother, Nicholas's blood ran cold. He wanted to bolt up, reach through the bars, and strangle Simon. But he didn't move. Simon wouldn't dare whip his mother, not without cause. Even with contrived charges against her, Simon wouldn't harm her in such a fashion. Doing so would only bring him great censure from the nobility and bishop alike.

No, this was an idle threat. At least, Nicholas fervently prayed it was so.

At the ensuing silence, he guessed his ruse was working.

"He appears to be breathing," said the guard. "But he's unconscious and won't be confessing to anything."

Simon muttered a curse.

"Should we come back for him later, my lord?"

"Throw several buckets of cold water on him and try to wake him." Simon's heavy footsteps plodded away from the cell. "If that doesn't rouse him, then we'll wait and try again later."

Nicholas had positioned himself so his back was facing the wall. He couldn't let them see that he had salve on his wounds. Not only would that implicate his mother, but the guards would realize his wounds weren't festering, were in fact beginning to heal. He didn't know how that was possible, but the salve was like nothing he'd ever experienced and had even helped ease the pain.

He could only think of one person who had given his mother such a potent medicine. Lady Marian Durham. She was growing more renowned throughout the area for her medicines and cures. Perhaps she'd learned of his fate and had delivered the gift to his mother.

Whatever the case, he was still weak, but he wasn't lying at heaven's gates the way he had been yesterday when his angel made her appearance.

As the door closed and darkness fell back over him, he pushed up to his elbows. If only he could figure out a way to pick the lock on the cell door. But he had nothing useful or small enough to fit into the keyhole.

He was stuck and would have to wait for the guards to return with the water. When they opened the door to wake him, could he overcome them? Or would he do better to wait until they came for him later in the day? If he did, he would afford himself a few more hours of healing to regain his strength.

The truth was, none of his planning could come to fruition if Simon kept using his mother to manipulate him.

His only hope was that his angel would make another appearance and lend him her aid.

She was beautiful. More so than any earthly maiden. Her long, dark hair had been loose the last time she'd visited and had fallen across his arm when she knelt beside him, silky and thick and tantalizing. She'd been wearing the strange tight tunic again and leggings, leaving little of her figure to the imagination.

In fact, when she'd bent over him and her generous curves had brushed into him, he'd nearly forgotten all about the fire racing up and down his back. He'd also been distracted by the way her leggings had stretched tight, giving him a perfect view of her rounded hindquarter.

Much to his dismay, the feel and images of her body had lodged at the forefront of his mind. Even though he didn't want to lust, he hadn't been able to cease thinking about how desirable she was and how he wanted to press up against her and run his hands over her body.

"Curses upon me," he whispered, closing his eyes and picturing the way the sun's rays tinged the treetops in the Weald at sunrise. The hues of pink and purple and blue were a feast for a man's soul. The splendor of the woodland in the spring, the earthiness of freshly plowed loam, the wide eyes of a doe in the new growth of a coppice.

Yes, the Weald was unrivaled in its beauty and was where he needed to focus his thoughts. Not upon Sybil nor upon any woman.

If only over recent months he hadn't been struggling with the lusts of his flesh. But his urges had been steadily increasing, against his better efforts to stave them off. The more his urges flared, the more he loathed the prospect of becoming like his father and Simon, using women with little consideration or kindness in return. His father had been married four times and Simon three so far. In addition, they'd both taken advantage of the maidservants, always bringing a different one to bed whether she was willing or not. He'd once witnessed Simon accost a maidservant in a hallway, leaving her crumpled on the floor and crying afterward.

Nicholas had vowed he'd never force himself upon a maiden. He hadn't needed to. The fairer sex had always been more than agreeable to being with him, and he'd never been without a woman during the years he'd been quartered in London. After he'd met Jane during one of his missions to the coast, he'd revised his waywardness and stayed faithful to her. She'd been only sixteen, and he'd been willing to wait to marry her—had waited three long years.

They'd been on the cusp of their wedding when the French had attacked Rye . . .

He lay back on the ground and closed his eyes at the grievous memories. All that had happened didn't consume and torture him the way it had in the days following the death and destruction. But after losing Jane, he hadn't wanted anyone else, in spite of Simon's efforts to form financially beneficial unions for him.

Maybe with the grief of her loss fading into the past, his desires were reawakening. Now he was feeling needs he hadn't in years. Needs he'd been denying. But how much longer could he hold off?

If he survived this attempt on his life, should he take a wife?

He expelled a taut breath, as if that could somehow expel the tension in his body from the encounter with Sybil. She wasn't someone he could allow himself to be attracted to.

If he had another encounter with his angel, he'd think of her and treat her like a sister and nothing more for the few brief moments she was with him. He was strong. He could do it.

At the clang of a door and the call of voices, he returned to the same position as earlier, forcing himself to relax and pretend he was unconscious. He didn't relish the prospect of being soaked with cold water, but if doing so extended his life, then he had no choice.

He had to endure for as long as possible and keep hoping for a miracle.

- *10* -

SYBIL AWOKE WITH A CRICK in her neck and a pounding in her temples.

She opened her eyes to blackness. Where was she and what had happened?

For a moment, she could only blink, trying to sort her way through the fog in her head.

"No," came a man's voice nearby. "We'll be waiting until the lord returns."

"But if we haven't succeeded in waking Sir Nicholas, the lord will whip us instead."

"No sense in rousing him only to have him nod off again."

Sybil sat forward with a start, the events of the past couple of days rewinding and then flashing forward at double speed. Finding the test tube with a droplet of holy water. Overlapping to the dungeon and meeting Nicholas—twice. Dawson's hurtful rejection. The failed attempt to overlap again. Then the decision to drink the holy water and travel to the past.

Had she made it?

With a strange sense of anticipation, she quieted her thoughts and let her senses take over. Slight light was coming in the cracks of the square doorway of the closet. This door wasn't solid. Instead, it had slats with several gaps.

The mustiness was back more powerful than ever, as was the dampness and chill in the air. A clawing near her boot told her she wasn't alone in the closet. Perhaps a mouse or rat lived here.

She kicked at the vermin, and it scuttled away.

Her fingers were stiff around the hilt of the dagger she'd taken from the study. Thankfully, she still had the weapon. She set it aside, then wiggled her hands to bring feeling and warmth back to them. At the same time, she skimmed her fingers over the floor beside her. Her mobile wasn't there.

Was she solidly in the past this time? If so, how long had she slept?

"I say we at least take him out to the whipping post." A man spoke again, and this time, Sybil cocked her ear closer to the door to listen to the conversation. "We can leave him hanging there."

"What if one of the servants loyal to him cuts him down?"

"We'll tie the fellow up right along with him."

"Nay, we'll wait. Can't risk it."

Sybil knew they were referring to Nicholas, and her heart gave a leap of hope. Was it possible she still had time to protect him from another beating?

She curled her legs up and out, stretching her limbs and muscles as best she could in the small confines. She needed to be at her best when she exited the closet and engaged in combat with the men.

Except for the clatter of dice, silence descended outside the door. She inched up cautiously into a crouch that allowed her to peer out one of the cracks in the slat.

In the faint light of a sconce, two men sat on stools on either side of an overturned crate, oddly numbered dice, shells, and coins spread out between them. They wore thigh-length coats of mail. But their necks, heads, as well as their legs were unprotected. From what she could tell, they each had a sword on their weapons belts.

One of the men was young, thin, and without facial hair. She guessed he was the one who'd suggested taking Nicholas out to the whipping post, his fear of the master driving him to protect himself at any cost.

The other man's back was facing her. But from the gray strands in his hair as well as the stoop of his shoulders, she guessed he was middle aged and had remained loyal to his lord these many years by doing whatever was asked of him—no matter how beastly.

Such a man would have fighting experience and wouldn't hesitate to kill her. She'd have to disable him first. The younger one might not join in the skirmish right away, might believe his companion would be able to easily bring her down.

For several more minutes she studied the men, planned her method of attack, located the keys hanging on a hook near the door, and attempted to discern how quickly she could put into effect the rescue before more guards heard the commotion and came down to investigate.

Finally, after studying the latch on the door and using the tip of the dagger to pry it loose, she took a steadying breath. It was time to venture into 1382.

As she pushed open the door, she was surprised when it

didn't creak and draw the guards' attention. In fact, she had time to stand and position the knives in both hands behind her back before the younger man caught a glimpse of her.

His eyes widened, and he jumped up from his stool, tipping it over in his haste. "Holy saints. Where did you come from?"

The older guard was on his feet in the next instant, his sword drawn. His face was leathery and covered with a short graying beard. As he took her in, his gaze lingered first on her tight shirt and then on her jeans. A flare of lust rushed in to replace his surprise, and his lips curled into a grin, revealing graying teeth in dire need of a dentist's attention.

"What have we here?" He sheathed his sword, clearly not anticipating the threat she posed.

All the better. She'd have a straighter shot at knocking him out with the first kick.

"Lord Worth sent me," she said quietly.

The middle-aged guard's smile widened. "See, what did I tell you, John? We've got nothing to worry about. The master's rewarding us for our faithful duty."

The young man—John—was still staring, his eyes holding more fear than desire. Clearly he recognized she hadn't approached from the stairs, and he was trying to make sense of where she'd come from.

"I get a turn with the wench first," the older guard said, his gaze raking over her again.

She waited, needing him to take just one step closer.

"You aiming to do this nicely?" His nostrils flared, and he lowered his voice. "If not, I don't mind a little screaming and clawing."

Sick pervert. Apparently, they existed in the past the same as they did in the present.

As he took his next step, she leapt, kicked her leg out, and aimed for the nerve bundle below his ear. Her boot connected, snapping his head sharply.

"Definitely not nicely," she said as he toppled backward. The momentum slammed him into the wall, and he slid to the floor unconscious. "You're next." She motioned to the younger guard. "Come and get me."

He stared at his companion, then at her. He swallowed hard, unsheathed his sword, and began to advance.

She had to give the kid credit. He wasn't running at the first sign of danger.

"You're a witch from the devil." His grip wavered. "There's no other explanation."

She removed her hands from behind her back, revealing her weapons while circling around. She couldn't let him trap her in a corner. She'd have more flexibility if she fought out in the open.

Keeping her focus upon him, she read his expression and eyes to anticipate his next move. When he lunged at her, she was ready and sidestepped.

Before he could spin and swing again, she landed a kick in his lower back and then the bend of his knees. Both moves sent him stumbling into the opposite wall. Before he could steady himself and raise his sword, she dropped her knife and threw a punch into his temple, one hard enough to knock him out.

Like the other guard, he slumped against the wall and crumpled to the ground, unmoving.

From past experience, she knew she had less than five minutes before they began to gain consciousness. She made quick work of retrieving her knife and stripping them both of their weapons. Then she dragged them together and used a set of discarded shackles to immobilize their feet.

Without wasting further time, she unlocked the door and jogged toward Nicholas's cell.

He was waiting at the iron bars of his cell, obviously having heard her fighting with the guards. Even though the darkness shadowed him, there was no disguising the solidness of his frame and the power in his bearing.

"You are unharmed?" His gaze skimmed over her, as though he was searching for any injury.

"I'm fine." She jabbed the key into his door, the faint light from the opposite end giving her sufficient illumination. Even so, she fumbled as she had with the other lock, not accustomed to the old style.

"Let me." He pushed aside her hand, twisted the key, and in the next instant swung the door open.

"The guards did not accost you?" His tone held a deadly note, one that told her what he'd do to the men if they had hurt her.

"No. They didn't touch me."

As he stepped out and was but centimeters from her, his presence was even more overpowering, but not in a way that repelled her. Quite the opposite. He felt safe. He was the one suffering, but instead of focusing on himself, he was more concerned about her. So unlike Dawson.

She gave herself a mental shake. Now wasn't the time to

think about her feelings. She had to stay focused and act.

"They won't be out for long." She started back down the passageway at a jog. "Let's move them into the cell to keep them from alerting anyone of your escape."

He was on her heels, and as they entered the area by the stairs, he halted abruptly, his eyes rounding upon the guards shackled and unconscious where she'd left them. "You disabled them without drawing blood?"

Obviously. But she bit back the word.

His attention shifted to her and then dropped to the dagger she still held. "You have my knife."

A strange energy coursed through her at the realization that of all the knives she could have chosen from the wall in the study—ancient knives that had been preserved for hundreds of years—she'd picked his.

Surely Providence was somehow drawing them together. What other explanation could there be for how she'd ended up with his dagger?

She handed it to him, unable to keep from admiring his bare chest. The light of the sconce highlighted the perfection of his muscles. He was buff.

Her gaze drifted upward, taking in the dark scruff on his chin and jaw. His firm mouth and straight, narrow nose. His bottomless dark eyes.

As with the last time, he seemed to be trying not to let his sights drop beyond her chin. He apparently had more manners than she did.

Pressing his lips together, he crossed to the younger guard and pulled his mail off none too gently. With his back facing her, she had a full view of his mangled flesh. His wounds glistened with the salve she'd gloped on yesterday, bright crimson, some still oozing blood.

Inwardly, she shuddered, could only imagine the pain he was in. How was he even moving? If her back looked like his, she'd be delirious or crazy or both.

They didn't have time to stand around and strip the guards, but maybe Nicholas assumed they'd be safer wearing the mail as they made their escape. Whatever his intentions, she had to stop gawking and join in his efforts to speed things along.

She crossed to the older guard and hefted the chain mail over his head. As she dropped the cloak of linked chains to the ground, one of his hands snaked around her neck and the other gripped her upper arm, drawing her flush.

"You decided to give me a turn after all." The stench of his breath came from rotting teeth. Or maybe it was his rotting soul. She'd smelled it before, and he didn't frighten her. She slipped out her knife, but before she could disable him, Nicholas rammed the hilt of his dagger against the man's head, jarring him and forcing his grip to loosen around her throat.

She fell back a step, in time to see Nicholas lift the man's hand and stab it to the wooden doorway of the stairway closet. She wasn't sure whose knife it was, suspected it had been the guard's and that she'd missed confiscating it when she'd searched him previously.

The man released a cry, but Nicholas quickly silenced him with a fist to the mouth and a choke hold around his throat. "Next time you lay a hand on her, Potter, I'll chop it off."

Nicholas squeezed hard, and the man's eyes bulged, radiating fear.

She'd witnessed plenty of violence over the years, but this fury in Nicholas was swifter and more severe than she'd ever seen.

As Potter nodded frantically, Nicholas released his hold on the man's throat.

"I could have taken care of him myself." She crossed her arms and spread her feet.

Nicholas gave a curt nod toward a long, plain shirt he'd taken off the younger man. "Put it on."

"What about you? You need something more than—"

"You cannot go anywhere without donning clothes, or you will encounter more of the same vulgarity."

She *was* clothed. But apparently by the standards of the Middle Ages, she was nearly naked. As much as she wanted to argue, they couldn't waste the time. She swiped up the shirt, caught a whiff of the sourness of body odor, but yanked it over her head anyway. As she tugged it down over her leather jacket and jeans, it fell almost to her knees, like an oversized nightgown. She looked ridiculous in it, but now was neither the time nor the place to fret about how she appeared.

"Let's get the guards into the dungeon cell." She reached for the younger guard.

"No. We must be on our way."

"But they'll yell and draw attention—"

Nicholas slapped his hilt against the older guard's head, knocking him unconscious again. He straightened, wrapping a weapons belt around his waist and grimacing as the leather made contact with his open wounds.

She held out her hand. "Give it to me. I'll wear it."

He slanted her a sideways glance but continued fastening it.

Was her offer inappropriate too? Or was he stubborn?

When finished, he nodded toward the stairs. "Follow me."

As he strode away from the guards, her attention fixed upon the older guard's hand still pinned to the door. "Shouldn't we release his hand?"

"After his threats to you, he is fortunate I am allowing him to keep it."

Nicholas was clearly a man accustomed to brutal methods that didn't play a part in modern law enforcement. She hesitated only a moment longer before trailing after him, hoping she hadn't misjudged him and put herself into greater danger than she'd anticipated.

~ *11* ~

THANK THE SAINTS HE WAS FREE. And thank the saints, Sybil was clothed.

Nicholas paused at the base of the steps. She hadn't seemed uncomfortable in her state of undress, but immodesty would draw undue attention from other men like Potter. It was drawing his attention, too, and would only add to his trouble with lust when he needed to abolish it.

She was still indecent in the tunic, but it would have to suffice for now. Maybe he could also grab a cloak on the way out of the castle.

If she was still with him.

As she approached, he had the urge to pull her close and hold her, as if that could somehow keep her from disappearing. She'd been here with him much longer than she had previously. That could only mean she would be leaving any second.

Her eyes were troubled, likely because he'd left Potter's hand pinned to the door. Simon's lackey would free himself from his knife soon enough and would have no lasting damage. Little did she understand how fortunate Potter was. After his threats to her, Nicholas wanted to punish him much worse and probably would have if she hadn't been present.

Nicholas guessed he still harbored an unholy rage from all that had happened to Jane, from the way she'd been sorely abused. Regardless, he had no tolerance for men like Potter.

Sybil halted beside him, and he couldn't keep from studying her face, needing to memorize it before she faded from him, maybe this time forever. After all, she'd finished what she'd come to do and had no need to stay. He could make his way out of the castle now without her.

Her features were as delicate and beautiful as the last time, maybe more so now that he wasn't in so much pain and could focus better. Her hair was pulled back, sleek and smooth and flowing in a long mane down her back. Her dark eyebrows and long lashes framed her eyes and made the green seem brighter. She had a cut on her chin that hadn't been there during her last visit. It wasn't bleeding, which meant she hadn't sustained the injury while freeing him. So how had she been hurt?

"What are we waiting for?" she whispered, peering past him up the stairway.

Her mouth, her lips. They were full and rounded and beckoned to him. It wouldn't hurt to steal one tiny kiss from this angel, would it? Before she disappeared? Yes, he'd told himself he wouldn't get involved with a woman. But since she wasn't staying, he didn't have to worry about the ramifications of kissing her.

His muscles tightened with need.

"What?" she asked again, turning her attention upon him, her eyes filled with trust.

She trusted him to protect her. How would he be any

better than Potter if he stole what wasn't his to take?

"I wanted to thank you before it was too late." His words came out slightly more passionate than he preferred.

If she noticed, she didn't react. "Too late?"

"I keep thinking I shall turn around to find that you are gone back to heaven."

"Oh, right." She fidgeted with the tunic, and it slipped down one of her shoulders. "I won't be going anywhere soon this time."

"Then you are here to stay?"

"For a while."

Relief swelled in his chest—a relief he didn't understand. He sensed her tale was complicated, and he would like to hear it. But for now, he needed to get them both out of the castle and to safety.

From the light at the top of the stairway, he could tell eve hadn't yet fallen but was close. Simon had apparently not returned from wherever he'd gone. Or if he had, he had yet to make the summons for the next whipping.

The castle staff would be busy with preparations for the evening meal. Some of the guards would already be supping, which meant not as many would be standing along the battlements. Even so, he and Sybil would need to move swiftly and cautiously.

"Let us be on our way." Before he thought to stop himself, he captured her hand in his. At the contact of her slender fingers within his, the same surge of protectiveness from before filled him, when he'd been waiting at the cell door, knowing she was fighting the guards and he'd been unable to come to her aid.

He didn't want that to happen again.

She stared at their clasped hands as though she wasn't sure about the connection. As she began to pull away, he held her fast. "We must not become separated."

The excuse came out easily enough. And it held some merit.

She ceased her extrication and nodded.

He settled his grip more firmly, then started up the stairs. Her tread behind him was silent, so much so that he guessed she had some practice at stealth. But how, and why?

When they reached the top, he motioned silently to a dark alcove nearby. He didn't want to be out in the open for long, and he knew all the hiding spots along the way to the battlements. As he moved from one to the next, she stayed right behind him as soundless as she'd been on the stairs. He halted at the top of the tower that overlooked the part of the moat closest to the cover of the forest.

They would have to jump, then swim the distance. Since there was still sufficient evening light left, it wouldn't take long for the soldiers on duty to spot them and rain down a volley of arrows. He didn't want to chance Sybil getting shot the same way Ellen's father, Arthur, had during their escape.

After the earthquake, Arthur hadn't wanted to leave Ellen behind in the dungeon. But she'd been buried too deeply in the rubble for them to find, and with the growing light of day, Nicholas had finally threatened to toss Arthur over his shoulder and carry him out. Arthur had agreed to go only when Nicholas assured him that he'd return for Ellen.

As they'd raced to get out of the keep, Arthur had stopped

to hide two bottles of holy water in a cabinet, letting Nicholas know he might have need of them when he retrieved Ellen. As it had turned out, Arthur had needed them more after an arrow pierced very near his heart. By the time Nicholas arrived at Chesterfield Park with Arthur, he'd believed the old man was dead. But thankfully, Lord Durham had more holy water to spare and had saved Arthur's life just in time.

The next day, when Nicholas left to retrieve Ellen in the dungeon, Arthur had not only been alive but had also been recovering from his arrow wound. Nicholas had spoken briefly with Lord Durham about the need to secure a safe hiding place for Arthur until the accusations of him being a witch could be proven false.

Now all he could do was pray Arthur remained unharmed. And he prayed someday Arthur would be able to forgive him for failing to rescue Ellen.

No matter what had happened on his last escape, this eve would be different. He had to be more careful and couldn't allow any harm to befall Sybil. Maybe he should have stopped and retrieved the remaining bottle of holy water from the closet under the stairs before leaving. Lord Durham had given him the two for Ellen as a precaution, which was just as well since Arthur's in the cabinet had already disappeared.

Nicholas had stored the bottles under the stairs before starting his digging through the debris, hadn't wanted to chance Simon finding the holy water and using it for ill gain.

He had no doubt Sybil had taken the one, and he didn't begrudge giving it to her since her brother had clear need of a miracle. However, 'twas too late to go back for the other now.

He pried open the tower door a crack and surveyed the battlement. The guard was walking away, his back turned. At this time of the day with fewer men on duty, he and Sybil would have a little over a minute ere the guard returned.

It wouldn't be long enough to jump and swim across the distance of the entire moat, which was wider on the sides of the castle that didn't have the drawbridge. But hopefully, they would be able to cross most of the way before the guards noticed them.

"Ready?" he whispered.

"What's the plan?"

"Jump into the moat, and I shall swim us across."

"I can swim for myself."

"You can?" Not many men could swim, and he knew of no woman with such skills. But Sybil had already proven to be different than most.

"I'll be fine. Don't fret about me."

Too late for that. He would worry about her every step of the way. He peeked out again and watched the guard turn a corner. "Now." He pushed open the door. Still holding her hand, he tugged her out onto the battlement that bordered the castle gardens and orchard. No one appeared to be out, but he didn't have time to scan the area thoroughly.

Instead, he released Sybil's hand and climbed into the nearest crenel. The gap between the two merlons was wide enough for both of his feet. As he crouched to assist her up, a guard came around the tower from the opposite direction.

At the sight of the two of them, his face registered surprise, then he gave a shout of alarm and lunged for Sybil. Nicholas unsheathed his dagger from Potter's sword belt. But before he could raise it and force the guard away, Sybil spun, aimed a punch into the man's temple. The blow was hard and accurate, but rather than felling the guard, he stumbled backward against the tower door.

"Make haste!" Nicholas held out his hand, intending to hoist her up and jump while they had a brief respite. But Sybil went after the man again, hopping up high enough to land a kick into his neck. It was swift and severe, knocking the guard to the ground, this time unconscious.

Suddenly Nicholas understood how she'd disarmed Potter and the young guard who'd also been on duty. He would have stared at her in amazement if another nearby shout hadn't sounded.

Someone else had spotted them. Erelong every guard on duty—and even those who weren't—would congregate on the battlement and attempt to halt them.

"We need to go. Now." He thrust his hand out to her again.

She wrapped her fingers around his wrist, creating a grip that allowed him to easily pull her up. Then without waiting for his signal, she jumped.

His pulse tapped a rapid protest, and he swung himself over and off directly after her. Even if she knew how to swim, she'd likely never done so amidst an onslaught of arrows. He would need to hover over her and provide a shield as best he could.

She landed with a splash seconds before he hit the water. As he went under, the pressure against his wounds sent fire racing along his nerves. He bit back a cry of agony and forced himself to focus on finding Sybil. Though the water was murky, he glimpsed her but a hand's length away, divesting herself of the tunic.

Before he could reach her, she propelled herself up to the surface.

He kicked his feet and followed. As he broke through next to her, he assessed the situation on the wall. Already the guard on duty had returned to the spot. He was shouting out and, at the same time, nocking an arrow into his bow.

"We'll need to swim deep," she said, easily treading water, "to stay out of range of the arrows."

"Very well. If you are able."

Again, without waiting for his permission, she pushed under the water and dove low.

He sucked in a deep breath and did the same.

She was quick, darting away ere he could reach her. With strong strokes, he chased after her, trying to keep a hand close to her boots as she kicked her feet in strong thrusts. Above, the evening light glowed against the surface of the water, revealing the arrows that were beginning to fall. They penetrated but slowed upon impact and didn't go deep enough to reach them.

After long seconds, his lungs began to burn with the need for air, but she kept going. Just when he didn't think he could make it another moment, she pushed up to the surface. He followed and popped up next to her.

They were close to shore, only a few strokes away.

A glance behind toward the castle showed at least half a dozen guards firing at the moat. Now that they'd been spotted, the guards' shouts grew louder, and they shifted their aim. He grabbed Sybil's hand and dragged her back under. They were far enough away that the guards would have a difficult time hitting them, but he didn't want to take any chances.

This time he led, and his grip upon her was unwavering. When they reached the edge of the moat, he climbed up the rocky incline, holding her steady as she scrambled next to him.

Arrows landed just behind them, most pinging against boulders.

"This way." He maneuvered her in front of him, towering over her, one eye on the arrows still aimed at them and one eye on the woodland ahead.

She didn't hesitate and plunged into the shrubs, shoving aside branches and hopping over windfall as though she knew the area as well as he did.

When finally they came into a clearing beside a worn grassy road, she paused and studied both directions. "Where to next?"

She was dripping wet with dirty moat water, but she didn't seem to mind. Instead, her body was tense, her gaze taking in every detail of the area.

He didn't want to be the bearer of bad news, but she might as well know the truth before they went any farther. "We will have to run a distance ere we reach a place in the Weald where we might hide. If we are fortunate, Simon's soldiers will not pick up our trail right away."

"And if they do pick up our trail?"

"They will be on mounts, and we will have but a short lead."

She shivered. Though the eve was warm for spring, the breeze was cool and sent chills over his wet skin too.

"I'll follow you." She gave him a push, as though to force him to go.

"If you cannot keep up, you must tell me."

"I'll keep up."

Everything about this woman astounded him and attracted him all at once. As before, his attention fell to her mouth, and desire hit him swiftly and powerfully. He wanted this woman. Wanted to have her like he had no other woman before, including Jane. Was that sacrilegious since she was an angel? Even though she was very womanly, she was an angel, wasn't she? The angels in Scripture had sometimes taken on human form, so it was possible that had happened to her.

He tore his gaze from her and started across the path. Whatever the case, he had to control his thoughts.

Though he didn't allow himself to look at her again, he could both hear and feel her closely behind. As he plowed through the overgrowth, his heart pumped with a strange new energy, one he couldn't remember feeling before, one that told him this woman was special, someone he didn't want to lose. Not now or anytime soon.

~ 12 ~

NICHOLAS COULD RUN FAST. But since Sybil had been training for a CrossFit competition that involved both running and swimming, she'd stayed on his heels for what seemed to be about three miles. Her breath came in gasps, and her muscles burned, but she kept pushing herself, especially at a faint shout behind them—one that told her their pursuers weren't far behind.

The shadows of the coming night were lengthening, and the forest was growing steadily thicker and more overgrown. It was unlike anything in modern Kent, which was mostly cleared of its forests and consisted of rolling hills, winding streams, patches of heathland, and a few farmsteads.

She'd been flabbergasted since the moment she'd stepped out of the tower on the castle wall and taken in the endless trees and the unaltered land without power lines, motorways, traffic lights, and subdivisions. Even the castle had been in full form, its walls still standing, the gardens growing in profusion, and the air laden with a smoky, earthy scent.

In some ways, she felt as if she were in a fantasy world. If not for the pressure in her chest, the sweat beading upon her forehead, and the blister forming on her toe from where her wet sock was rubbing against her boot, she might have believed she was in a coma and dreaming.

But as with the previous overlaps, the physical reality was much too vibrant for her to attribute her experience to a coma-dream.

"There!" Nicholas pointed ahead to a ravine. It was steep and would be tricky to climb. But if they could manage, they would be able to buy themselves time as the men on horseback looked for another route to continue the chase.

Upon nearing the chalky outcropping that rose along a hillside, she mentally prepared herself for the ascent, picking out hand and footholds. When Nicholas launched himself up the rock wall, his long legs and arms took him to the top effortlessly.

She leapt and began scrambling up the steep incline.

He was already leaning over the edge and reaching down for her. "Grab on."

She wanted to prove she had the same abilities he did, that she could make it to the summit without his aid. But the crackle of brush and more shouting behind them told her she didn't have time to show off.

Using his arm to hoist herself, she scaled the ravine as he half-lifted her.

"You are a good climber." He pulled her away from the ledge into the tall grass. "Is there anything you cannot do?"

She was exceptional at her job and had honed her body to handle the rigors of whatever she might encounter. But never in her wildest imagination had she believed she'd use her conditioning as she raced for her life in the Middle Ages.

"I'm terrible at horse riding." She gulped in several breaths.

"I should offer to help you improve your equestrian skills." Bent at the waist, he breathed heavily too. "But then I shall perhaps lose the one thing I do better than you."

Delight shimmied through her at his roundabout compliment. He was stronger and faster. There was no arguing the fact. But she was satisfied with how she'd been able to match his effort, never lagging behind. "I suppose you're not used to a woman who is able to keep up with you."

Still bent and resting his hands on his thighs, he cast her a sideways glance. "I assure you, I have never met a woman like you."

Everything about him was magnetic, even the briefest of looks. And her body seemed unable to resist the draw, flushing with a warmth that had nothing to do with the physical exertion.

With calls only a dozen paces away down the ravine, he motioned for her to follow him again and started through the brush up an incline. As they reached the pinnacle of the hill, Nicholas crouched behind a boulder and pulled her down next to him. A finger to his lips urged her to silence, and she tried to quiet her breathing and heartbeat.

Down the hill, the shouts were impatient.

"They are riding due south," he whispered, "but will soon be on our trail once more."

"How long?"

"Within the quarter of an hour."

"Alright, then let's keep going."

"You are rested enough?"

She pinned him with a sharp look. "If you are."

His lips quirked up the hint of a grin.

What did he find so humorous? Her competitive spirit?

He reached for her hand as he'd done several times already. As before, she was tempted to resist to show she was strong and capable and didn't need a man's help. But as his fingers closed around hers and their palms pressed together, something about the connection drew her. Maybe it was how physically attractive he was. Or maybe it was because she was in the past and this was all so temporary, so fleeting, which meant she didn't have to concern herself with repercussions.

Besides, he probably didn't mean anything by the contact, other than to ensure that she didn't get lost.

He kept low, pushing aside thorny branches and holding them back for her. "We should be able to reach a hiding place before they find a way around the ravine."

"And how do you know of the hiding place?"

"I wandered the Weald as a boy and am more familiar with it than most."

She suspected that wasn't the entire reason for his familiarity with the area. And with every passing moment, she wanted to know more about this strong and fascinating man she'd helped to save.

She'd had full view of his back for most of the getaway. Though his wounds were deep and would leave his posterior disfigured, the salve seemed to have provided a healing relief. The oily coating had also acted as a barrier against the filthy moat water. During the swim, she'd tried not to think about what kinds of waste had been dumped into the water. But from the stench coming from her garments, she could guess easily enough.

Rather than the full-out run they'd maintained before, he guided her with a slower jog that allowed for conversation.

"Is there a river or stream we can rinse off in before going into hiding?"

"And why would you wish to do that?" His tone hinted at humor.

"I suspect you'll enjoy being with me better if I don't stink."

He was silent a beat. "Not true."

Something in the way he spoke sent her blood racing a little faster. "Well, I'll enjoy being with you better if *you* don't smell like a sewage pit."

"When we are together, I shall guarantee that you will not be thinking on sewage pits."

Again, his tone had an almost seductive quality to it. Had he misunderstood her? When she'd said he would enjoy *being* with her, did he think she'd meant physically?

No doubt he already had many women at his beck and call. If he thought she would be one of them, he was in for a surprise. She wasn't a loose woman. In fact, even if her faith in God wasn't what it used to be before Mum disappeared, she hadn't given up her morals. She'd never slept with a man before, not even Isaac.

"I'm guessing a man like you has a woman in his life." She hadn't seen a wedding band on his hand, but that didn't mean anything since she didn't know if men in the Middle Ages even wore rings after marriage.

"A man like me?" The note of humor tinged his question again.

She wasn't a flushing woman, but she didn't know how to respond. "Yes, a man like you."

He didn't push her to confess her true thoughts about him, that he was likely the handsomest man she'd ever met, along with one of the most physically fit. Not only that, but he was smart, courageous, and kind.

"No, I do not have a woman," came his soft response.

She waited for him to expound, but he said nothing more. The silence combined with sadness was another clue, that he'd loved deeply and the loss had been dreadful. "Whenever you want to talk about her, I'm a good listener."

He ducked under several branches and cleared the ever-thickening growth for her. "I would not guess that angels are given into marriage."

He'd called her *angel* on a previous visit. Was that what he thought she was? An angel? She supposed that provided the most logical explanation for why she'd appeared and disappeared randomly right in front of him.

"I'm not an angel."

"A saint?"

"No, most certainly not."

"A witch?"

"Of course not. Just an ordinary person."

"Then you came to me through visions?"

"Something like that." How could she explain time crossing to him when she could hardly make sense of it for herself?

"So you have affections for another?"

Her thoughts sprinted to Isaac. Since the breakup, she'd gone out on a few dates, but she'd never felt any sparks with any of the men.

Nicholas's grip on her hand tightened. "Who is he?"

"There's no one anymore."

"Then this man is no longer involved in your life?"

"We still work together on occasion."

The muscles in Nicholas's arm flexed. Didn't he like the idea of her being with another man?

She gave herself a mental slap. Of course Nicholas wasn't jealous. He barely knew her. "I don't have feelings for him the same way he does for me."

"Yet he still pursues you."

"He's a good and kind man and would never push for anything."

Nicholas stopped abruptly so that she almost slammed into him from behind. His hand landed upon her hip to steady her, but in the next moment his fingers splayed, telling her he liked touching her, that he liked her.

She could feel him studying her face, and she didn't dare look up into his eyes, didn't want to see anything, didn't want to feel anything. As gorgeous as he was, she hadn't come to the past to have a fling with this man. She'd come to save him. That's all. She'd make sure he was secure, and then she'd start her efforts to find holy water and return to the present.

She twisted free of his hold easily with a maneuver she'd learned in one of her self-defense classes. Then she pushed forward through the brush ahead of him, not sure which direction she needed to go but guessing from the dampness beneath her boots that they were nearing a stream.

A few seconds later, she halted at the edge of a swiftly flowing creek. It was about three meters wide and appeared to be only a dozen centimeters deep. Although the water wasn't clear, it was translucent enough to see the pebbles and stones at the bottom.

They didn't have much time to spare for rinsing off, had to hide before their pursuers caught up with them. Without wasting another second, she stepped in, sat in the middle, then leaned back. The water was cold, but she let it flow over her, rinsing away the filth from the moat. She twisted her hair tie loose and dunked her hair too.

Splashing beside her, Nicholas lowered himself into the water. As he ducked under, she couldn't stop herself from watching the way the water cascaded over his bare chest, flowing into the valleys between his pecs and abs and all his other muscles. He slipped his hair out of the strip holding it in place, releasing shoulder-length dark hair. With his head submerged, he combed his fingers through his hair before scrubbing at it vigorously. He rubbed at his arms and his chest, then lifted his head. Before she could look away, he caught her staring.

She jerked her attention back to her own body and splashed water over her jeans. But she couldn't keep her sights from straying sideways and watching him stand, every glorious muscle in his body showcased by his wet garments.

He paused and peered through the forest the way they'd come, then reached out a hand to her. "We must proceed with all haste."

This time, she didn't hesitate to place her hand in his. As he helped her stand, the breeze wrapped icy tendrils around her, making her shiver.

"I would give you my cloak to warm yourself if I had one," he said.

"And I'd refuse the offer, no matter how kind, since you'd need it."

"Then 'twould appear we are quite the honorable pair."

They weren't a pair. But before she could argue the fact, he glanced again at the forest behind them. "Simon's men fear returning without me. Their desperation lends them fortitude." He started upriver, pulling her along against the current. They sloshed hard, and her toes turned numb within minutes.

He was likely attempting to wash away their footprints and any trace of their scent so their pursuers wouldn't know which direction they'd gone. Whatever his reason for staying to the river, she hurried to match his pace, her wet hair flopping against her cheeks. At least the exertion would warm her back up.

The forest hung more thickly above them, shutting out most of the view of the sky until it seemed darkness had already descended. When they'd waded another mile or so, he directed her out of the creek and up the bank. The way was difficult, the branches clawing at her clothing and hair.

When finally he shoved aside a tangle of brush to reveal a rounded opening in another chalky ravine, she climbed inside what appeared to be a cavern. The space was only slightly bigger than the stair closet in Reider Castle's dungeon. The stone ceiling didn't allow room enough to stand, but she could kneel comfortably.

Nicholas crawled in after her, then positioned the branches and brush in front of the entrance, concealing it and providing a refuge. And plunging them into darkness.

As she felt for the wall, her hand skimmed Nicholas's chest. "Sorry."

"Here." He clasped her arm and guided her to the wall. "I regret 'tis not comfortable, but 'tis one of the places here in the Weald that will keep us secure from Simon's men."

She sat back, stretching out her wet jeans and boots, wishing she could take them off and dry out. But if merely wearing her modern clothing was taboo, then shedding them even in the darkness would be too much.

As Nicholas situated himself beside her, his warm exhalations brushed her ear. He stilled, his breath catching, as though he recognized how near they were.

There was most definitely an undercurrent between them.

She remained motionless, for what she didn't know.

Finally, he shifted and winced, no doubt the pressure of the wall uncomfortable against his wounds.

She started peeling off her leather coat. "Use my jacket as a cushion for your back."

"No, you need it for warmth."

She released a scoffing sound. "It won't keep me warm when it's wet."

Before he could protest any more, she finished divesting herself of the garment and pressed it against his chest. "Take it."

He didn't move. "You are already unclad enough as it is."

"It's dark in here. You can't see anything."

Slowly, reluctantly, he took hold of her coat. If he thought she was immodest in her T-shirt and jeans, what would he think of the way other modern women dressed—movie stars with their gowns cut to their navels, teenage girls with short-shorts that barely covered their bums, beaches full of bikini-clad women?

She didn't like or agree with the modern fashions that too often turned women into sex objects. She'd never bought into the ideology that a woman baring her body showed confidence and comfort with her sexuality. Such a philosophy ignored the fact that men—and even women to a degree—had visceral reactions to the beauty of the human body.

Whatever physical reactions Nicholas was feeling, it was clear he didn't wish to take advantage of her—unlike the guard in the dungeon. She scooted away, putting a few centimeters between them. "There. No seeing or touching."

"Very well." His comment contained steely resolve, as though he was making a vow to himself.

She leaned her head back, and for the first time since awakening in the closet under the stairway, she replayed all that had transpired. Orchestrating Nicholas's escape had all gone so swiftly and had been so dangerous that she hadn't had time to think about what she was experiencing.

Was this real?

The goose bumps on her wet skin, the water dripping from her straggly hair, the tight rub of her jeans against her inner thigh—how could she fabricate everything?

She pinched her arm and gave a start at the bruising pain.

"Why did you do that?" he asked.

Could he see better in the dark than she could? Maybe his eyesight adjusted to the dark more readily than hers since she was accustomed to having light whenever she needed it.

"I'm checking to see if I'm really here."

"Do you feel this?" His fingers skimmed along her arm.

"Yes." The caress was light, exquisitely so, yet it seared her skin, making her keenly aware of his calluses and the pressure of his hands.

He drew a line to her shoulder. "And that?"

The stroke scorched her deeper, sending heat all the way to her middle. She closed her eyes, not sure whether to savor the delicious sensation or to fight against it. "I thought we just agreed on no touching."

His fingers found her hair, and he twisted a strand between his thumb and forefinger. "I am only helping you determine that you are no longer a vision but are here with me."

Not once had he seemed disturbed by her appearances, easily accepting that a spiritual realm existed and that she had been a part of it.

"Is it helping?" His voice dropped low.

The timbre reverberated inside her, echoing in her chest and ricocheting to every nerve. It sent a hum into her blood—a hum that was exciting and yet at the same time dangerous.

Were his caresses helping? No, they were only confusing her. Because now she had the strangest urge to reach out and touch him in return, wanting to let her fingers roam wherever they pleased. She'd start with his abs.

She gave herself a mental slap. Why was she acting like a hormonal teen around this man instead of a respectable twenty-seven-year-old?

She twisted away from him, forcing his hand away. She couldn't let him cross the line they'd established. Maybe this was all normal flirting for him. But she never flirted. Never had, not even with Isaac. And she wouldn't start now.

- *13* -

NICHOLAS FISTED HIS HANDS ON HIS THIGHS. What was wrong with him? He'd agreed with her about not touching. But then only seconds later, he'd touched her anyway.

Curses upon him. "My apologies. Please forgive me."

"You're fine."

When he'd first met her, he'd determined to treat her like a sister and nothing more. But he had to concede that he couldn't view her in a that way. 'Twas impossible. He was simply too attracted to her.

He pressed his fists to his eyes. If only his desires had remained buried with Jane. But 'twould seem the recent encounter with Lady Ellen had started a storm. Perhaps the suggestion they wed had increased the intensity of the squall. Now his encounters with Sybil were clearly stirring his yearnings into a raging whirlwind.

Could he resist the storm? Did he even want to?

He was, after all, twenty and nine years. Most men his age were long since married. Some men had even been married multiple times.

The question clanged inside his head as it had previously: Was it time to take a wife? If he did so, how would he be any different than his father and Simon, wedding a wife for what he could gain from her? Using her for his own satisfaction and for begetting sons?

He loathed the prospect of being like his kin. He'd wanted to have a different kind of marriage, one based on mutual respect, loyalty, and love. He supposed in some ways, that's why he'd wanted to marry Jane, because he'd shared a heart match with her that he'd never witnessed in his father or brother with any of their wives.

Once Jane was gone, he'd given up hope he'd ever love another woman. The odds of having another heart match were unlikely. But could he at least find a woman he cared about and who cared about him? Maybe they wouldn't share love, but they could share respect and loyalty. Couldn't they?

He'd do best to wait until that kind of maiden came along. Yes, he had to resist this storm of desire that seemed bent on overcoming him. And that meant keeping his hands off Sybil.

The simple truth was that he had to control himself. He wasn't sure how much longer she'd be in his life. She'd indicated she was only here temporarily, and during her stay, he didn't want to hurt her or cause her to have any regrets.

"Why is Simon trying to kill you?" Her question was direct. Though he'd given her a vague answer about why he was in trouble during their first encounter, he sensed this time she wouldn't be satisfied with anything less than a truthful answer.

"There are many reasons." He situated her jacket against the cave wall and leaned against it gingerly, trying to minimize the pain.

She waited in silence. Even though the cave was dark, he could see her outline and that she'd crossed her arms to ward off the chill from rinsing in the river.

"Foremost, Simon wants me to reveal details about fortifications along the coast. The French have paid him to give them useful details as they strategize an attack, and he grows desperate to deliver. Since I am a courier for the king, he believes I am relaying important information to the coastal towns."

"And are you?"

"I am carrying news of the plague throughout Kent."

"While you carry the news, you're also relaying fortification instructions to the coastal towns."

"'Tis what Simon believes."

"He's correct."

"He is a cunning snake. In order to deflect suspicion away from himself, he has accused me of being a spy for the French."

"He believes if he tortures you, you'll share what you know in order to prove yourself loyal to the English."

In so short a time, she'd obviously picked up on many clues. How had she so quickly deduced the current predicament?

"He has smeared your good name," she continued, "and now you are on the run for your life."

"Precisely."

"Is there a way to prove he's the one spying for the French and to clear your name?"

"I have memorized a secret code from a French missive I found on his writing table. If I am able to decipher it, I may be able to establish his involvement."

"And if you fail to prove he is a spy?"

"I shall have little choice but to live out my days as an outlaw of the Weald."

"Then there are other outlaws living in the Weald? And you will join forces with them?"

"Many of the outlaws are people I know well already."

Her curt questions came to an end although he suspected she had more she wanted to ask.

There was so much he wanted to know about her as well. But where did he start his questions without overwhelming her? Could he inquire about her brother and why he needed holy water?

Before Nicholas could formulate a question, a call echoed in the forest outside the cave. He'd been careful to camouflage the opening. He didn't think anyone would be able to find them. But for now, they needed to stay silent.

He leaned against her shoulder and tilted his mouth toward her ear. "Simon's men are near."

She nodded.

He didn't push himself away from her. Resting lightly against her eased some of the strain against his back. As though sensing the same, she did nothing to dislodge herself, allowing him this contact.

For long minutes, she didn't move or speak. And he was impressed again by her ability to remain calm under such trying circumstances.

When the voices drew closer and stopped outside the cave, he inched his dagger out only to find that she'd also withdrawn her knife. He hadn't seen a woman use a knife proficiently before. Most were ignorant of how to protect themselves with a weapon or otherwise. But Sybil held the knife correctly, and likely was as skilled with it as she was with everything else.

Perhaps if Jane had been trained in some basic weaponry, she would have been able to defend herself better. . . .

He closed his eyes and tried to block out the image of her lifeless and battered body after he'd recovered it. Her brother Eric had been the one to discover their mother. Both women—among many others—had been weak and defenseless, unable to protect themselves.

After discovering the abuses and atrocities perpetrated by the French during their destruction of Rye, Nicholas had taken a band of archers and gone after the raiders. They'd met up with the enemy at Dover while the rest of the French fleet waited offshore. They'd easily decimated the raiders, repaying them twice over for all they'd done.

But the killing of his enemies hadn't brought him peace. Rather, it had only added to the torment in his soul—a torment that had stayed with him ever since.

Sybil didn't take her attention from the opening.

Even after the voices faded, she remained motionless and alert, as if she was prepared for a diversionary tactic, where the guards pretended to go away to lure them out.

They waited soundlessly for the better part of an hour. Nicholas suspected the guards were well on their way out of the Weald. Even with torches to light their path, the superstitions surrounding the woodland were too numerous. They wouldn't want to linger any longer than they had to now that darkness had fallen.

Even so, Nicholas didn't plan to take any chances tonight, lest a remnant had stayed behind.

Finally, he sheathed his dagger. As he did so, Sybil must have taken that as the sign that they were safe, for she slipped her knife into a casing inside her boot.

"We shall remain for now," he whispered near her ear as he had before.

"Good call."

He started to push away from her, needing to put the proper distance between them again.

She stopped him with a touch of his arm. "You can keep leaning against me . . . if that's more comfortable for your back."

He should have guessed she'd notice his discomfort. She didn't seem to miss a single detail.

Was he wise to consider her offer? Surely, the contact for a short while longer wouldn't compromise his resolve to keep his hands off her.

"Thank you." He situated himself again so that his shoulder was propped against hers, easing the pressure of having to lean his back against the cave. "Since I have informed you about my brother, now you must tell me about yours. Did the holy water heal him as you had hoped?"

Her muscles tensed against him as though in protest of the topic.

"Unless you would rather not discuss the matter—"

"He refused to drink it."

"Then he has no wish to be healed?"

She expelled a sigh, one laced with frustration. "He told me he doesn't want my help and to leave and never come back."

"That is why you do not know how long you will stay here?"

"It's complicated."

"I should like to know how the visions of you come and go. You claim you are not an angel or saint or witch. But from whence do you hail? From heaven or someplace in between?"

"Neither." She paused as though trying to figure out how to explain in a way he could understand. "I'm from a different time and place altogether. Drinking a little bit of the holy water allowed me the short visits with you. On the last occasion, I drank more, and now I'm here until I'm called back."

"The holy water is indeed powerful. 'Tis another reason Simon seeks my death. I inhibited him from having control over the St. Sepulchre wellspring that contains the holy water."

"Then you believe me that I'm here because the holy water brought me?"

"I have heard of its healing power. But naught of this visiting from another time and place. Nevertheless, I have no reason to doubt you."

"Thank you."

He wished he could prevent her from leaving. "Does your brother have the power to call you back to your time and place?"

"Only if he has the holy water to do so, which he doesn't."

A kink of tension eased from Nicholas's shoulders.

"Even if he did have it, he made it clear he doesn't want me in his life anymore." Her whisper this time was drenched with despair.

He'd felt much despair in his life and knew platitudes wouldn't make the feeling disappear. Instead, he gathered her hand in his. She didn't stiffen as she had the other times he'd held it. Perhaps she was growing accustomed to his hold. Or perhaps she needed the comfort of having someone understand her heartache.

"The distance away will help him realize how valuable you are."

"Am I valuable?"

"You have been to me. If you had not liberated me, I would be a dead man."

"Even if Dawson never misses me, I knew I had to come and help you."

Her whisper tickled his neck. That meant her mouth was close—close enough that all he had to do was shift a fraction, and he could lay claim to her lips. He had no doubt she would kiss with the same intensity that characterized everything she did. There would be no timidity or coyness or reluctance.

Just the thought of such a kiss sent a jolt of heat through his blood.

No. This wasn't the time or place to let his mind stray. He had to think of something else. "Did Dawson give you the cut on your chin?"

She hesitated. "He didn't mean it, wasn't himself, wouldn't have considered throwing things at me before Mum disappeared."

He pictured her chin, her lips, then kissing those pretty lips. Again.

Curses upon him. "Tell me about your mother."

"Only if you tell me about yours."

"Anything." Anything to distract him from doing something he'd regret.

- *14* -

S$_{\text{YBIL}}$ LOVED TALKING WITH HIM. In fact, she couldn't remember ever talking so much to one person in a single setting. Not even to her mum.

But she conversed with Nicholas for hours about everything. She told him about her dad abandoning their family when she'd been five, how he'd run off with another woman and had never been a part of their lives after that.

She tried to explain her mum's work at tracking down and catching terrorists, but she found it difficult to help him understand the devastation and fear that modern people experienced with criminals who bombed public places or hijacked airplanes. It was equally hard describing her work as an investigator. But he was fascinated to hear about her training in kickboxing and in other defense techniques.

He told her about his mother, Lady Theresa, and his frustration that she had to live with Simon. As the youngest son, Nicholas wouldn't inherit any land or estates. If he made a good match to a wealthy noblewoman, then he might change his fortunes. But what he was hoping for was a gift from the king—land in the Weald for his devoted service over the past ten years. Then he could finally build a home of his own and give his mother refuge there.

But King Richard was busy, not only with the ongoing war with France, but he'd faced recent unrest with an uprising among the poorest laborers in the country. Nicholas recounted the details last year when bands of rebels had gone through the Kent countryside, forcing noblemen to join their cause. Eventually, thousands of rebels had gathered outside of London to meet with the king, but after several tense days of murdering and looting, the leaders of the rebellion had been caught.

Nicholas also told her about the plague that was beginning to ravage England and spoke about how it had devastated the country thirty years earlier. She remembered some details about what had become known as the Black or Bubonic Plague, but it was different hearing about it firsthand. Now with the new outbreak, people were panicking. She didn't blame them, couldn't imagine a life without modern medicine.

At some point she must have dozed. She wasn't sure how, since usually she struggled to fall asleep. But perhaps the fresh air combined with the physical exertion had worn her out.

She awoke suddenly to find strong arms wrapped around her and her head cushioned by a broad bicep. A broad, bare bicep.

For a moment, she attempted to gain her bearings. She was still in the past in the cave with Nicholas. Faint light slanted through the brush at the cave opening to reveal dawn.

Although cramped, they were both lying on the ground, and he was behind her, his arms surrounding her, the length of him pressed against the length of her backside.

Were they spooning?

A flush climbed into her cheeks. Yes, it seemed possible they were doing just that.

How had this happened?

No doubt he'd lain on his side to make himself more comfortable and to take the pressure off his injured back. And perhaps she'd curled up against him for his body heat in the dropping temperature of the night. In the process, he'd wrapped her up to keep her warm.

That was all there was to the spooning. Absolutely all.

Even so, she needed to extricate herself. With the attraction toward Nicholas that flared so easily, she had to put some distance between them.

She started to shift. But as Nicholas expelled a weary breath near her neck, she held herself motionless. With his injuries and the cold, perhaps he hadn't slept well. If he was finally resting, she couldn't wake him yet. She could wait for a little while before moving, couldn't she?

Allowing her body to relax, she replayed the last twelve hours of being in the past, marveling again that this all felt so real. But was it? If so, what was happening to her body in the present time?

When Isaac showed up for work and saw her car still parked where it had been yesterday, he would be worried. If her mobile still had any battery life, he'd be able to track her to the closet. If not, he probably wouldn't consider searching the castle for her, might even assume she'd been kidnapped by Dr. Lionel.

What would Dawson think when she ended up missing just like Mum? Would he regret his last words to her?

Her heart gave a beat of protest at the prospect of hurting Dawson. But then she pushed aside her concern. Her disappearance wouldn't bother him. She'd given him what he wanted—no more nagging or interference in his life.

Even so, she'd be wise to work out how to put more holy water into one of the hiding places so she'd be ready to go back if she found herself in too much danger. Maybe she'd search for the wellspring at St. Sepulchre Nicholas had mentioned. Yes, that's what she'd do. Once she made sure Nicholas was well away from Simon's men and safe from recapture, she'd venture onward to Canterbury.

Nicholas released another breath against her neck, and before she knew what was happening, his lips brushed against her pulse.

The caress was so light she could almost believe he'd done so unconsciously, shifting his head in his sleep and making contact without realizing it. The slight touch of his lips to her neck brought her to complete wakefulness. Rapid messages zipped along her nerve endings, making her keenly aware of him and his beautiful body.

One of his hands slid over her arm, and he rubbed gently, as if to chase away the chill there. The other slipped to her waist, and his fingers found the bare patch of skin where her shirt had crept up. The touches in both places roused a sharp but sweet need deep inside. But before she could make sense of the contact, his lips pressed against her neck again, this time fully.

Pleasure coursed through her, almost explosively. She nearly gasped but closed her eyes and willed herself not to react.

His lips didn't linger. Instead, he mumbled softly and incoherently, confirming that he was still asleep, that he didn't realize he was overstepping the boundaries they'd established.

Was he thinking about her in his sleep? Or someone else?

"Sybil," he whispered, answering her question. His fingers at her waist slipped upward, grazing underneath her shirt near her ribs.

She gave a start and placed her hand over his to halt his exploration before he moved too high. As she did so, he released a soft moan and brought his mouth against her neck more forcefully. The pressure was hot and hungry, and it sent a charge of electricity through her veins that lit her whole body with need.

Although he might be half-asleep and not aware of all he was doing, she was wholly cognizant and had to put a stop to this interaction.

"We can't," she whispered, but somehow her voice came out low and full of wanting. As much as she knew she needed to break the connection, she couldn't force herself to move, didn't want to leave his arms.

He made her feel things she hadn't experienced in ages too, maybe never.

At the rustle of the nearby brush and sudden light pouring over them, she froze. Nicholas stilled too, and his breathing changed.

"And what have we here?" came a voice with a thicker accent, like someone from West Midlands with a Brummie dialect.

Nicholas relaxed and laid his head back against her

bunched-up coat, which apparently he'd used as a pillow. She felt the cold hilt of his dagger as he rested it against her hip. She hadn't noticed him unsheathing it. In the next instant, he had it hidden again, which assured her that the newcomers posed no threat.

"Ye clarting about in there, Nicholas?" Rounded eyes amidst a fleshy face peered at them. A middle-aged man with a mostly bald head. A kind face but one that was rapidly turning red.

"No, we're not doing anything, Father Fritz." Nicholas attempted to extricate himself, but in the process he landed on top of her, his body pressing down, making them appear guilty of indulging in intimacies.

"Then why, my dear son, are ye both stripped down to nothing?"

More curious faces filled the mouth of the cave, taking in their sleeping arrangement, which she could admit looked compromising.

"I can explain," Nicholas said.

"No explanation needed, sire." One of the men guffawed. "We all know well enough how things work."

His bawdy comment brought more laughter.

"Stand back." A command boomed from outside the cave. The men staring inside disappeared, and another man poked his head inside, his face thin and severe. He swept his gaze over them, then shook his head curtly. "God's bones, Nicholas. What are you doing?"

"It be plenty clear." Father Fritz spoke just outside the cave. "Nicholas is fornicating."

Nicholas released a long sigh. "I am not fornicating."

Sybil could only stare up at him. He was still perched in a compromising position above her. A part of her wanted to laugh at the situation. Another part of her burned with embarrassment that these men assumed she and Nicholas had engaged in sex.

The man with the severe expression pinned a hard look upon Nicholas. "Is this woman your wife?"

"No—"

"Then she will be soon."

Nicholas glanced down at her, and his eyes held an apology.

She bit back a smile, the unraveling of their predicament growing more ludicrous by the second.

"Now, get dressed." The severe man glanced over his shoulder warily. "We need to be on our way before Lord Worth's men return." He pulled back from the entrance and barked several orders to the others outside to give Nicholas a chance to get decent.

Nicholas shook his head and pushed away from her. Even then, in the tight space, the process of sitting up was tricky without touching each other.

"I am heartily sorry, Sybil," he whispered as he combed his fingers through his loose hair and began to tie it back with the leather strip. Every muscle in his chest and arms rippled as he did so. The dark scruff on his face was thicker, making him more gorgeous in the morning light—so much that her stomach flipped end over end.

She attempted to work her fingers through her own hair,

but the strands were still damp and tangled. She wound it into a knot and secured it in place with her hair tie, hoping she could find a brush at some point. Were brushes invented yet? Or were there only combs?

Nicholas finished with his hair. "I vow, I shall do my best to repair your reputation."

"I'm not worried about it." She supposed in the Middle Ages, she would be seen as a loose woman for having spent the night with Nicholas. But it didn't matter what people thought when she and Nicholas knew the truth.

She reached for her coat, but he shook his head. "Ralph," he said to the severe man who had positioned himself with his back facing the cave opening, clearly guarding their privacy. "Will you please find a cloak for Sybil?"

The man shouted out a question to the others, and an instant later, he tossed two thick gray garments into the cavern.

Nicholas handed one to her. "Put this on."

She didn't argue with him, especially since her coat was still damp. As he wrapped a cloak around his shoulders, she followed his lead, the wool scratchy and containing a smoky scent. But it was heavy and warm. And after being chilled for the past hours, the covering was blessedly welcome.

She followed Nicholas out of the cave into the brush alongside the river and was surprised to see at least a dozen men with bows hanging from their shoulders and quivers at their belts. Two of them were now cloakless, but the rest wore matching gray cloaks with their hoods up. Except for the man Nicholas had addressed as Father Fritz. He was attired in a long robe, and a leather belt circled his rotund waist.

All eyes settled upon her, and she did her best to keep a casual and calm stance. In her profession, she was used to being the only woman in a group of men. But being the lone woman here unsettled her. When Nicholas didn't release her hand, she was more relieved than she wanted to admit.

The commander of the group—Ralph—stared at her as openly as the other men. But instead of curiosity, his narrowed eyes held suspicion. He was an unusually tall man—close to two meters—and slender and wiry. His face was marred by several large scars and a misshapen nose. With his blond hair threaded with white, she guessed he was in his midlife. Like the others, he had a bow hanging over his shoulder.

The bows were longer than usual, almost as tall as the men themselves. Although she didn't know much about bows and arrows, she suspected they were using longbows.

Nicholas straightened, pulling himself up almost regally. She was fascinated that she could so easily see the differences in their social classes just from the way the men held themselves. Nicholas was nobly born. And Ralph stood with a bearing of someone who had rank. But the rest were common folk with rougher skin and stooped shoulders of men accustomed to hard work.

"We received news of your capture only yesterday." Ralph was the first to speak. "When we got word that Lord Worth's men were in the forest, we suspected you'd escaped."

"Sybil is the one who set me free." Nicholas caught her gaze, his eyes filled with gratefulness.

Ralph watched Nicholas an extra second before turning his attention upon her. "Thank you."

She nodded.

His silent questions filled the air. Who was she? Where was she from? And how did she know Nicholas enough to come to his rescue?

She sensed in this man a keenness that matched her own and guessed it wouldn't take him too long to piece together the details and realize there was more to her story. He was obviously a friend of Nicholas's, but that didn't mean he would accept her.

Even now, his eyes turned to the sky and narrowed upon a flock of birds rising into the air. "We must go now."

Father Fritz was halfway up into the saddle of one of two horses, and Ralph nodded at the other. "Take my mount."

Nicholas shook his head.

Ralph's gaze slid to Nicholas's now-covered shoulders. "You are badly injured."

"Just my back. Not my feet."

"Then you would have one of the other men ride with your betrothed?"

Nicholas's jaw tightened as did his grip of her hand. "No other man will ride behind her but me."

"You are certain?"

"Let it be known." Nicholas's tone turned steely. "No man dare touch her without incurring my wrath."

Sybil was tempted to remind Nicholas she'd disarmed two guards in his dungeon by herself and didn't need him to threaten the men. But the possessiveness in his tone silenced and weakened her all at once. She didn't understand it, but it only added to the growing awareness of this man.

Ralph nodded. "Very well. Then take her with all haste to the village."

As he turned away from Nicholas, Sybil glimpsed a slight quirk of Ralph's lips. Was he pleased with himself for manipulating Nicholas into riding the horse? Though she would have preferred to run, she respected his concern for Nicholas. She wouldn't complain about having to ride if it spared him the exhaustion of out-racing Simon's men again.

Within moments, she was seated in the saddle with Nicholas directly behind her, her body wedged tightly against his. When he reached around her for the reins, his chest pressed against her back. His chiseled Greek-god chest that she couldn't stop thinking about.

"I apologize again for this misunderstanding with my men." His soft comment near her ear sent flutters through her abdomen.

"You want them to believe I'm your betrothed?"

"'Tis for the best."

"Why?" Was she baiting him, trying to get him to admit that he liked her? "Never mind. It doesn't matter."

"It matters to me." Again, his voice rumbled next to her ear, much too intimate, reminding her of the delectable kisses he'd placed on her neck before he was awake. She was embarrassed that she wanted to feel his lips there again.

"You saved my life." He dug his heels into the mount's sides. "Now 'tis my turn to make sure you are safe. Whatever that entails."

For a reason she didn't understand, his explanation disappointed her. She didn't want him to be with her because he was repaying her. Strangely she wanted more, though she knew she shouldn't.

~ 15 ~

NICHOLAS PURPOSEFULLY SLOWED THE MOUNT for the last league of the journey, not ready for the time with Sybil to end.

Even though it was a form of ecstatic torture having her sitting in front of him, his thighs gripping her, his arms encircling her, his chest brushing against her, he wouldn't give this ride over to any other man. He wouldn't give *her* to any other man.

In fact, the more he'd considered anyone else having her, the harder his heart pounded in protest.

Though they'd ridden hard for several hours, it hadn't been so vigorous as to prevent conversation. Father Fritz on his mount had lagged a short distance behind, allowing them some privacy. As with the previous night, she'd been curious and had asked many questions. This time, she'd wanted to know about the Weald, the band of archers expertly trained by Ralph de Legh, and Devil's Bend, the village where hopefully they would be able to avoid Simon's searches.

She shifted again, as she'd been doing more over the past hour. Since she wasn't accustomed to riding a horse, her hindquarters were likely sore. He'd considered stopping and allowing her to have a respite, but they were nearing the end of their journey, and she would be free from the saddle soon enough.

All morn and through the afternoon, he'd pushed onward, an urgency driving him to cross through the bishop's land and enter the deep Weald. Though Simon's men might venture through the outer perimeter of the forestland in spite of their superstitions, they would never enter the heart of the Weald that many believed belonged to the devil. At least he hoped so.

She twisted to watch a doe grazing with its mother in a hedge. "So, most of the men who live in Devil's Bend have been wrongly accused and aren't true criminals?"

"Father Fritz was convicted of being a spy for the French."

"That seems to be a common crime."

"London's prisons are filled with many alleged spies."

She paused, contemplating his sad statement. "And what of Ralph? Is he an outlaw?"

"His son, one of King Richard's archers, was accused of stealing royal jewels by the man who committed the thievery. He was taken out to the gallows to be hanged, and Ralph intervened."

"Now he's a wanted criminal too?"

Nicholas nodded. "His son was wounded during the escape and only lived a fortnight."

She fell silent, likely moved by the weight of the injustice every bit as much as he'd been. He liked that she was compassionate and felt things deeply. He liked that she didn't have to fill the lull in moments like this with needless chatter. He liked that she could oft make conclusions for herself without him needing to tell her every detail.

The truth was, the longer he was with her, the more things he liked about her. In fact, the list was growing quite lengthy.

Did he dare contemplate Ralph's declaration that he marry her once they arrived at Devil's Bend? Ralph hadn't needed to say aught for Nicholas to understand the man's reasoning. The time alone in the cave had damaged Sybil's reputation, especially because they'd been in a state of indecent attire. He'd made things worse by practically jumping on top of her.

In addition, his own reputation was at risk. He'd spoken against men using women to sate their lusts, had opposed and punished archers who did so during warfare, and made sure that no outlaws remained in the deep Weald who abused women.

If he didn't marry her, would he be guilty of violating his own rules? Would he lose the respect of those who held him to a higher standard?

Why not wed her this very night?

Heat circled low in his gut at the prospect of sharing another night with her, but this time as her husband, with nothing holding him back from letting his hands roam where they pleased and kissing her anytime he wanted.

But even as his desire twisted within tightly, he despised himself for having such feelings and thoughts. He'd resolved not to marry a woman to fulfill his own urges. And here he was, selfishly considering it.

No, if he made Sybil his wife, he'd allow for mutual affection to develop, and he would wait until she was comfortable with him before consummating.

After all, he'd waited three years for Jane. Surely he could be patient now, too, so that he didn't turn into a brute.

She fiddled with her cloak, scratching her neck where the wool rubbed. He could tell she wanted to take the cloak off, had even started to at one point as the day had grown warmer. But he'd stopped her with a touch to her arm and a nod toward Father Fritz.

"Since you weren't an outlaw until recently, how did you become connected with the deep Weald and Devil's Bend?"

"I grew up in the Weald—"

"The real reason, Nicholas."

Her directness always sent a strange thrill through him. But not this time. This time, he didn't want to answer. How could he? The truth was too complicated, too horrific, too devastating.

Splashes of sunshine broke through the leafy canopy overhead as if to dispel his dark thoughts. The chatter of the thrushes and blackbirds softened the tension within him as did the sight of the wildflowers in the meadow ahead. If only someday he could have a home in a place like this. He could easily picture a manor house tucked away on the edge of the meadow with sheep grazing nearby. He'd have goats and geese and a cow. And he'd have tenants to grow crops and help with the shearing.

He wanted a simple life away from the peril that threatened on every side, a place where he could keep his family safe, a refuge he could finally give to his mother, a home where he could prevent anyone from hurting those he loved.

"It has to do with the woman you lost." Sybil spoke quietly and with certainty.

She'd already guessed about his lost love during a prior conversation. He might as well admit it. There was no reason not to. "Yes. It has to do with her."

"And you loved her?"

"Very much."

Silence settled between them, but it wasn't awkward. Instead, just the small amount of sharing seemed to have lifted a portion of the burden he'd been bearing by himself. What would happen if he gave himself permission to share it all? She'd said she was a good listener.

As they crossed the meadow and plunged into another portion of the forest, his stomach gurgled with hunger pangs that had been increasing with every passing hour. Except for the one meal his mother had brought to him in the dungeons, he hadn't eaten in days. Although Sybil hadn't complained, he guessed she was hungry too.

"In addition to horse riding," she said, as he maneuvered the horse up a rocky ascent, "you must teach me how to use a bow and arrow."

The incline pressed her more fully to him, and he relished the weight of her body against his. "What if I am a terrible at it?"

"Then you wouldn't be leading a band of archers."

"Ralph is the leader—a Cheshire bowman, one of the best in all the land. His father was recruited by the Black Prince as one of the first mounted archers, and he helped bring victory to the English in Poitiers. 'Tis said the archers drew so fast and furiously that the sky became dark with the thickness of the arrows."

"I didn't know arrows were effective against plate armor."

"An ordinary bow, no. But a longbow is powerful enough to pierce iron, leaving knights at the mercy of a skilled archer. That makes a bowman worth ten regular soldiers."

As they reached level ground, she continued to recline against him, clearly lost in thought, probably processing all that he was telling her and drawing conclusions of her own.

He liked her interest in the subject. But it was unusual to be having this kind of discussion with a woman. "Ralph's father claimed that in the Battle of Crécy, the longbow archers killed two thousand French knights and the English lost only fifty men."

"If that's so, then maybe people stay away from the deep Weald because they fear the archers more than the devil."

"Perhaps 'tis some of both." He bent and let the loose tangles of her hair brush his face. The strands had long since dried, and he wanted to let her hair loose from the knot she'd fashioned. Instead he wrapped the reins around his hand more securely to keep himself from doing so.

She dropped her gaze to his fisted hand on his thigh before training it on the forest ahead. "You've yet to tell me how you became good at the longbow."

"You are assuming much."

"Then prove me wrong." Her voice contained a low challenge.

Something about it shot raw desire through him like an arrowhead hitting the center of a target. Saint's blood.

He uncurled his fingers with the need to press a hand to her hip and hold her more possessively. But at the sight of

Father Fritz drawing alongside them, he rested his hand against his thigh once more.

"Praise be, we're almost there," the priest called. "This noggy body can't take what it used to when I was in my prime."

"Tell me, Father," Sybil said. "Who is the best archer in the Weald?"

Father Fritz released a merry laugh. "Why, yer riding with him, bab."

Sybil shifted enough that Nicholas could see the start of a smug smile upon her lips. "I'll look forward to my first lesson."

Had he seen her smile yet? He couldn't remember one. Was this as close as she came? "If I give you archery lessons, then you will teach me your kickboxing."

"Right."

Did her easy acquiescence mean she wouldn't be in a hurry to travel onward from the Weald? And if she did, where would she go? He couldn't imagine allowing her to just walk away. Even if she was able to defend herself proficiently, she'd only find herself in trouble sooner or later.

All the more reason to consider marrying her. Then she'd have no reason to leave.

"Ye will be needing a place of yer own now, my dear son." Father Fritz fanned his flushed face as he rode beside them. His wide forehead was dotted with perspiration, and his tonsured hair stuck to his head, the heat of the day proving to be the most summerlike they'd had yet.

"I shall stay with Ralph and Beatrice like I usually do."

"Ye can take my home. Ye'll be wanting the privacy."

Father Fritz glanced pointedly at Sybil and then made a kissing motion.

The sight of the portly man's puckered mouth and rolled eyes would have made Nicholas laugh under any other circumstance. But at the insinuation that he'd want to be alone with Sybil while he took her to bed, flames skimmed through him, scorching him.

Father Fritz ended with a knowing nod. "It's sure good to see that yer gawking over a woman. Can hardly keep those hands to yerself, can ye?"

Nicholas pressed his lips together to stop from reprimanding Father Fritz. The rebuke wouldn't do any good since it never had previously. The priest was helplessly outspoken.

"Mighty fine to see you agog for once."

"Gawking?" Sybil murmured, another smirk playing at her lips. "Agog?"

He shot a glare at Father Fritz.

The priest's smile only widened, and he made kissing motions in the air again, this time loud enough so that Sybil could hear them.

She ducked her head.

"Father," Nicholas whispered harshly, as if the whispering could prevent her from hearing his conversation with the priest. "Cease the lewdness at once." He kicked his horse ahead of Father Fritz's, his gaze sliding back to Sybil. "I apologize—"

He expected to behold blushing cheeks, wide surprised eyes, even mortification crinkling her forehead. Instead, she was shaking with muffled laughter.

The humor in her gaze and the turned-up corners of her mouth made her more beautiful than before. After a moment, he allowed himself to grin, relieved she hadn't been offended and had instead found the same amusement in the priest that he oft did.

Before he had a chance to say more, the forestland gave way to a clearing and a cluster of thatched wattle-and-daub cottages. In the common lands beyond, the flocks of shorn sheep were grazing, their bodies bare except for the tufts left around their feet and head.

After living with and visiting the outlaws of Devil's Bend from time to time over the past five years, he'd learned a great deal about the wool industry, the main way the community earned money to buy and trade for the items they couldn't produce themselves.

There were no signs of the pigs that had already been put out to pannage to feast and fatten by autumn slaughter. But the geese wandered about the meadow, many with goslings waddling close behind.

At the sight and sound of their horses trotting toward the village, calls rose, and women stepped out of their doorways or rose from where they were kneeling in their herb and vegetable gardens. The handful of children who lived in the village ceased their duties or play. Curious but wary gazes settled upon Sybil.

Nicholas slowed his horse to a walk as he passed by the first of the homes, all of them with smoke curling up from a center hole in the thatched roofs, their shutters open to allow in the freshness of the spring day.

When he reached the middle of the village, he halted. He

had no choice, not with Beatrice blocking the grassy road, both hands on her ample hips. In a simple tunic and wimple, she was a plain woman with a dusting of freckles on her face. Her stature stretched wide, with thick arms and shoulders. No one dared to contradict Beatrice. And no one wanted to face her wrath.

She cupped a hand over her eyes to shield them from the sunshine. "So the men freed you, did they?"

"I have Sybil to thank for the rescue."

At Sybil's name, Beatrice shifted her attention. As she took in the half-open cloak along with Sybil's immodest attire underneath, her brows drew together.

Although he'd kept his hands to himself the majority of the ride, he reached for Sybil's waist, his fingers fanning over her possessively. The move was almost instinctual, and he did it without thinking about why, except that he wanted to protect her from anyone who might question who she was and what she was doing with him.

Immediately Beatrice focused on his hold of Sybil.

He pressed his lips together, hoping Beatrice could understand his silent message that he expected the village women to treat Sybil with respect. Yes, the situation appeared to be indecent, and Sybil looked like a woman of ill repute. But if Beatrice accepted and treated her kindly, then everyone else would take that as their cue to do likewise.

"Sybil." He spoke as formally as he could. "This is Beatrice, Ralph de Legh's wife. She is like a second mother to me, and I pray she will become that to you as well."

Beatrice's gaze darted between Sybil and him several times

before she settled upon his face. After a moment, she broke into a grin, revealing the wide gap between her top front teeth. "Nicholas Worth has finally found himself a woman."

~ *16* ~

NICHOLAS'S WOMAN?

Sybil opened her mouth to refute the claim, but Father Fritz, who had reined in next to them, spoke before she could. "Aye, Nicholas is agog with the sweet bab."

Agog. She nearly smiled again, especially when Nicholas squeezed her, as if to remind her of Father Fritz smooching at the air just a few moments ago. She didn't need reminding. The image of Father Fritz's portly lips puckering passionately at nothing was burned into her memory.

She glanced at Nicholas.

He lifted his brows, giving her full view of his rich brown eyes, which were twinkling. Even though he wasn't grinning, she could sense the barely banked smile.

Father Fritz began to dismount. "He's so agog, he'll be marrying her before the day is through, that he will."

Before the day is through? Yes, the men had alluded to her being betrothed. Ralph had insinuated that she and Nicholas should get married. But no one had mentioned actually having a wedding today. She started to protest, but in the next instant Nicholas leaned in to her ear.

At the warmth of his lips, the rasp of his breath, the

pressure of his mouth—her protest died, and she could suddenly think of nothing else but his nearness.

"Only if you agree to it," came his earnest statement.

This man. Her body melted into him. How could she do anything but agree to whatever he wanted?

She gave herself a mental shake. What was happening to her? Where was the solid sense of reasoning she'd always prided herself in having?

Beatrice was watching her and Nicholas with keen interest, likely reading too much into their interaction.

"Have no fear," Nicholas whispered against her ear again. "I shall never force anything upon you."

He'd proven himself to be noble and true. And she didn't have any fear of him. In fact, she wanted to lean her head back and let him go on whispering in her ear forever.

But at Beatrice's growing smile, Sybil forced herself to break the connection with Nicholas.

"I'm tickled pinker than a piglet's belly." Father Fritz finished dismounting and positioned himself next to Beatrice. The two beamed up at Nicholas and her as if they were staring at the king and queen.

Sybil had to put an end to this nonsense before it got further out of hand. She started to slip her leg over the saddle intending to descend the way cowboys did in the movies. But her foot caught in the cloak, tangling her, so that she tumbled against Nicholas's broad chest again.

He steadied her, then he slid down with a grace and ease that put even the best cowboy to shame. When he reached up for her, he settled his hands on her waist. As he lifted her down, she held her breath, expecting him to take advantage of the closeness by brushing against her. Dare she admit she was hoping for the contact?

Although his eyes turned to dark brown liquid fuel, he set her down a respectable distance away. He didn't immediately release his grip on her waist, and for a second he seemed to be waging an inner war, forcing himself to let go and take a step back.

All the while, Beatrice and Father Fritz continued to watch them with goofy grins.

"I agree, Father Fritz." Beatrice stepped up to Nicholas and patted his cheeks like a proud mother would do. Maybe in some ways, he'd been a son to her after she'd lost her own. "After all these years and all the heartache, you deserve some happiness of your own."

Nicholas didn't contradict Beatrice. And Sybil guessed this again had to do with the woman he'd lost, the one he'd admitted he'd loved. Did he still love her?

Beatrice turned to face Sybil, bringing large hands up to her cheeks and patting them just as she'd done to Nicholas's. The woman's fingers smelled of onion, as though she'd just come from the cutting board. But Sybil remained where she was, sensing Beatrice's acceptance was important in this outlaw community.

"You come with me now." Beatrice clutched Sybil's arm. "I'll take good care of you and get you ready for the wedding."

Was this woman really serious about a wedding today? She couldn't be. Things like this didn't happen, did they?

Nicholas caught Sybil's gaze and nodded, his eyes

reassuring her as his words had a moment ago that he wouldn't force himself or a marriage upon her no matter what anyone else might say.

She blew out a breath and allowed the woman to pull her along toward the open door of a home that reminded her of the displays at the living history museum in West Sussex. Gone were the bright-white paint, smooth walls with perfectly aligned beams, and neatly woven thatch. Instead, the daub—the hard mixture of clay, dung, and straw that covered the home—was rough and grainy and even crumbling in places. The wattle posts were coarse. And the thatch was misshapen, straw poking out at odd angles.

"Sustenance first, Beatrice." Nicholas's statement held the authority of one used to ordering people around. "She has not eaten all day."

"I'm guessing you haven't eaten all week," Beatrice quipped over her shoulder.

"I would not turn down a meal."

"Then come in with you, and I'll feed that bottomless stomach of yours." Beatrice spoke with false exasperation, since it was obvious she doted on Nicholas and would give him every crumb in her house.

As Sybil entered the dark interior, a pungent scent greeted her, like bacon fat but much stronger. Though the day was warm, a low fire burned upon the center hearth. There was no chimney to capture the smoke. Instead the haze lingered throughout the room, appearing to exit out windows as well as a hole in the roof.

"I was nearly finished making rushlights." Beatrice crossed

to a kettle where some of the rushes were still soaking. She gathered them up and laid them next to the others drying on a rack.

From what Sybil could quickly glean, the rushes somehow accumulated the fat in the hollow pith. She guessed that once lit, the tallow inside burned similar to a candle.

Nicholas entered the cottage behind them, and Beatrice nodded at a trestle table with benches on either side. "Sit down, and I'll have some pottage heated in two shakes of a lamb's tail."

The home was about the size of Sybil's bedroom in her flat, with only crudely made furniture and the barest of kitchenware. There was no sight of a bed, and she guessed Beatrice and Ralph slept on pallets on the earthen floor.

Instead of crossing to the table, Nicholas came directly toward Sybil, only stopping when he was but a hand's length away. In the low lighting and with the tight confines, his presence was overpowering and yet strangely exciting.

"Sybil will sit and eat with me." As he spoke the words to Beatrice, he held out a hand to Sybil, both his words and actions setting in place a precedent, one that said he considered her his equal and positioned her in a hierarchy above Beatrice.

Sybil hesitated. "I can serve myself."

"As my future wife, you are a guest here just as I am."

Future wife. Did he want to marry her?

His eyes were dark, and the dim lighting kept her from reading them.

Regardless of this marriage issue, she had to make a choice. How did she want the people to view her? As nobility? Equal to Nicholas?

She didn't exactly like that prospect. Having had a single mum while growing up, she'd never had much extra. She'd learned to work hard for everything she accomplished and earned. The truth was, she could relate better to Beatrice's and the other laborers' way of life than to Nicholas's.

Nicholas didn't wait for her to protest again. Instead, he placed his hand on the small of her back and guided her to the table. Once she was situated on a bench, he took the spot next to her.

All the while Beatrice heated the pottage, she peppered them with questions about how they met and how they managed to escape. Sybil let Nicholas do most of the talking, curious how he would explain her presence and where she'd come from. He didn't mention the holy water or his visions of her, only that she was a family friend staying at the castle and had been able to use her fighting skills to throw the guards off.

Nicholas left his cloak on, but Sybil was suffocating under the wool. Not only was it scratchy, but it was heavy and hot. As Beatrice set mugs of a frothy liquid and bowls of pottage in front of them, Sybil shrugged out of the monstrosity and placed it on the bench beside her.

Beatrice halted midsentence and stared at Sybil's tight T-shirt and jeans. Nicholas darted a sideways glance her way before setting both elbows on the table and focusing intently on his meal.

Sybil stirred the rich mixture that seemed to have a bit of everything—barley, onions, peas, and pieces of meat that looked like chicken but were likely some other wild fowl that made its home in the forest.

"You will find Sybil appropriate attire, will you not?" He directed his question toward Beatrice.

"Of course." Her reply was stricken, and her face contained a pained look. "Did Lord Worth's men . . .?"

Sybil paused in her stirring. "No. Nothing like that. Lord Worth's men didn't harm me in the least."

Beatrice's shoulders heaved, and she pressed a hand over her heart.

"I'm fine. Really."

"I was there with her," Nicholas cut in between bites. "And Sybil is quite good at defending herself."

Beatrice regarded Sybil a moment longer, as though trying to decide whether to believe their assurances. "If you're sure, then I'll go see about borrowing clothes. I think Kat has an extra outfit."

Borrow? Extra outfit? Did that mean most people who lived here in the Devil's Bend only had one set of clothing? Sybil wasn't a huge shopper, ordered most of what she needed online. But still, she couldn't imagine not being able to run to the store to purchase whatever she wanted whenever it suited her.

Beatrice crossed to her and lifted the cloak about her shoulders. "Until you and Nicholas are married, I want you to keep your clothes on."

Nicholas kept eating, his gaze still trained upon his bowl. He didn't seem to show any signs he'd heard Beatrice except that his chewing slowed.

Sybil merely nodded, guessing before long she was going to end up in a skirt whether she wanted to be in one or not. She'd only ever worn a skirt twice in her life—once for an award banquet she'd attended with her mum, and the other time . . . well, it had been for the funeral they'd finally had for Mum when everyone said Cecilia Huxham had been gone too long and the possibility of her surviving was slim, that she was most likely dead.

Sybil stifled a sigh. She most certainly wasn't the feminine sort. But if she didn't wear the appropriate attire for women in 1382, how many more people would assume, like Beatrice, that something horrible had happened to her? Or squirm with discomfort, like Nicholas?

As Beatrice exited, Nicholas let his spoon grow idle. "I meant what I said. We do not have to get married."

"I can't imagine doing so—"

"I can." He stared at his spoon, twisting it absently.

"What? You can't be serious."

"I am entirely serious." His low tone did strange things to her insides, a reaction to him that seemed to only be growing in frequency.

She stared at his profile—the hard jaw, his rigid chin, his firm mouth. If she were ever to consider marrying a man on looks alone, he would win the contest. But after spending close to twenty-four hours with him, she knew he was so much more than a handsome man. Her first impressions of him had been right. He was a man of strong principle and character.

"You may not wish to be married to a knight who is now considered a traitor to his king and country."

"You aren't a traitor."

"I intend to prove my innocence, but it will take some time."

"I know." Was it possible she could help him? After all, this was what she was good at. Investigating, digging up clues, uncovering what no one else could.

He fiddled with the spoon again. "I may not be able to give you many worldly possessions."

"I'm a simple woman and don't need much." Why was she trying to convince him of her worth? She wasn't actually considering marrying him, was she? When she was in a coma in the modern day?

Of course, she'd heard stories of people remaining comatose for years, some even for several decades. But she didn't want that to happen to her. She wasn't in the past to stay. She had to return to her life and Dawson eventually. And she'd left unfinished business with her work. She needed to bring Dr. Lionel to justice for his crimes.

Besides, she'd only just met Nicholas. Even though the chemistry crackled between them, that wasn't enough of a reason to marry him.

"Why?" Her question slipped out.

One of his brows rose as though he didn't understand what she was asking.

"Why would you want to marry me?"

He dropped his attention to his pottage. "You are beautiful and desirable and intelligent and kind. What man would not want to have you?"

"But why you?"

"I am but a man." His voice was full of insinuations.

She wasn't a prude, but she suddenly felt as though the temperature in the room had increased by twenty degrees. She wanted to fan her face, but she kept her fingers wrapped tightly around her spoon.

"While I may have needs," Nicholas spoke hurriedly, "I have no wish to become like my brother, who uses women to feed his lusts. Instead, I should like to be a decent and respectful husband."

Did he not consider that a woman might also have needs? That a marriage could be mutually satisfying? Obviously, she didn't have a great example of that with her parents' marriage, but she'd witnessed others—like Harrison and Ellen—who reveled in a beautiful love and passion together.

"To that end," Nicholas continued, "I would not pressure you to share the marriage bed—until you are comfortable, and we have developed mutual respect and caring."

So, he was telling her they would spend time getting to know and love each other after they wed? Wasn't that what dating was for? Or courtship? She wasn't up on the customs of the Middle Ages, but she guessed that couples had limited opportunities to spend time together and entered into marriages for many reasons other than love. Even so, this proposal was hasty. The entire conversation was absurd.

"I have always wanted children and a family of my own." His voice turned soft. "But over recent years, I could not imagine being with any woman . . ." He fell silent and his expression turned contemplative.

She had no trouble guessing the direction of his thoughts. "Except for her."

He nodded. "I have not considered the possibility of another woman until . . ." He shifted to look at her, and the intensity of his gaze made her breath snag in her chest. He lifted a hand as though he would caress her face, but then reached for his mug instead.

A dozen questions and concerns swirled together and demanded answers. If she was honest with herself, she'd longed to have a family of her own too. Now that she'd lost Dawson, the need pulsed within her even more acutely.

But she couldn't possibly consider staying, getting pregnant, and having children in 1382. What would happen if she woke from her coma in the present day? Or if she died? She wouldn't want innocent children to suffer the loss of a parent on account of her. She already knew how painful that was.

"Why now?" she asked. "Why not wait and spend time getting to know each other first?"

He took a sip of what appeared to be watery beer. "Regrettably, your reputation was tarnished after we stayed together last night. When the men return shortly, they will tell tales and word will soon spread."

"Does that matter?"

"Even without such tales, 'twill be difficult enough for the women to accept you, even if Beatrice takes you under her wing."

"Then they're shallow."

"They would forgive us if we right the wrong we have done."

"But we haven't done any wrong."

"They will not see it that way."

"I'll work it out." Even though she was hungry, the conversation was taking away her appetite.

"You have no home, no protector, no means to survive. I shall offer that to you."

"I'm independent and can fend for myself."

"And where will you live? How will you earn money for food?"

His words gave her pause. She hadn't thought too far ahead, had only considered finding the holy water and placing it in one of the hiding places. But how would she survive while doing so? He was right that she would have no way to buy food or pay for lodging. Even if she searched for temporary work, women didn't hold jobs or have professions in the Middle Ages the same way they did in modern times. She guessed some women partnered with their husbands in a family business. But as a single woman alone? What could she do?

"You will have no recourse but to take to the streets of London selling your body." His tone turned gruff. "And I would lock you up and make you my prisoner before I let that happen."

Even if he was right, surely she didn't have to rush into a marriage. There had to be other options. "What about living with one of the families here in the village and assisting them?"

He hesitated, glancing around.

She followed his gaze. The home reeked of poverty. She doubted Beatrice and Ralph could afford to have her live with them. Could any of the families in the village? They likely wouldn't be able to pay her or even feed her without bringing hardship to themselves.

He took several more bites of pottage before washing it down with the remaining contents of his mug. Then he stood, his back rigid, his eyes on the door. "If you truly have no wish to marry me, I shall make arrangements for you to reside with Beatrice and Ralph."

Was he hurt by her rejection? How could he be when they barely knew each other?

Even so, as he crossed to the door, she sensed his frustration, even his disappointment.

"This doesn't have to do with you, Nicholas. I really do like you."

He halted inside the doorframe but didn't turn to face her.

"But this is all so sudden," she rushed to explain. "And the decision is too important to jump into quickly."

He stood unmoving for a moment, as though waiting for her to say more. But what else could she say?

As though coming to the same conclusion, he ducked outside and strode away.

The moment she was alone, her heart flooded with longing. For him.

- 17 -

"OH, MY HEAVENS." Beatrice stood back from Sybil and placed a hand over her heart. "It's no wonder Nicholas is so taken with you."

Sybil fisted a hand in the coarse woolen cloth which was a dark green. The tunic—as Beatrice had called it—fell to her feet, nearly dragging on the ground over her combat boots—which she'd refused to exchange for other shoes. The sleeves were long too, dangling beyond her wrists.

It was difficult to imagine how women could wear the heavy clothing all throughout the spring and summer. She'd only been attired in the garment for a minute and already she was perspiring and had never wished more for shorts and a T-shirt.

Thank goodness she hadn't put on the linen smock underneath. The cumbersome undergarment would have made the new outfit worse. Her sports bra and panties were fine, even if Beatrice had been scandalized at the sight of Sybil wearing such scanty attire.

"You are so beautiful." Beatrice pressed a hand to Sybil's cheek, her eyes shining with tears. "I never thought I'd see the day when Nicholas would find a maiden to capture his heart.

But it's clear you have done just that."

Had she really captured Nicholas's heart?

"Yes, you have," Beatrice insisted, as though Sybil had spoken her question aloud. "In all these years since losing his beloved Jane, he's never once taken an interest in anyone else."

Jane. So that was *her* name.

Sybil tried to imagine what she'd been like but felt only a strange pang at the idea that Nicholas had loved Jane so deeply and so loyally. Could he ever love like that again?

Attraction and love were two different things. Nicholas was obviously physically attracted to her. And kindly enough, his offer of marriage had come with an abstinence phase, a time of getting to know one another before sharing further intimacies. She respected that. Most men wouldn't have made such a concession.

He hadn't said much about his family but had shared enough for her to know he was motivated by the need to be different from the brother he despised including how he treated women.

"You're going to make Nicholas very happy." Beatrice maneuvered Sybil until she was sitting on the bench at the table. Then she fingered a strand of Sybil's snarled hair, now hanging down her back.

"I don't know." Sybil watched out the open doorway, hoping for a glimpse of Nicholas, but she hadn't seen him since he'd walked away nearly an hour ago.

"It's easy to see you care about him too."

"Is it?"

"Clear as a summer sky."

"We've only just met."

"My parents made my marriage arrangement." Beatrice gently unraveled a knot of hair. "Ralph and I had but a day to get to know each other before we wed."

"Just one day?" That's all she and Nicholas had so far. Was it enough?

"Then a week later, he left to fight in France, and I didn't see him again for another year."

"That must have been dreadful."

She shrugged. "I didn't become acquainted with him until after he returned and we had our son. Now, after thirty years, we've learned to love each other."

Learning to love. What a foreign concept in modern relationships that so often started with feelings of love that dissolved as time passed. If couples went into marriage with the mindset that it would take a lifetime to learn to love, would more marriages survive the pull toward divorce?

"Your affection for Nicholas will grow with time," Beatrice said confidently. "He's an easy man to love."

"I don't doubt you."

"Good." She continued to untangle Sybil's hair, almost as if in doing so she was helping to untangle Sybil's thoughts. "I always said the maiden who ends up with him will be very, very lucky. He's the kind of man who pours out his heart and soul for the people he loves without reservation or thought to himself."

A deep place in Sybil ached for someone to love her that way and to reciprocate in return. But giving in to her attraction to Nicholas would be selfish, especially since she didn't know how long she'd live in the past. It wouldn't be fair to him to start a relationship only for her to be yanked back to the present without a moment's notice.

At the sudden calls from outside the house, Beatrice paused and peered through an open window. "Looks like the rest of the men are back. Ralph will be hungrier than a wild boar."

Sybil expected Beatrice to rush outside as she'd done when Nicholas had ridden into town, but instead she picked up the comb she'd placed on the table next to a linen head covering—which Sybil had no intention of wearing. The gown was enough, and she would let Beatrice know it.

Regardless, Sybil was grateful the kindly matron was willing to continue helping her smooth out the snarls. This time Beatrice worked in silence, inclining her ear to the conversations of the returning men, to their tales of outmaneuvering and outwitting Simon's men.

At the sound of Nicholas in the fray, Sybil's pulse picked up speed. A moment later when his voice drew nearer, she sat up straighter. What would he think of her in the tunic? No doubt she looked as ridiculous as she felt.

"We should have the wedding as soon as possible," Ralph said as he stopped just outside the cottage door.

"Not today," came Nicholas's low response.

"Then on the morrow?" Sybil could see Ralph's tall frame, his baggy garments, and his hair tied at the back of his neck. He held his bow in one hand and cap in the other.

"I cannot say when." Nicholas spoke as calmly as if he were discussing when to plant crops. Was he no longer frustrated and disappointed? Or perhaps Beatrice had been wrong about

Nicholas's desire for her. Maybe he'd changed his mind and didn't want her after all.

Beatrice halted the comb halfway through a strand, clearly not wanting to miss a single word of the conversation.

"I would give her time to adjust first." Though Nicholas's words were hardly more than a whisper, they echoed loudly through Sybil's mind and chased away any remaining doubts about Nicholas. He was a good man. That was clear.

Ralph shuffled, then dipped his head. "I don't need to remind you that her reputation will be smeared."

"I shall order the men to keep silent about what they saw."

Ralph shook his head. "Your reputation too. They'll lose their respect for you if you don't set this wrong to right."

Sybil stood abruptly. Nicholas hadn't mentioned he needed to marry her to protect his own reputation. If the incident in the cave would put him at risk with his men and this community, then she needed to consider marriage, didn't she? Doing so seemed like the wisest move for everyone, especially since Nicholas had all but offered her a marriage in name only. It would be temporary, without physical intimacy muddling things.

"I would be most grateful if you would allow her to stay with you and Beatrice." Nicholas's comment was so quiet she almost missed it. "I shall reimburse you handsomely for the favor."

For pity's sake. She couldn't allow Nicholas to pay for her room and board. After telling her of his desire to have a place of his own someday, he didn't need to waste his earnings on her. Straightening her shoulders, she started across the room.

"Just marry her, Nicholas." Ralph's voice was almost urgent. "I know you want to."

Nicholas didn't immediately respond.

Her steps slowed.

"I promised her I would do what she wants," he finally said.

"And what does she want?"

Sybil took that as her cue to sidle past Ralph and make her presence known.

Nicholas was standing with his arms crossed, a lightweight white tunic falling to his thighs over dark brown trousers. A belt hung low on his hips containing both a sword and his dagger. His gaze swept over her hair hanging in long waves over her shoulders, then traveled down the length of her shapeless gown.

She twisted her fingers in the loose fabric at the hem of the sleeve. She looked terrible, should have stayed in her jeans or maybe just changed her shirt.

His eyes flew back to her face, and the brown darkened with something she couldn't name but that told her he liked what he saw.

"I'll marry you today." She spoke before she lost her nerve.

He didn't react. Instead, he studied her as if trying to understand why she'd changed her mind. But she didn't know if there was one reason she could give him. No doubt she'd change her mind again before this was all over.

Ralph's thin face with all his scars regarded her as severely now as when he'd first met her. She had the feeling he didn't like her but was accepting her for Nicholas's sake.

"We need not rush into a marriage," Nicholas said gently, as though speaking to a child.

"I'll do it."

"You are certain?"

Ralph clamped down on Nicholas's shoulder. "She said yes, so quit arguing with her." In the next instant, he curled his tongue and emitted a piercing whistle.

The commotion throughout the village ceased, and all eyes turned upon the tall archer.

"Gather round," he called. "We're having a wedding."

~ *18* ~

"A WEDDING ANON?" Nicholas waited for Sybil to show signs of protest or hesitation or dismay. But he saw none of those things.

"Make haste!" Ralph bellowed. "Get Father Fritz now!"

Nicholas held her gaze, the green made brighter by the green of her tunic. Something light and warm replaced the usual intensity within her eyes. When her attention slid to Ralph barking orders at the top of his lungs, as if the village were being attacked by the French, her lips twitched with a smile. And when she surveyed the men scrambling around at top speed trying to obey him, one side of her lips quirked up.

Nicholas couldn't keep his own lips from curving, a shaft of happiness filtering through the darkness that had lived inside his soul for so long.

When she caught him smiling, he coughed and covered his mouth, trying to smother his mirth before Ralph realized he was the object of their humor. She shifted just slightly away, enough for the tunic to curve around her body, to hint at what lay beneath. Somehow the hints were more alluring than the full view of the curves he'd witnessed in her other garments. The modesty gave him only a glimpse of what was meant for the sanctity of the marriage bed, teasing him with promises of pleasure, building anticipation within him.

Not that there would be pleasure any time soon. He intended to honor his word and everything he'd spoken earlier, especially that he wouldn't pressure her into the marriage bed. In fact, 'twould be best if he refrained from physical contact until she made it clear that she would welcome it.

Within mere minutes, the entire town, including men, women, and children, were assembled in front of the chapel.

"Where is Father Fritz?" Ralph asked sharply.

Beatrice was standing beside Sybil, fussing over her hair and smiling as though Sybil were her own daughter. The sight warmed Nicholas's heart. The dear woman deserved more than life had given her, but she had learned to make the best of what she had.

"Father Fritz?" Ralph boomed. Nicholas wasn't sure what had gotten into Ralph and why he was rushing everyone around to have the wedding, but he wouldn't protest, wanted to make the most of Sybil's acquiescence before she had second thoughts.

At the house near the end of the street, the door burst open and the priest stumbled out, one of the men pushing him along. Father Fritz was stuffing his arms into his cowl and yawning loudly.

"Quit yer mithering!" The priest turned and smacked the poor fellow tasked with collecting him. "I was sleeping like a wee tot, that I was."

"Come on with you, Father Fritz!" Ralph called. "Can't you see we're all waiting?"

At the sight of the entire town perspiring and breathless, Father Fritz halted, and his mouth fell open. "What the blimey is going on?"

"Nicholas and Sybil are getting married." Beatrice patted Sybil's cheek.

"Nicholas, my dear son." Father Fritz scratched his protruding belly. "Mighty eager to be with your woman, aren't you now?"

Titters and guffaws came from the crowd.

Nicholas half expected Father Fritz to start making kissing motions in the air again, and when he caught Sybil's gaze, she was holding back another smile, as if she'd been thinking the same thing.

"Ye could have held yerself together for a few more hours, couldn't ye, Nicholas?"

"I am holding myself together just fine, Father." Just as long as he didn't get too close to Sybil or look at her for any length. Whenever he did, he couldn't seem to control his reactions as well as he wanted to.

Father Fritz finished tightening the belt at his cowl. But he'd donned the garment upside down so that a large swath of material had bunched up at his shoulders, giving him the appearance of a hunchback.

"Ah, well, what's done is done." Father Fritz stumbled, and the man accompanying him reached out to assist him, only to have the priest swat him with the prayer book.

"This is a blessed day indeed," Beatrice called to Father Fritz. "Our dear Nicholas has found love, and for that we must truly celebrate."

Love? His feelings weren't love. At least, not the same kind of love he'd felt for Jane. Even so, his attraction to Sybil was strong. Was it disloyal to Jane? Moreover, what would Eric say after returning with the other hunters to find him married to someone else?

A sliver of unease pricked him, and he peered beyond the grazing sheep to the forest. Maybe Eric would come running out at any second and demand that the wedding be halted.

Nicholas fisted his hands. What should he do? Should he wait and discuss the matter with Jane's brother first?

Ralph reached for his shoulder and squeezed it. His severe gaze held Nicholas's and seemed to transfer a measure of calm and certainty into the growing turmoil inside. Was that why Ralph was hurrying the wedding along? So Eric wouldn't be able to step in and disrupt anything? Or speak with Nicholas and convince him not to go through with it?

"Come now, Father Fritz," Ralph called again. "Let's begin."

Grumbling under his breath, the portly priest hastened his steps until he reached the chapel. "I'm coming. I'm coming." He halted several feet from another young couple, closed his eyes, and began to recite a prayer.

"Father Fritz," Ralph growled. "Over here."

The priest's eyes popped open, and he shot Ralph a glare.

"Wrong people." Ralph returned the glare before cocking his head at Nicholas beside him.

Father Fritz glared at the man and his maiden in front of him as if the mix-up was their fault before pivoting and crossing the last of the distance. "There ye are, Nicholas, my dear boy." He smiled at Sybil. "And don't ye look lovely, bab. Not that ye didn't without yer clothes on. Ye looked very fine then too."

Sybil's eyes widened.

Nicholas almost choked on a laugh.

This time when Father Fritz closed his eyes and began his prayer, Nicholas stepped closer to Sybil. He wanted to reach for her hand, to twine his fingers through hers. But he didn't have a reason to do so, not when they were no longer running for their lives. Besides, he would fulfill his resolution to be chaste if he limited the contact with her.

Father Fritz began to read the rite of holy baptism until Ralph whacked him in the arm. Nicholas guessed, as he had already many times previously, that Father Fritz's superiors at Walsingham Priory had trumped up the espionage charges because they could no longer tolerate his odd mannerisms.

He was odd, to be sure. But he cared about people deeply, and that was all that truly mattered.

As Father Fritz started reading again, this time from the correct rite, Nicholas tried to expel the tension growing inside, but it stuck in his chest like a snagging blackthorn branch wrapping its wickedly long thorns around him. By the time the priest had finished praying and reading Scripture and began a soliloquy, Nicholas's insides were punctured, and he was having difficulty drawing in a breath.

"Move things along faster, Father," Ralph, standing next to Nicholas, murmured under his breath. "Can't you skip ahead?"

Father Fritz paused and scowled at Ralph. "I suppose ye would like me to have Nicholas kiss his bride before the vows?"

"Yes."

Father Fritz's brows shot up.

Nicholas's did too. Beside him, Sybil stiffened.

Ralph didn't say anything more, but Beatrice clapped her hands. "What a fine idea, Father Fritz. You always seem to know just what everyone needs."

The irritated lines in Father Fritz's face dissolved, and he nodded gravely. "Of course I do. Nicholas has been going plumb barmy with need. Now is the perfect time to let him have his way with his bride."

Nicholas started to shake his head in protest, but at an elbow from Ralph, he bit back his confusion and hesitations.

"Get on with ye, my dear boy." Father Fritz motioned between Sybil and him. "Do it now before I change my mind and make you wait." Or before he suggested something else entirely inappropriate and embarrassed everyone present.

Nicholas pivoted slowly toward Sybil.

She stared straight ahead, her back rigid.

Maybe she'd never shared a kiss with a man. And maybe she was afraid.

He lifted a hand and brushed at the hair on her shoulder. He'd show her that she had nothing to fear. Especially from him.

She flicked a gaze at him but didn't turn.

He slid his hand deeper into her hair. As his fingers tangled in the thick waves of silk, a swift rush of heat pulsed through him. Guiding her head around with one hand, he slipped the other to the small of her back. As his fingers flattened in the hollow spot just below her waist, he allowed his other hand to graze her neck.

She sucked in a short breath, one that only pumped more heat into his blood and turned his body taut with need.

How was this simple interaction able to set kindling aflame within him—at least flames on his end?

She stood still, her eyes now fixed upon his mouth, as though she was preparing herself for more.

He would give her more. Heaven help him, but he would show her exactly how much more could exist between them when she was ready for it.

As though she was the sunlight he needed after a dark winter, he pressed against her and fused his mouth with hers, basking in the rays and luxuriating in her warm sweetness.

She hesitated for a moment, then rose on her toes. As she opened her lips and kissed him back, there was nothing timid or uncertain or fearful in her response. Just as there was nothing timid or uncertain or fearful about her. Instead, she was a bright light, breaking through all the cracks in his broken soul. She poured in a delicious blaze that spilled through the shards and spread all throughout his chest.

"Beautiful. Absolutely beautiful." Beatrice's voice cut through the haze that had wrapped around Nicholas and drawn him against Sybil more fully so that he could feel her curves and the rapid thud of her heartbeat.

She broke away first, almost shoving him back. As she spun to face Father Fritz, a flush marked her cheeks. Her eyes were wide, as though the kiss had taken her by surprise. And she pressed her fingers to her lips—lips that were moist and swollen and made for him to kiss.

He had the overwhelming urge to grasp her and kiss her again. The need rocked him, and he tore his attention away from her lest he give way to it and embarrass himself in front of the village.

Father Fritz's eyes were round, and he swallowed hard. "Well, now. After watching that, I think we're all needing a cloudburst of cold rain to be dousing the heat."

Laughter rang out around them.

"Continue with the vows, Father," Ralph barked. "They're ready now."

"Wagging dog tails, ye be right about that."

More laughter followed.

Nicholas wanted to reassure Sybil that the jesting was all in fun and she needn't worry. But the moment he glanced at her, his attention went straight to her mouth.

She was nibbling at her lower lip.

Saint's blood. He wanted to be the one nibbling her lip. But he crossed his arms to keep from grabbing her and taking her lower lip his prisoner.

Father Fritz was grinning like he planned to jump into a song and a dance. But Ralph clamped a hand down on him, pinning him in place.

"The vows, Father."

Father Fritz held up the prayer book, which somehow was upside down. He cleared his throat to speak, dropped his attention to the page, then squinted in confusion.

With a heavy sigh, Ralph rotated the book.

Father Fritz peered at it again and nodded solemnly. "Nicholas, wilt thou have this woman to be thy wedded wife, to live together after God's ordinance in the holy estate of matrimony? Wilt thou love her, comfort her, honor, and keep her, in sickness and in health; and forsaking all others, keep thee only unto her, so long as ye both shall live?"

"I will." The words spilled from him with no prodding.

"And Sybil, wilt thou have this man to be thy wedded husband, to live together after God's ordinance in the holy estate of matrimony? Wilt thou obey him, and serve him, love, honor, and keep him, in sickness and in health; and forsaking all others, keep thee only unto him, so long as ye both shall live?"

She hesitated, drew in a breath, and then spoke. "I will."

"Ye won't regret it," Father Fritz whispered, leaning in. "Ye can ask for no better man than our Nicholas."

Nicholas prayed Father Fritz was right. He wanted to be a good husband, didn't want her to have any regrets about her decision. And he wanted her to eventually care about him enough that she would want to stay with him forever.

The rest of the ceremony passed quickly. Within minutes Father Fritz was making the sign of the cross above them where they knelt in front of the chapel door. As they rose, Nicholas took hold of her arm and assisted her to her feet. How was she feeling? Relieved? Or was she already regretting so hasty a decision to marry him?

Father Fritz reached for their hands and placed them together, setting Nicholas's on top of Sybil's. For a moment, he worked at spacing Nicholas's fingers evenly apart, as if the presentation was vitally important.

When satisfied with his work of art, he filled his lungs with air and called out in an overly loud voice: "For as much as Nicholas and Sybil have consented together in holy wedlock, and have witnessed the same before God and this company, and thereto have given and pledged their troth each to the other, and have declared the same by the giving and receiving of a ring—"

He paused, frowned, and then shook his head. "Never mind that. We don't have the ring yet. Ye'll be getting her a pretty little one, won't ye now, Nicholas?"

"It's alright." She started to draw her hand out from under his, but he held her fast.

"I shall have one made." As soon as 'twas relatively safe, he'd ride to the coast where he would commission a goldsmith friend.

"Fine then." Father Fritz patted their hands. "By the joining of hands, I pronounce therefore that they be man and wife together, in the name of the Father, Son, and Holy Ghost. Amen."

Nicholas whispered an "Amen," and as soon as he did, the villagers clapped and cheered and whistled.

He'd done it. Come what may. He was a married man.

Now he just prayed Eric could accept it, that they would both be able to move on with their lives without any regrets.

- *19* -

SYBIL WASN'T USED TO BEING SURROUNDED BY WOMEN. But when tables and benches were pulled outside, she found herself segregated with Beatrice and the other females as they chattered with each other and prepared the meal—slicing rounds of cheese and bread and making a salad of leeks, parsley, and even primrose.

She felt terribly out of place, not only in the long tunic but also in trying to keep up her end of conversations. She'd never been good at small talk, especially with women, unless the discussions centered around their workouts and competitions.

She had no idea how to add to the talk about which geese were still broody, how to keep maggots from growing in the sheep's hind parts, or the amount of crushed ale hoof that was required to treat a chill.

Instead, her attention drifted to the men who, after starting a fire and setting mutton to roast, moved to the edge of town for a knife-throwing contest. She easily put together the details—the few broken arrows lying about, the circular targets held up by mounds of earth, and the patches of worn grass—to know the villagers had created a shooting range.

Nicholas had explained during one of their discussions

earlier in the day that archery laws had been in place in England for over a hundred years, requiring the training on weekdays. About twenty years ago, King Edward III had added to the law by commanding obligatory practice on Sundays and holidays for every man between fifteen and sixty.

She was fascinated to learn that most towns and villages took the law seriously and had established target practice areas known as the butts.

She would have preferred to watch the men practice their archery, but clearly a competition with bows and arrows was too boring, too commonplace. The knife throwing was apparently more festive.

Nicholas and Ralph were easily the best. As the rest of the men were eliminated, only the two remained. When Nicholas took his place at the edge of the field with a knife in hand, she could no longer hide her interest in their competition. She didn't mean to turn her back on the women and stare at Nicholas, but she ended up that way.

He stood straight and tall, his entire body taut with intensity. His dark hair was loosely tied back, leaving his chiseled face free for admiring. And admire it she did. She couldn't help it.

How was it possible this man was her husband?

The realization didn't send fear racing through her the way she'd assumed it would. Instead, it filled her with a sense of wonder that of all the men, she'd ended up with one like Nicholas, who was as attractive on the inside as he was on the out.

Even though she'd already told herself that everything she

was experiencing was too real to be merely a dream, she kept waiting to wake up at any moment.

"Can't keep your eyes off him, can you?" said Gemma, one of the younger women standing beside her watching the competition. Eighteen, maybe nineteen, she was fair-haired, slender, and pretty.

The introductions after the wedding had been so rapid and to so many people that Sybil hadn't been able to remember everyone. But she hadn't been able to forget Gemma, mainly because of the longing in the girl's eyes whenever she stared at Nicholas.

Not that the girl's infatuation with him was anything worth fretting about. He hadn't noticed Gemma once, not even in passing.

"I'm interested to see who wins the contest." Sybil tore her attention from Nicholas as if she could somehow prove Gemma wrong. She could take her eyes off him whenever she wanted. He held no sway over her.

But even as she cast a glance at Gemma, her sights wandered back to Nicholas. As he aimed, his tunic—now covered by a vestlike garment called a doublet—stretched tightly around his arm. His fingers gripped the hilt with practiced proficiency. His strong, skilled, and sturdy fingers.

She could almost feel them splaying across her lower back and sliding through her hair from their kiss. His lips had clashed with hers, like a knight commanding an army, thrusting in and taking her prisoner in one swoop. She hadn't put up any resistance, had capitulated, had let him willingly invade. In fact, she'd eagerly welcomed him, surrendering herself. She was even embarrassed to admit that if he'd swept her up in his arms and continued to kiss her, she would have let him. She wasn't sure how she would have had the strength to stop.

Even now, the imprint of his mouth seemed to linger upon hers. And every nerve was attuned to him, the need inside her like a barely contained fire greedy for oxygen.

She willed him to look her way, wanted to see if his longing matched hers. But since their parting ways after the wedding in front of the chapel, he'd been busy with the men and hadn't sought her out, almost as if he'd forgotten she existed.

If only she could as easily put him from her mind. But it was as if the more she watched him, the more she wanted him. She'd always scoffed when other women became obsessed with a guy. But now it had officially happened to her—she'd gone crazy over a man.

Falling for Nicholas had happened fast—maybe too fast. But she was a grown woman and knew what she liked in a man . . . and Nicholas was more than she'd ever expected.

"To be honest," Gemma said almost wistfully, "I'm surprised he's taken an interest in you."

Nicholas's knife hit the center yellow band, one of five colored rings, with red next, then blue, white, and finally black on the outside circle.

"Your appearance is nothing like Jane's. And neither is your temperament."

At the mention of Jane, Sybil's attention snapped to Gemma. The young woman was waiting for Sybil's reaction, a sad smile upon her lips—one that wasn't entirely genuine.

Had Gemma known Jane personally? For just a second, Sybil was tempted to ply Gemma with questions about the mysterious love of Nicholas's life. But if and when Nicholas was ready to talk more about Jane, he would.

"I'm not replacing Jane in his life." She'd never ask him to stop loving Jane. "Maybe Nicholas likes me because I'm different and don't remind him of her or his past."

"Or maybe the rumors are true that you seduced him."

Sybil clamped her lips together to keep from saying anything else. Gemma was immature and jealous, or maybe she was trying to protect Jane's memory. Either way, Sybil didn't intend to give the girl the satisfaction of seeing her riled up.

Ralph threw his knife next, embedding it into the target close to Nicholas's. As the two retrieved their weapons, Ralph's stern voice carried toward them. "Since it's your wedding day, I let you win. Didn't want to embarrass you with your bride watching."

Sybil held her breath, waiting for Nicholas to shift his gaze and seek her out amidst the women. In the middle of sheathing his knife, his attention snagged directly on her without having to search. Even though the glance was only a second long, it was enough for her to see his interest.

A sweet sense of satisfaction settled inside her.

He was more cognizant of her than he was letting on. Maybe he wasn't as hyperaware of her every move the way she was of his, but he was most definitely keeping track of her whereabouts.

Throughout the rest of the evening and as darkness fell, she did her best to minimize staring at Nicholas. Beatrice was a helpful distraction, never without something to talk about, mostly gossip about each of the families who lived in Devil's Bend.

"Nicholas, he does his best to uncover the truth about each man." Beatrice sat on the bench beside Sybil as they finished their meal.

One of the matrons across the table pushed aside her wooden plate. "He's getting one more confession from those who are vouching for my Kenric's innocence before taking the case to the hundred court."

Over the course of the meal, Sybil had learned that Kenric, with his wife and two children, had fled into the Weald after he was accused of stealing fourteen bushels of wheat from the abbot of St. Augustine's. The bailiff had been the one to orchestrate the thievery but had placed the blame on Kenric—merely an innocent bystander who had been in the wrong place at the wrong time.

Kenric had no way to refute the charges, so he'd run away before the bailiff could arrest him. The poor man had been hiding in the Weald for the past year with no hope of clearing his name . . . until Nicholas had taken up his cause. Nicholas had found witnesses who had been with Kenric on the night of the crime as well as others who knew of the bailiff's stealing and were willing to speak out against him.

The more Sybil learned about Nicholas and his kindness to the people of the Weald, the more she admired him. He had no reason to involve himself with their cases, no reason to defend them, no reason to see justice brought about. But he did so anyway, without accepting compensation.

Of course, as the women unfolded their tragic stories, Sybil had learned that some—like Beatrice and Ralph—would never be able to leave the Weald. Even though Nicholas had tried to help them, they had no way to prove their innocence.

"Poor Nicholas," Beatrice said as she licked her fingers clean from her second portion of mutton. "He's been helping everyone else find justice. But now there's no one to help him."

Nicholas stood near the firepit where the other men were congregated, now drinking a home-brewed alcohol that was stronger than the watery ale everyone consumed in place of water—which Sybil had learned wasn't purified or safe for drinking.

He was listening to one of the men and was as powerful as always with his arms crossed, feet spread, and head slightly inclined toward the man. The firelight illuminated the strong lines of Nicholas's face and the gravity of his expression. She guessed the man was sharing another tale of injustice and that Nicholas was trying to figure out a way to solve the problem.

His work investigating crimes wasn't so different from hers. In fact, since starting at ABI, she hadn't done anything quite as noble as Nicholas, except for her case with Harrison. She'd always dreamed that she would fight crime and injustice. But the majority of her cases as a private investigator had to do with disgruntled husbands or wives trying to uncover evidence to use against their spouses in divorce court.

Maybe when she returned to the present, she'd apply for a new job—something that made a true difference, something like Nicholas was doing in defending the innocent. In fact, what if she could help him while she was in the past?

As if sensing her intense question, he tilted his head just a little, enough that she was in his line of vision. His dark gaze collided with hers, and for the first time all night she could feel his desire. It shot straight through her, embedding deep, loosening longing inside her and spilling it through her body.

As though sensing his effect upon her, his lips cocked up on one side.

She dragged her attention to the table and the women. But she could no longer hear what any of them were saying, could only think of Nicholas and the connection with him and the overwhelming desire to kiss him again just like she had at the wedding. Kiss him and hold him and have him whisper in her ear.

She gave herself a mental slap. What was coming over her? She couldn't let herself get carried away with her thoughts and feelings for Nicholas. If she did, she'd make everything about this trip into the past more complicated. For now, she had to remain objective and couldn't repeat the kiss from the wedding.

At a shout of greetings coming from the edge of town, Beatrice pushed up. "Here we go now. Let's pray we don't have a brawl tonight."

A group of six men strode out of the forest toward the center of town. Two were carrying a buck tied between poles. The others were holding torches that cast light upon the bulging sacks slung over their shoulders. No doubt the sacks were filled with smaller game—game the women had spoken about salting and drying.

Sybil climbed up from the bench too, her legs tangling in

her tunic. "Why would there be a brawl?"

"Jane's brother Eric is back."

A sliver of unease shimmied up Sybil's spine, and she rubbed the long sleeves of her gown. "What can you tell me about Eric?"

"He won't be happy to find Nicholas has taken himself a wife."

"That's putting it mildly," said another woman at the table.

Sybil studied the group of hunters and guessed the man in the forefront was Eric. Blond-haired and with thicker features that reminded her a little of Isaac, the man strode with heavy purpose in each step. He seemed to be in his mid to late twenties with lines grooved into his face that spoke of heartache and tragedy.

Why would Eric be upset that Nicholas had gotten married? Were they still grieving over Jane's loss?

From the way Nicholas referenced her, Sybil had assumed the woman had died many years ago. But perhaps it had been more recently.

"How long has Jane been gone?" she asked.

"Almost five years," one of the women replied.

"Right." Five years was plenty long to grieve. Nicholas had every right to move on.

"We've been wanting them both to find happiness again," Beatrice said in a hushed tone as the conversations began to taper to silence. "But neither has been able to let go of what happened."

Eric and his companions neared the fire. "What is the cause for making merry?" he asked as he dropped his load.

The men with the buck lowered it to the ground. As they straightened, the only sound was the pop of sparks from the fire.

Nicholas stepped away from the other men. All eyes swung to him, including Eric's. A part of Sybil wanted to walk over and stand beside Nicholas to present a united front. But another part sensed this was his battle to fight and that she needed to refrain from aiding him.

"I have taken a wife." Nicholas spoke the words evenly, as though he had no regrets and nothing to hide.

Eric stared at Nicholas, his jaw turning rigid.

"This is our wedding feast." Nicholas glanced her way, singling her out.

Of course Eric followed his gaze. And as he studied her, his eyes remained cold and unwelcoming.

She resisted the urge to rub her arms again. Instead, she held herself with unflinching stillness, unwilling to allow anyone to intimidate her. She hadn't done so in her other life in the modern era and wouldn't start now.

Eric jerked his attention back to Nicholas. "Who is she?"

"She came to my rescue and saved my life."

"And?"

"And I desire her."

The bluntness of Nicholas's statement sent a flush through Sybil.

Eric didn't immediately respond. Everyone seemed to be holding their breaths in anticipation of his reaction. What would he do? Lash out at Nicholas?

Her muscles tensed, and she flexed her fingers, ready to go

for her knife still strapped inside her boot.

"You've disrespected her memory," Eric finally said, his tone radiating with anger. "And you've acted rashly and dishonorably."

Sybil didn't need anyone to spell out who Eric was referring to. The fact that he thought Nicholas was dishonoring Jane's memory by getting married was ridiculous. But loss and grief could make people irrational. She'd witnessed that all too often, not only as a PI but also when she'd worked for Kent Police. Maybe she'd even witnessed it with Dawson. He'd let his grief control him so that he lost himself in the process.

"We have paid for our transgressions long enough." Nicholas's voice was hard too, and he didn't let his attention swerve from Eric, as though he anticipated Eric might attack him. Surely the young man wouldn't do that, would he?

"I'll never atone for my mistakes. And neither will you. I thought we stood together on that, you and I."

"I may never atone for her death. But I am no longer dead inside and cannot deny the need that flows through me."

Eric released a scoffing laugh. "You're pathetic. I thought you were stronger than that."

Nicholas didn't respond except to press his lips into a tight line.

Again, the crackling of the center bonfire was the only sound. Eric glowered at Nicholas for several more seconds before he spun and stalked off. Only after he entered one of the cottages and slammed the door did anyone move. Even then, the conversations were low, and people began to clear away the remnants of the feast.

Beatrice wound her arm through Sybil's. "Come now, I'll get you settled into your home and help you into bed."

"I'll be fine." She didn't want to disturb Beatrice any more than she already had. "Point me in the direction, and I'll settle myself in."

Beatrice didn't let go and instead ushered her forward, a rushlight in one hand, guiding their way as they moved out of the bonfire's glow. "Nicholas has tasked me with being your servant while the two of you live in the village."

Sybil halted. "My servant?"

Beatrice's face creased with distress. "Is it so difficult to believe I was once a lady's maid?"

"It's not that." Sybil scrambled to find the right words. She didn't want to offend her ally. "I'm sure you're a fine lady's maid."

"I'm one of the best."

"I believe you. It's just that I'm used to taking care of myself."

Beatrice studied Sybil's face before patting her arm and tugging her along. "From everything I've seen so far, you're as helpless as a babe. In fact, I don't think I've met a lady quite as in need of a maidservant as you."

She wanted to protest that her ignorance had to do with the difference in eras not in their differences in station. But she was smart enough to know she needed to stay silent about the matter or risk having these people think she was a madwoman.

"Besides," Beatrice said, "if you send me away, you'll make Nicholas think you're ungrateful for his thoughtfulness."

"Right."

"He's being very considerate and only giving you what you're due as a lady."

A lady? Sybil almost snorted but held back her scoffing. Beatrice was right. Nicholas *had* been considerate toward her since the moment they'd met, thinking about her needs above his own. Besides, she could benefit from Beatrice's instruction while she accustomed herself to living in the Middle Ages.

As they arrived at a cottage on the outskirts of the village, the one Father Fritz lived in, Sybil hesitated in the doorway. "I don't want to take away Father Fritz's home."

"Have no worries." Already stepping inside, Beatrice flicked a hand to dismiss her concern. "He'll stay with some of the other single fellows and find great enjoyment in doing so."

Sybil swallowed the rest of her objection. It would do no good to say anything to Father Fritz. The quirky priest would probably respond with something entirely embarrassing.

Beatrice held up the rushlight to reveal a simple interior much like her cottage, except there was a bed against one wall. Made of a square wooden box frame, it seemed both too short as well as too narrow. But it contained a lumpy mattress as well as blankets—which was more than Ralph and Beatrice had.

A rough-hewn table with stools stood against one wall. The wooden shelves above it were crowded with an assortment of dishes, crocks, and jugs. A cloak hung from a peg on the wall above a chest with several clothing items folded on top.

Sybil had expected it to be less tidy, even disgusting like Dawson and Acey's flat. But the one room was surprisingly clean.

"Sit down with you." Beatrice pointed to the stool at the

same time she rushed to answer a knock on the door. A bright-eyed young woman peeked into the house at Sybil before smiling shyly and handing a sack to Beatrice.

When they were alone again and the door closed, Beatrice began to empty the contents on the table—what appeared to be soap and salves and an assortment of linens. "Time to get you ready for your first night with that handsome husband of yours."

So that's what this was. Beatrice believed this was her real wedding night, that she would sleep with Nicholas. At just the thought, Sybil flushed and pushed up from the table. "Can't."

Beatrice laughed lightly as she guided Sybil back to the stool. "After that kiss at your wedding, yes you can. You'll have no trouble."

Sybil was afraid of that. She didn't need Beatrice making her more appealing so that the resisting would be even harder.

"Now first, let's get you out of your tunic." Beatrice began to tug at the sleeves.

Sybil examined the linens on the table and on the chest. "Will I have a nightdress of some kind—"

"Of course not. Why would you need anything?"

"I need *something*."

"I have your nightcap here." Beatrice held up an oddly shaped piece of material.

Did Beatrice really expect her to get into bed naked wearing only a silly hat? "Oh no. I really can't."

"Don't you worry. Nicholas is a sensitive man. Knowing him, he'll be very careful—"

"Sweet holy mother." Sybil jumped up and paced away,

pressing her hands to her overheated cheeks.

She wasn't sure why the conversation was so mortifying. She wasn't naïve and knew everything there was to know about sex already. With the way sex was flaunted in modern times, she would have expected herself to remain unruffled at Beatrice's almost-birds-and-the-bees talk. But for a reason she couldn't explain, the suggestions of Nicholas and her being together intimately only charged her nerves with a strange energy she didn't want to dwell on.

"Please find me a nightgown, Beatrice. Please."

Beatrice laughed again. "Very well. But you've got nothing to fear. Now come here and let me do what I was trained for. It's been too long, and I'm excited to take care of you."

Sybil nearly groaned out her protest. She wasn't about to get ready for Nicholas, and she also couldn't imagine sitting down and letting Beatrice pamper her with strange products. She didn't wear makeup except a little mascara once in a while. She'd never had a manicure in her life. She didn't follow the fashions. And she kept her hairstyle simple.

But how could she deny Beatrice this opportunity to care for someone again the way she used to?

Sybil bit back words of refusal and returned to the stool, praying that somehow, someway, she would be able to keep her sanity during the long night ahead.

~ 20 ~

"Thought for sure you'd be abed with your bride by now." Ralph's voice rumbled from beside Nicholas where he leaned against a tree in the shadows.

"I decided to take first watch." He kept his gaze trained on the dark shadows of the forest, searching for anything unusual. But so far, the only movement had been from bats, a hedgehog, and an owl swooping down to catch a field vole. He'd heard nothing but the trills of spawning toads and the occasional whine of a distant fox.

"Any other man would've taken watch for you tonight."

"True, but I brought this peril upon us." During the feast, the men had discussed the threat Simon now posed to the village. They'd decided to keep watch for the next few days, just in case Simon's guards ventured farther into the Weald.

Ralph rested a shoulder against the opposite side of the tree. He spat into the long grass at the edge of the meadow while gazing up at the sky that was lit with a million stars.

The night had taken on a chill, but Nicholas was counting on the cold air to keep him awake.

"I have decided I must move on from Devil's Bend." He'd contemplated the matter a great deal throughout the eve, especially as he'd watched the villagers eat and make merry, putting aside their own troubles to celebrate with him.

The people here had become family to him in a way that his own kin had never been. They'd already suffered enough as outcasts, and he didn't want to bring them more harm and hardship. But the truth was, his presence amongst them posed a threat to their quiet and simple existence.

"I understand what you're saying." Ralph seemed to measure each word carefully before responding. "But all of us here are dodging the law in one way or another. It could come creeping up on us at any time."

"None are a menace like Simon." Even if most outsiders were frightened of the deep Weald, his brother's men had no choice but to pursue him if Simon threatened them badly enough. "I shall leave on the morrow and attempt to divert their attention elsewhere."

"No. If they come, we'll stick together and fight."

Nicholas shook his head. "This place is a refuge to those who need it. Where would everyone go if the village was discovered?"

Ralph turned quiet.

Nicholas's gaze strayed to the cottage. The shutters were closed, and there was no sign of light within. Sybil was likely already slumbering. Nevertheless, his pulse quickened as it did every time he thought about her being inside and in bed.

"Will you take her with you?" Ralph asked.

Had his friend caught him peeking at the cottage and sensed his desire for Sybil? She would be safer here, away from his lusts.

"I shall return for her once Simon has given up the chase."

"I suppose you'll be heading down to Dover as soon as you're able?"

"Yes, but tell no one of my destination."

Nicholas rolled the set of strange numbers through his head again as he did several times a day in order to keep from forgetting them. Other than Sybil, Ralph had been the only one he'd told about the numbers from the missive he'd discovered on Simon's writing table.

Ralph had agreed it was a message from the French. But Nicholas wasn't skilled in ciphering and needed to visit his friend Walter in Dover, who was an expert at uncovering secret codes. If it was a treasonous message, Nicholas would take it directly to the king and prove his loyalty and therewith absolve himself of all charges of espionage—or at least he hoped he could absolve himself.

"I gave Beatrice a week after our wedding before I left. You can spend a few days with your wife. She deserves that."

Nicholas shook his head and started to speak, but Ralph cut him off. "Simon won't regroup immediately anyway."

Nicholas pushed away from the tree and straightened. He wasn't sure what Simon intended to do next. But Ralph was right. Sybil deserved more from him so soon after their wedding. And truthfully, he wanted more too. He wanted a few days to be with her at the least.

Ralph spat into the grass again. "We'll take care of her until you come back."

Nicholas knew Ralph meant the words to reassure him, but they stirred unease within him. He'd already left one woman behind, and the results had been devastating.

"You'll have nothing to fear," Ralph said, clearly sensing the direction of Nicholas's thoughts. "I'll protect her with my life."

Nicholas felt his throat closing up not only with gratefulness to his friend but also with a whole host of emotion for Sybil. Why had he allowed himself to care about her so deeply already? Hadn't he learned his lesson with Jane? The heartache of losing her had nearly killed him. How could he survive losing another woman?

Maybe Eric had been right, that they hadn't atoned for their mistakes and never would. The ache in Nicholas's chest pulsed at the picture of the agony in Eric's eyes when he'd held his mother in his arms, when they'd both realized they'd been too late. After that day, they'd only had each other.

Whatever the case, he was married now. And he'd meant what he'd told Eric—that he was no longer dead inside and couldn't deny the need flowing through him.

"Go on now with you." Ralph straightened. "I'm taking your watch."

Nicholas's muscles tensed with the desire to make the most of the little time he had left with Sybil. He let his attention drift to the cottage again, and his heart reared like a war horse, kicking its legs, eager for the charge. He'd promised her he wouldn't pressure her to consummate their marriage. And he'd promised himself he would wait until they had more substance to their relationship before giving in to his physical desires.

Could he go in and remain chaste while still spending a night with her?

"God's bones, man." Ralph shoved him. "You'll regret it if you don't go to her."

Nicholas stumbled forward. Once his feet were moving, he couldn't stop. He strode directly to the cottage, his heart picking up pace with the need to spend every minute with her that he could.

As he took in the position of the moon, he silently cursed himself for wasting so much of the night already. If he was honest with himself, he'd also been holding himself back from returning to the cottage because every time he'd looked at her throughout the feasting, he'd thought about kissing her again the same way he had at their wedding. And he couldn't kiss her again, could he?

He hesitated at the door. Could he remain strong enough?

Huffing a breath of exasperation, he pushed his way into the cottage and at the same time pushed past his cowardice. The woman inside was his wife in the sight of God and man. If he wanted to kiss her again, it would be within his rights to do so.

As he closed the door, the blackness of the room enveloped him. Even so, he'd been in Father Fritz's home enough to have a general idea of where the furniture was located.

He crossed to the table and braced himself while he removed his boots. He unstrapped his weapons belt, then he worked at the laces of his doublet and shed the garment quickly. He started to lift his tunic up, then paused and lowered it. Surely he would do better at holding his urges at bay if he bared himself no further.

What about her? What if Beatrice had put her to bed

entirely bare? Just thinking about it conjured images he didn't need to dwell on. In that case, he'd sleep on top of the covers.

Making his way to the bed, his heart thudded with anticipation, and he had to silently remind himself of his resolve. He would hold her. Maybe kiss her. But that was all.

As he bumped into the wooden bed frame, he heard her shift against the straw-filled mattress.

Had he roused her with his entrance? Or had she been awake, waiting for him?

He lowered himself to the edge.

"I can sleep on the floor if you'd like the bed," came her whisper.

"No." He slipped down onto the mattress.

Again, she moved. Was she starting to sit up—or perhaps crawling off?

He reached out to stop her, and his hand grazed her arm. The bare skin of her arm.

His gut clenched. Had this been a mistake?

"I didn't think we were going to . . ." Her voice was soft and filled with embarrassment.

"I am not intending to break my promise to you. But since you are bare, you will need to stay covered."

"I'm wearing a chemise. I asked Beatrice for a nightgown, and this is what she came back with."

He skimmed his fingers up the rest of her arm and found a thin linen strap upon her shoulder. He traced the strap down to the loose material that covered her bosom.

She'd stilled at his touch, was hardly daring to breathe. Did she like it, or had his forthrightness frightened her?

He returned his hand to her arm, a slightly safer location. But even there, before he could stop himself, he dragged his fingers down the length of her arm, the silky skin too hard to resist.

She sucked in a sharp breath.

At the sound, desire ripped through him. Saint's blood. This was harder than he'd expected. He pinched his eyes closed, held himself still, and then drew his hand away. "Wrap up in a blanket." His command came out tersely.

Thankfully, she didn't question him and began shifting and turning until finally she lay still and silent.

This time when he reached for her, he found the thick wool of a blanket surrounding her, leaving no bare skin and cutting him off from any access to her body. Even though his gut gave a kick of protest, his reasoning told him he would be a happier man in the morn for remaining honorable.

He closed the distance between them, drawing her against his chest and wrapping his arms around her before tucking her head underneath his chin. Her hair was mostly contained within the blanket too, which was just as well. If he began combing his fingers through it, he wasn't sure where that would lead.

She held herself stiffly, as if still uncertain what to expect from this, their wedding night.

"I do want you," he whispered, hoping to reassure her. "And I will have you. But not this night." Not anytime soon. But he wouldn't tell her of his plans yet. Thus far, she'd proven to be a levelheaded woman. But Jane had always sobbed when he mentioned needing to leave, and the parting had been difficult.

"Have you been with many women?" Sybil's question wasn't laced with jealousy, only curiosity.

Even so, it took him by surprise. "Your question is too bold."

She gave a slight shrug. "You've just given me your answer."

As usual, her sharpness sent a thrill through him. But in the same moment, an intense shaft of jealousy pierced him. "And you? Have you . . .?" He couldn't even force himself to say the words.

"Your question is too bold." Her tone hinted at humor.

"Fair enough."

"It may seem odd that a woman of my age is still a virgin. Or maybe it's not so odd here. But I was waiting for the right man."

He relaxed against the mattress and relished the length of her against him. Even with the blanket acting as a protective barrier, she was warm and soft and curvy and fit against him in all the right places. "Then I shall prove to you that I am the right man."

"You're doing a good job so far."

"Am I?"

"I've never met anyone like you." Her words were soft, almost as if the admission had come out unexpectedly.

He pressed a kiss to the top of her head, wanting to kiss so much more than that. But he intended to go slow and use self-control. "I regret I have been with other women. If I had remained chaste, perhaps I would not struggle now to contain my desires."

"I admit, I don't like picturing you with anyone else."

He smiled at her confession. "I did not take you for a jealous woman."

"I'm not normally."

"Just with me?"

She shrugged.

"I own freely that I am a jealous man." He tightened his hold of her. "No man will dare to look at you now that you belong to me."

"Belong?" Her tone held a hint of scoffing. "Do you think you own me? Like I'm your property?"

He only had to think of his father and Simon's treatment of their wives to understand how such a legality must feel to Sybil. "As my wife, I may do with you as I please. But I would that you belong to me not only in body but also in soul and spirit."

"No woman should ever be owned by a man."

"You are mine." He couldn't keep his tone from turning rough with possession and was surprised by the force of his need. Perhaps this was what drove Simon. And perhaps it led him to lash out in an effort to be in control.

She pushed at his chest and started to move away.

"Wait." He loosened his hold, needing to be different from Simon, needing to be a better and more caring husband, needing to relinquish his desire to bend her will to his. "You are mine, but I shall be yours."

She ceased her efforts to free herself and stilled.

Yes, he wanted her to possess him every bit as much as he possessed her. "I vow to be yours in body, soul, and spirit."

When she expelled a breath, he drew her back against him but tenderly. The bond between them was yet tentative, and he sensed it could be easily broken if he wasn't careful.

"I vow I shall be a good husband to you."

"Then you must know that I'm your equal and not your possession."

He hesitated. Such a declaration defied everything he knew to be true about women.

"I'm not like the other women."

"'Tis why I am drawn to you. I would not have you be like them."

"I won't be content to be left behind to do menial things. I'll help you with defending the innocent from their accusers."

He didn't know how she could help him. But he wouldn't say so now. "I cannot help anyone else until I help myself."

"I'll help you too." She spoke with such confidence and longing that he wanted to promise her she could do anything she wished. Was it possible she could grow to care about him, that eventually they would have a solid and loving marriage?

"I would see you safe above all else." Which was another reason he needed to leave. If word spread that he'd taken a wife, Simon might decide to capture and use Sybil as bait. Nicholas couldn't abide the thought of what Simon might do to her in order to lure him in.

Maybe he'd been too rash in marrying her. Maybe she would have fared better without a connection to him. And yet, the connection was undeniable. He hadn't been able to keep his attraction to her a secret from anyone.

"I have to prove Simon is a traitor. Until then, he remains a threat."

"Tell me everything about Simon. I need to know every detail."

He hadn't planned on spending his wedding night discussing his evil older brother and his devious behavior. But Sybil was persistent, wanting to hear about Simon's various wives, his methods of punishment that led to their deaths, Simon's strengths and weaknesses, the number of guards he had as well as their loyalty.

As usual, she asked astute questions like she was gathering data to use against Simon. And as usual, one conversation led to another so that Nicholas found himself telling her more about his childhood and his training as a knight. He spoke of his time as a page in the household of a kind neighboring lord and how that had helped to shape him into a man of honor. Without it, he feared he would have followed more closely in the footsteps of his brother and father.

Although Sybil was as good a listener as she'd claimed, he wanted to find out more about her too and pressed her to share more about her past, which led to more talk about Dawson and her mother. He could sense as he had previously that she cared for people deeply and had been wounded deeply as a result.

When hours had passed and she finally drifted to sleep, he closed his eyes too, contentment filling him. What he wouldn't give to have many such nights in his life, lying beside his wife and whispering about their pains as well as their hopes for a better future.

~ 21 ~

SYBIL STRETCHED AWAKE TO FIND ARMS tightening around her.

Instantly, she was alert. She assessed the situation as quickly as always, noting that she was still in the past with Nicholas, that his thick arms were the ones surrounding her and his hard chest like a shield protecting her. Within the confines of his body, she felt as if she could truly sleep in a way she hadn't been able to in years. Both in the cave and now in the bed, she'd rested soundly, without any trouble from insomnia.

Perhaps without all the stress of her present-day life, she'd been able to fall asleep easier. Or maybe the quiet of the cottage had helped. As she'd lain in bed waiting for Nicholas, she'd been struck by absolute silence, which was so different from her flat, where she could hear the neighbor's TV through her wall, the rumble of delivery lorries passing by, and the cranky stuttering of her old fridge.

The complete darkness had been intense, too, without the digital light from her alarm clock or the flash of a notice on her mobile or headlamps from a passing car.

Whatever the case, her sleep had been dreamless and peaceful, and now the light of day was slipping past the cracks in the doors and shutters enough that she could see the outline of Nicholas's shoulder and a stretch of his neck and jaw.

How was it possible she was still here with him? She guessed a part of her had expected to awaken to find that she was back under the stairs in Reider Castle. Although it seemed like ages since she'd gone into the closet and ingested the holy water, it had only been two days. Did that mean today was the first of June?

She could see how it would be easy to lose track of time in the past without the access to a calendar or news sources or work schedules. She had to admit, she rather liked the simplicity and could get used to a life without the constant hurry to get from one activity to the next.

She also hadn't missed any modern conveniences—at least not yet. She'd only camped a time or two while growing up, and this rustic way of life felt partly like that. Maybe once she had to do her own laundry or make her own food, she'd feel differently. But for now, she wasn't put out, not even by the lumpy straw mattress in the wooden box bed.

Her blanket had loosened enough that she easily drew out an arm. The chill of the room sent goose bumps over her skin, a glaring reminder of another difference in the past—no heater to kick on when the night temperature dropped. They would likely have to light a fire in the center hearth to chase away the chill.

As if sensing her coldness, Nicholas drew her closer, enveloping her with his warmth.

Maybe she wouldn't need a fire after all.

The steady rise and fall of his chest told her he was still

sleeping. Breathing in deeply of the air that seemed permanently laden with woodsmoke, she closed her eyes, a new but pleasurable satisfaction welling up inside. She had no place she had to be and nothing demanding her time. This was the only thing she needed or wanted—to be right here, lying beside Nicholas, wrapped in his arms. In fact, she could do this all day. Maybe she would . . .

His words from last night sifted back through her mind: *"I do want you. And I will have you. But not this night."*

He wanted her. But he'd refrained, just as he'd promised. Somehow that restraint made him even more appealing.

She rested her head against his chest and breathed him in, the scent of leather and spices filling her senses. Since arriving in the village, he'd had someone put more salve on his back on a couple of occasions. And she guessed she was smelling the herbs that were part of the salve.

He smelled as good as he felt. And the sight of him . . .

She opened her eyes again, leaned back slightly, and let herself take him in. His lashes were long and dark, and a strand of his hair fell across his forehead. The scruff on his jaw only seemed to highlight the ruggedness of his face, lending him an aura of danger that drew her in.

She wanted to touch his face, wanted to feel his stubble, wanted to test whether his jaw was as rigid as it looked.

Did she dare?

Before she could overthink the situation, she lifted her hand and let herself graze him, lightly so she wouldn't wake him. The outline of his jaw, his firmness, the nearness—it all sent a delicious tremor through her.

Every time she looked at him, he seemed to be more handsome than the last, probably because the more she got to know him, the closer she felt to him. She saw who he really was inside, and the whole Nicholas package was an absolutely tremendous deal.

As though waking, he shifted.

She paused her perusal, watching his expression. When he remained peacefully at rest, she let her fingers roam again, this time up the scruff to his cheekbones. How was it that she was leisurely touching him? How was it that he was holding her so possessively, as though he had no intention of letting her go? And how had she ended up married to him?

She had to be going mad. It was the only explanation for how her life had changed so drastically in such a short time.

As she skimmed even higher, she smoothed the strand of his hair back. His hair was unruly and thick and beckoned to her. She wanted to keep exploring, comb her fingers all the way through. But she held herself back, marveling that she had any right at all to touch him.

She lifted from him altogether, but before she could go far, his hand shot up and gripped her wrist. His eyes opened halfway, and he regarded her through heavy lids. In the next instant, before she could tuck her arm back under the blanket where it belonged, he brought her hand to his lips and brushed a kiss across her knuckles.

The warmth and pressure—and the way he was looking at her—unleashed a flurry inside her stomach.

He kissed her knuckles again, his eyes holding hers, heating her all the way to her core. He made no attempt to disguise the desire he had for her. His wanting was thick and heavy. But it wasn't suffocating. Instead, it seemed to spread through her, like melted honey, so that all she wanted to do was give way to him and let him cover her with sweet kisses.

As though sensing her acquiescence, he kissed her hand again, this time higher, on her wrist. His lips lingered there against her rapidly beating pulse. A moment later, he began to make a slow trail up her inner arm.

His kisses were feathery, exquisite—so that her breath hitched with each teasing touch. Until finally he reached her collarbone. He grazed her shoulder with his thumb almost reverently before bending in and pressing his lips right in the center near the strap of her chemise.

This time his kiss came down forcefully, and she couldn't keep a gasp from escaping. In the next instant, his mouth caught hers just as powerfully. He dragged her close and at the same time plunged her off a cliff into oblivion. The air around them gusted, and heat rose to engulf them. But still she fell hard and fast, unable to brace herself, not even wanting to. Instead, she arched into him, longing to stay with him, needing to be closer.

Somehow her blanket fell away, and his hand splayed flat across her stomach, searing her through the chemise. As one of his legs tangled with hers, he deepened the kiss, taking her captive—body, heart, and soul.

She wanted to take him captive too. Needed to get closer to him. She fisted a hand in his tunic and tugged it up.

He grew motionless and broke the kiss, his breathing heavy and ragged against her lips. As his dark eyes met hers, she found herself lost in them.

He heaved an almost-shuddering breath and tore his gaze from her. Then with an agonized groan, he rose, releasing her and forcing her to let go. She was tempted to snag on to him, jerk him back down, and press her lips to his again. But he stood and stalked away from the bed until he was at the table, his back facing her, heaving up and down.

Only then did she realize her chest was rising and falling with equal swiftness, that they'd kissed so intensely they'd forgotten to breathe.

"Curses upon me." His whisper was filled with self-loathing.

She pushed up to her elbows, trying to make sense of why he was angry. "What's wrong?"

He held his shoulders stiffly while he rubbed a hand down his face.

In her inexperience, had she done something wrong? Maybe she shouldn't have grabbed his tunic. "You didn't like kissing me—?"

"Saint's blood, Sybil," he said harshly. "'Tis the opposite. I like it too much."

"But . . .?"

"I take full responsibility for my overzealousness."

Oh. So he was upset at himself because he thought he was moving too quickly and breaking his vow that they would remain chaste for now. "You didn't act alone, Nicholas." Somehow her voice came out sultrier than she'd intended.

He glanced over his shoulder at her, then quietly cursed himself.

"I was kissing you too."

He shook his head. "Cover up in the blanket."

She sat up and looked down at herself. The chemise wasn't silky and slinky like modern lingerie. While it showed her arms and lower legs, it was modest. But apparently seeing her in it presented a temptation for Nicholas.

A part of her wanted to defy him, to throw the blanket off the bed. But another part of her respected his desire to wait, although she couldn't quite remember why it was so important to him.

He dragged a hand through his hair, his fingers shaking.

Was he trembling because of the strength of his desire and his efforts to restrain himself?

She reached for the blanket, and as she wrapped the blanket around her shoulders, he expelled a noisy breath.

Two days. She'd only known him two days. And even though the chemistry between them rivaled a detonated explosive device, she knew he was right—they would do better to be patient, spend more time together, and get to know each other first.

He held himself rigidly for another moment before he swiped up his doublet off the table where he'd discarded it last night. He made quick work of donning it, snatching up his weapons belt, then striding to the door.

She waited for him to speak again, but he exited without another glance back.

Once he was gone, she fell back into the mattress and let out the tension that had been building.

He was fighting demons she couldn't see, and if he lost the

battle, he'd only despise himself. That meant she had to be on his side and help him win. That also meant for now, they couldn't share the bed. Not until he'd made peace with his past, whatever that might be.

"No," she whispered into the now-lonely cottage. "You can't sleep with Nicholas, not now, and not ever."

They were already getting close, and she had to put on the brakes to keep things from getting out of hand. Especially because she had no idea whether she'd live another day in the past or wake up in her modern-day life.

He'd been wounded once deeply when he'd lost Jane. And if she allowed a closeness to develop with him, he'd only be deeply hurt again. That was the last thing she wanted to do to him.

She needed to act honorably too. She couldn't let herself get carried away by these new and exciting feelings that were developing. She had to keep a level head, remain objective, and maintain a distance from him.

Such a plan would be best. For both of them.

~ 22 ~

"NOCK. MARK. DRAW." Nicholas whispered the command and then loosed an arrow. The familiar twang of the bow vibrated near his ear even as his fingers fumbled to find another arrow in the quiver he'd strapped onto his belt. But it was empty. He'd fired off every single one.

He lowered his bow. As he did so, one of the youth who stood on the sidelines of the butts ran toward the target to retrieve the arrows.

Nicholas counted those at the center. Even with the early morning sun glistening off the dew and blinding him, he'd hit the yellow central bands with every shot.

At the opening and then closing of the door of the cottage where he'd left Sybil, he tensed. He'd thought a little target practice would help release his pent-up energy, but at the prospect of her watching him, his body began to heat again as it had when he'd kissed her in bed a short while ago.

He was surprised he'd made it as long as he had lying in bed with her. But their conversations had been pointed and real and open, and he'd liked talking with her just as he had every other time.

When she'd dozed off, he'd contemplated giving her a kiss

then. But his own eyes had drooped with weariness, and in no time, he'd fallen asleep too. He'd slumbered lightly, his body too aware of her nearness, so that as she'd begun to caress his face, he'd easily awoken.

He'd been waiting and wanting to kiss her again. It was his right to kiss her in their marriage bed whenever he so pleased. But the moment their mouths had fused, he'd known he wouldn't be able to stop with just one kiss. Her lips moving against his, the way she'd pressed against him, the tug of her hand in his tunic—all of it had been like tossing dry grass on a fire.

If he'd allowed himself one more moment with her, one more kiss, one more touch, he would have combusted. He hadn't expected so strong a reaction just from kissing her. But the kiss had been more than just a kiss. It had been an experience, one in which she'd been as fully present as he was. And that only made the connection all the more powerful.

He couldn't kiss her again. At least, not like that.

From the corner of his eye, he could see that she'd started across the distance toward him. His heart picked up its pace, but he didn't turn, didn't give himself the pleasure of taking her in. Instead, he focused on the youth as he ran back to him with the arrows.

"Twelve per minute, sire," the boy said with a grin.

"I shall make it fifteen." He let the boy help him replenish his quiver, made sure the lad stood well back, then lifted his first arrow. An expert bowman was trained for speed in battle. He could easily shoot fifteen, sometimes more per minute when he wasn't distracted by thoughts of the beautiful wife he'd left behind in his marriage bed.

She'd stopped a dozen paces away and was studying the way he was using the bow.

He would relish the opportunity to show her his skills. Nock. Mark. Draw. Loose. The commands from battle were etched into his head. He repeated them over and over, focusing on the target, until once again his fingers found nothing in his quiver.

When he lowered his bow this time, he allowed himself a glance her way.

"Impressive."

Strangely, her one word sent pleasure through him more than the accolades of a dozen men.

"I want to learn." She was taking in every detail of the bow as if picturing herself using it the way he had.

She'd donned the green tunic, but her head was bare, as it had been last eve during the wedding. Thank heavens at least she'd pulled her hair back into a knot so it was no longer hanging loosely around her, adding to her irresistible allure. He'd expected her to wait for Beatrice's assistance with her grooming, but Beatrice likely hadn't anticipated them rising so early, presumed the newlyweds would stay abed.

The village was only just stirring after the late night of feasting. A few women were out gathering tinder for fuel, and two men were drawing water from a well into large buckets that would be used to replenish the troughs for the oxen and horses.

"Will you teach me?" The green of Sybil's eyes in the morning light was filled with expectation and eagerness. She was serious about learning to use the bow and arrow.

He couldn't imagine any other woman wanting to learn. But he had no reason to deny her this. Having some skill with the bow and arrow wouldn't hurt her—might, in fact, help save her life.

"Find us a regular bow," he called to the boy retrieving the arrows. "And gloves."

"I'll use the longbow." Sybil crossed to him and reached for it.

He slung it over his shoulder away from her. "'Tis too big and heavy for a beginner. You will start your learning on a regular bow."

Her brows pinched as though she might protest, but then she nodded. "Let me watch you again. But this time go slower."

The boy brought him the arrows, and as he raced off to find a bow for Sybil, Nicholas went through the basics, showing her how to hold the bow, how to locate the points on the string protected by horn, and then how to nock into one of those points. He fired the arrows and answered her astute questions.

When the boy returned, Sybil wasted no time putting on the gloves and readying herself with the regular bow, positioning it, nocking an arrow, and then firing. She lacked power and the arrow fell flat only a dozen paces away.

As the sun rose higher, the villagers were soon hard at work doing their daily tasks for survival. With the plowing and sowing already completed in the cleared field, the men devoted themselves to other tasks. Some were repairing a wattle fence with more daub, while others created a dead hedge with hawthorn and brambles. Another man was in the process of steam bending hazel so the wood could be shaped for furniture, while yet another was shoeing a horse.

Several women were already using the walking wheels to spin the newly shorn wool, winding it into thread on a spindle. A couple of women were milking sheep and would use the liquid to make sheep's cheese. Still others were gathering geese eggs or were working in their gardens.

Except for Eric, who glared once in passing, and the village children perched on fence posts nearby, no one seemed to be paying particular attention to his shooting lesson with Sybil, although he suspected everyone was watching nonetheless. They didn't expect him to join in their work, but he had assisted from time to time on previous visits with whatever tasks were most urgent.

They wouldn't expect Sybil, as a nobleman's wife, to take up the daily tasks either, although she would find more fulfillment in accomplishing something rather than sitting around doing nothing. He trusted that Beatrice would aid her in filling her time productively while not taxing her unnecessarily.

Whatever the case, he relished teaching her archery. She was a quick learner and a hard worker. When she finally began to understand the technique, her arrows flew with more strength and precision, not hitting the target but at least going some distance. Never once did she complain, even though he guessed her arms ached from the repetition of pulling the bow and that her fingers were sore, even through the gloves.

Upon finishing with the archery lessons, she wanted him to show her how to ride a horse, and after that, she insisted on learning some basic sword-fighting maneuvers.

The day passed much too rapidly. At eventide, the villagers used his new marriage as another chance to feast together. When the feasting was over, he took the first guard duty shift. By the time he stumbled into the cottage in the early hours of the morn, he was tempted to crawl into bed with her again. But he refrained and spread out a blanket on the floor instead, knowing he wouldn't be able to resist her the next time he slept beside her.

The next day followed a similar pattern, and he spent nearly every waking moment with her in archery and sword-fighting practice along with more training with riding a horse. She was easy to converse with, and he never tired of being with her. In fact, the more time he spent with her, the more he began to dread leaving.

But upon speaking with Ralph and several other men, 'twas clear he could delay his departure no longer, especially because riders had been spotted in the Weald. He did not doubt the riders were Simon's men searching for him. Nicholas had to track them down, wherever they were, and let them pick up his trail so that he could lead them far away from Devil's Bend.

That night, again, he forced himself to sleep on a blanket on the floor. When he awoke, Sybil was already at the butts practicing with her bow, her arrows imbedding into the target ever closer to the center. He fell into an easy rhythm with her similar to the other mornings. But as the sun rose higher and the village began to awaken, he knew he had to be off.

He reached for Sybil's bow, but she shifted it away from him even as she pulled out another arrow. "You have worked hard enough for now." He spoke firmly. "Time to rest."

"I'm very close to hitting the center target. Just a few more tries, and I'll have it."

"Most boys must practice weeks before being proficient. You cannot expect to learn archery in mere days."

"I intend not only to learn it but to become one of the best." She held herself almost defiantly, her flashing eyes daring him to contradict her.

He wouldn't have been able to even if he tried. She was simply too beautiful, with her chin jutting out and her forehead lined with determination.

"Beatrice has delivered us a meal, and we shall go now and eat it." His stomach growled, confirming the need for the fare.

Sybil glanced to the cottage, as though surprised to see that the real world still existed all around her. She stared at the door for a moment, then shook her head. "You go. I'll continue to practice."

As she started to draw her bow, he swooped her up, bow and all, slung her across his shoulder, and carried her toward the cottage.

"What are you doing?" She didn't fight him. Instead, her voice almost sounded amused.

"Taking you home." *Home.* The word warmed him. Even if Father Fritz's cottage wasn't a permanent home, with Sybil beside him, it felt more like home than Reider Castle ever had. Had he put too much hope in a place of his own? For so many years, he'd believed that having an estate would solve his problems. Maybe it wasn't so much about where a man lived but with whom.

"You do know I am allowing you to do this, don't you?" she asked.

"Are you now?"

"Yes, I could fight my way free from you in two seconds if I chose to."

"Not two seconds from me."

"Yes, two seconds from you."

He tightened his grip. "I should like to see you try."

"And embarrass you in front of everyone? I'll spare you the indignity."

A grin worked its way up his lips. "And I shall spare you yours."

Her fingers grazed his back, and suddenly he was attuned to every lovely part of her body, especially the way his arm brushed up against her firm backside.

He increased his pace so that he didn't do something foolish in front of the entire village, like inch his arm higher. As he shoved open the door and ducked inside, the waft of pottage made his stomach rumble again.

He kicked the door closed behind them. And before he knew what was happening, she linked her arm around his neck in a tight vise while at the same time hooked his free arm behind his back, jerking it up painfully.

The sharpness of her maneuvers took him off guard, forcing him to loosen his hold. In the next instant, she was sliding down, turning around, and flipping him onto her back in the same move she'd made the first time he'd seen her in the dungeon.

This time, however, he was prepared. He wrapped an arm around her waist. Before she could gain momentum, he straightened and pulled her against him, pinning both arms to her sides.

With her back flush against his chest, he could feel her stiffen and prepare to break free. Before she could disarm him some other way with one of her interesting defensive techniques, he did what he'd been wanting to do since their wedding night. He bent in and pressed his lips to her neck, tasting her skin, breathing in her freshness, and feeling the rapid beat of her pulse.

She gasped and her grip slackened.

He let his lips linger there even as a warning clanged through him that he needed to be careful to remain restrained with this exchange.

"I see what you're doing," she whispered huskily.

"And what is that?" He skimmed his lips to the spot below her ear.

She dragged in another short breath. "You're trying to weaken me."

"Is it working?" He knew it was, but he wanted to hear her own to defeat.

She tilted her head, giving him permission to continue.

He didn't need her permission. To prove it, he laid a kiss against the hollow of her ear. "Do you concede to me?"

"If I accept defeat, what will you do to me?"

He would devour her if he could. But he cast aside that thought as quickly as it came. "I will command you."

"How so?" Her whisper was filled with longing.

This time he dropped a kiss to the soft hollow where her shoulder and neck met. At the kiss, she snaked a hand up behind his head, gripping him hard, as though to beg him to keep going.

A sizzle of energy coursed through him at the realization that he could command her with but the faintest of kisses. He pressed his kiss into the spot more firmly and let one of his hands skim up her arm. Even with the sleeve acting as a barrier between his fingers and her skin, the feel of her awakened him every bit as fully now as it did whenever he glimpsed her in her chemise.

He had the overwhelming urge to spin her around and kiss her on her mouth. This bantering, the soft kisses on her neck, the wanting . . . it was all leading to another passionate exchange, wasn't it? Surely he wouldn't be pushing her too much by sharing a few kisses this morn before he departed.

As he brushed a kiss against her jaw and dropped his hand to her hip, intending to pivot her, a banging resounded against the door. It flew open before he could release her.

Father Fritz took them in with rounded eyes, his cheeks flushing. "Beatrice, ye were right," he shouted over his shoulder outside. "They have their hands all over each other, that they do. Good thing I knocked."

With a start, Sybil broke away, ducking her head and crossing toward the table.

Nicholas folded his arms and narrowed his eyes at the priest. "What do you want?"

Father Fritz held up the same canister of salve that Nicholas had brought with him from the dungeon. "'Tis time for me to doctor your wounds."

The priest had been faithfully tending him morn and night. But now was not the time. "Come back later."

Father Fritz shot another look over his shoulder. "Blimey. Ye were right on that score too, Beatrice. Nicholas wants me to doctor him later."

Faintly, he could hear Beatrice's scolding voice calling out, "I told you to leave them be."

Sybil was stirring one of the bowls of pottage too fast, spilling some onto the table. Even as every muscle in Nicholas's body ached to pull her back against him and continue kissing her, he knew he was playing a dangerous game with temptation. Maybe this interruption by Father Fritz was for the best.

"I'll leave ye two lovers be." Father Fritz glanced at Sybil. Finding her back turned, he grinned at Nicholas, then waggled his eyebrows.

Nicholas deepened his scowl even though a part of him wanted to laugh. "You may as well stay and put on the salve, now that you are here."

"I don't mind coming back later, my dear son." Father Fritz's grin remained in place. "It's just that since yer leaving soon, I thought—"

"Leaving soon?" Sybil spun, the pottage now dripping from the spoon onto the floor.

How had Father Fritz learned of his plans? Nicholas scowled at the priest again, but it wasn't his fault. Likely Ralph had spoken to Beatrice. And once Beatrice had news, it wasn't long before the whole village was privy to it.

As Father Fritz took in the surprise upon Sybil's countenance, his grin slipped away. "Well, now, I guess I'd better get my noggy on my way. I be needing to attend to one of the villagers who's been urgently asking for . . . prayer . . . anointing . . . the Holy Eucharist . . . and possibly even baptism—"

"Stay." Nicholas no longer wanted to be alone with Sybil, not now that she knew of his leaving. Father Fritz would be able to help if she cried overmuch.

Nicholas pulled off his tunic and dropped to the bench at the table. Besides, Father Fritz was right. He needed another coating of the healing salve before he departed. Though the wounds didn't hurt nearly as much anymore, they still stung.

Father Fritz didn't move and neither did Sybil.

"Where are you going?" she asked quietly.

Was her question the calm before the storm? "Away. To keep Simon from tracking me here and thus exposing the village."

She set the spoon down on the table and pinned it there, as if she were afraid it would fly away with him.

Nicholas motioned Father Fritz in with a curt nod.

The priest's eyes only opened wider, and he shook his head.

"Saint's blood, Father Fritz. Put the salve on."

Father Fritz scurried toward him, not daring to look at Sybil.

Perhaps the priest would do no good after all. He seemed more frightened of her reaction than Nicholas.

"You're right." Sybil's voice was still much too calm. "You need to leave."

Father Fritz, in the process of opening the tin, paused and expelled a long breath. "There, no harm done—"

"And I'm going with you." Sybil lifted her chin and met Nicholas's gaze with a steely one of her own.

Something about her challenge, as previously, gave him a secret thrill. Even though he liked that she spoke her mind and wasn't afraid of peril, he couldn't take her. Or could he? If she came, then he wouldn't have to leave her behind and worry for her safety.

On the other hand, he had no guarantee that once he made himself prey to Simon's men he'd be able to outrun and outwit them. Having her along might slow him down and put her needlessly in harm's way—especially since she was only just learning to ride a horse.

She studied his face, as if reading his thoughts.

"I would take you if I could." It was the truth. He wasn't merely saying so to placate her the same way he'd done with Jane. Sybil was a stronger woman. She was capable and skilled and smart. And her words from several nights ago echoed in his head: *"I won't be content to be left behind to do menial things. I'll help you with defending the innocent from their accusers."*

Maybe someday she could ride with and help him. But not this time.

He braced himself once again for sobs and tantrums. But they never came.

Instead, she lowered herself to the bench opposite his. "What is your plan? How will you stay ahead of Simon's men?" Her eyes were dark and serious, and her question was just as purposeful, as though she had every intent of advising him on how to travel without getting caught.

With a cock of his head toward Father Fritz, who had begun to administer the salve, Sybil nodded, seeming to understand that he would do best not to reveal his plans. The marks on his back attested to how brutal Simon could be when attempting to extract information. And he didn't want to jeopardize anyone with information Simon might find useful.

They talked and ate their pottage while Father Fritz applied the salve. When finished, Beatrice made an appearance to clear off their meal, also offering to help Sybil with her hair and head covering.

Nicholas bowed out of the cottage to allow the women privacy and also to see about borrowing the swiftest mount possible. As he walked away from the cottage with Father Fritz babbling nonstop, Nicholas already missed being with Sybil after only minutes away from her. He truly wished she could accompany him, but he sensed this was a mission he would accomplish better on his own.

~ 23 ~

SYBIL WASN'T READY TO SAY good-bye to Nicholas. But as she stood on the edge of Devil's Bend with the gathering of villagers, she knew it was for the best. She couldn't ride a horse well enough yet. And sharing a mount with Nicholas would slow him down as he tried to outrun Simon's men and lead them out of the Weald.

He spoke in hushed tones with Ralph and several other older men. From the seriousness of their expressions, she knew they were all worried for Nicholas.

She tried to tell herself he would be fine, that he wouldn't allow Simon to capture him. But she only had to think about how badly he'd been hurt when she found him in the dungeon to know he wasn't a superhero. He could be captured, hurt, even killed in this dangerous era when the law and law enforcement seemed to be at the whim of a select few.

Even though her blood had been running cold since Father Fritz had spilled the news about Nicholas's leaving, she'd kept her emotions in check. Regardless, a part of her had started to panic. She'd come to the past to help Nicholas. How could she do that if he was far away from her?

She gave herself permission to study him openly a final

216

time, lingering over his strong profile. She'd learned much about him during their few days together as man and wife. Not only was he a patient teacher, but he was encouraging and giving and nothing ever seemed to ruffle him. He'd easily accepted her athleticism and desire to become proficient with his weapons. And he seemed to enjoy spending time with her as much as she had with him.

He'd remained true to his word to give them time to get to know each other and, after their first night, hadn't initiated any physical contact again until just a little while ago when he'd carried her back to the cottage. She could see now that the total abstinence had been wise, since just one touch, one kiss, hadn't satisfied her.

But she also knew why he'd allowed the contact—he'd known he was leaving and that the kisses wouldn't lead anywhere.

What if he didn't return? What if she never saw him again?

An ache formed deep inside, one of need for this man in a way that was almost frightening. The need pulsed swiftly and fiercely through her chest, nearly sending her to her knees with the pain of the longing.

Was this what falling in love felt like? Had she fallen in love with Nicholas already? It seemed impossible. But her desire for him was stronger than what she'd ever felt for anyone else.

She could only pray he'd return soon—maybe within a few days, at the very least a week. Yet even that might be too long. For if he survived, would she still be here when he came back?

She didn't know what was happening with her body in the present day. If no one had found her, would she die under the steps? Without IV fluids and monitoring, she wouldn't last but a few days in the closet. And if someone had discovered her and taken her to the hospital, what if Harrison and Ellen were returning from their honeymoon and figuring out a way to revive her? Maybe they'd located more holy water and had the dose necessary to bring a her out of the coma and a second dose to keep her alive.

As if sensing her gaze upon him, Nicholas glanced up. Something intense radiated in his eyes. Were his emotions the same as hers? Was he drawing as close to her as she was to him?

"I would have a last moment with my wife." He spoke with an authority that never failed to command action from the men.

The men bowed their heads. With a nod, he watched them walk away with the women. They were leaving her alone in the shadows of the woodland with a man who represented everything good and right in the world.

Nicholas stood a dozen paces away. He was holding the reins of his mount, but he was also holding her heart captive.

Birdsong and the chatter of squirrels filled the morning along with the laughter of several children playing together while watching the sheep.

"Be careful and be smart." She offered the words of advice she gave to her team members before an especially tricky investigation.

"I vow it." He seemed to give himself permission to take her in, starting with her face and then sweeping over the length of her. When his gaze met hers again, an undeniable heat darkened his eyes. "Be here when I return?"

She wished she could promise him as easily as he'd promised her. But she couldn't. "I'll do my best."

Apparently, her answer didn't satisfy him. He released his horse's reins and closed the distance between them swiftly. He grasped her hands first, then cupped her cheek. "You must be here." His voice was hoarse.

The desperation within it tugged at her heart. "I want to be with you, Nicholas, as I have for no one else ever before."

"And I you."

If this parting was already difficult, it was only bound to grow more so the longer they were together. What was she doing, encouraging this relationship and fostering a bond with him? She couldn't predict the ending of their story, but she suspected it involved much heartache. A strange sorrow took root in her chest—a sorrow she didn't want to think about at the moment.

As though sensing her sorrow, he slipped his hand around the back of her neck. "You will be here when I return, and we shall find a way to be together."

Before she could figure out a right—and truthful—reply, he bent and fused his mouth with hers. The taste of him was full of both sunshine and rain, wind and earth, joy and bittersweetness.

She gave herself over to him, unable to resist the pull to love him, even though she had to use caution. He allowed her little choice, plunging into the kiss with a fervor that pushed her to respond in the same, letting their mouths say everything words couldn't—that they were bonded, that this desire between them was more real than anything, and that they needed each other more than they needed sustenance.

How was it that being in the past, being with him, and being in love brought her to life in a way she'd never before experienced?

His kiss turned hard and desperate. He seemed to be offering her promises of the future, a lifetime of love and pleasure together, giving her a taste of all they would have when he returned.

She let her kiss grow just as desperate, her response telling him how much she cared about him and needed him and wanted to be with him always.

Then, without warning, he broke from her and stalked back to his horse. He mounted, flicked the reins, and nudged the horse forward.

Helplessness seeped through her—the same she'd felt whenever she visited Dawson. All she could do was watch Nicholas ride away. She had no power or ability to do anything else.

She willed him to turn around one last time and say good-bye. But he bent his head, kicked his heels into his steed, and disappeared into the forest. Within seconds, the woodland was still and silent, only the leaves whispering in the breeze.

Heaving a sigh of finality, she turned and gazed at the village. It was like a picture from a history textbook: quaint, simple, and pretty in the morning sunlight. The people were busy and didn't seem to be paying her attention.

What would she do here? Without Nicholas?

With heavy steps she made her way to the cottage. As she let herself in and closed the door behind her, the barrenness of the dim, dank room made her chest ache with a strange need to cry. This wasn't home without Nicholas.

She had nothing to do and nowhere to go. She couldn't flip on the TV to escape her sorrows in a crime show. She couldn't wander mindlessly on the internet, reading news and local crime reports. Not that she did those things all that often anyway. What she really wanted was to lose herself in a tough CrossFit workout. Or delve headfirst into a difficult new case.

Suddenly her whole body felt weighted down, and exhaustion swept over her. She'd gotten very little sleep over the past few days. Maybe she'd return to bed, curl up, and escape into oblivion through slumber.

That's what she'd do. And maybe when she woke up, she'd find this was all a dream.

She kicked off her combat boots and slipped off her belt. As she climbed onto the thin mattress and closed her eyes, her mind filled with the memory of Nicholas shedding his garments and then sliding into bed with her on their wedding night. His presence would have overpowered her in a king-size bed. But in a wooden bed box that was not much bigger than a single size, he'd been much too near. Even when he'd flopped onto the blanket on the floor the past couple of nights, his presence had been comforting, even exciting.

She drew the blanket around her more securely. She'd give anything to have his nearness now. Just one more day. Maybe one more night.

But would one ever be enough? Or would she be constantly wishing for more time with him?

In spite of her aching heart, she somehow fell asleep. The

sound of footsteps in the room woke her, and she held herself motionless. Even with her eyes still closed, she could sense the daylight pouring into the cottage and guessed she'd slept for a couple of hours at most.

The steps approached the bed, and she inched her hand toward her leg and the knife in her boot only to remember she'd taken her boots off.

As the presence hovered near, she caught a whiff of onions and allowed herself to relax. It was just Beatrice. The woman had probably come to check on her and see how she was doing now that Nicholas was gone.

But at the moment, Sybil didn't want to talk to anyone. Her heart ached too much, and she didn't have the energy to hide it.

Beatrice breathed heavily above her for several more moments, then she turned and crossed the room with firm steps. When the door clicked closed, Sybil released a sigh.

What was she doing here wallowing in a drafty cottage in the middle of the Weald in the year 1382? She needed to get up and start sorting out how to find holy water before she died either in the present or the past. Because once she died in one era, according to Harrison the body would also soon die in the other time period—unless she ingested holy water at just the right time to stave off death.

It was complicated, and the fact was, her chances of surviving this trip were slim. She could understand now why there were no records of people time traveling. They didn't live to talk about it. Those who did, like Harrison and Ellen, had barely survived.

The real question was—did she want to return to the present, or did she want to stay in the past?

Of course, she didn't want to leave Nicholas, didn't want to cause him grief again. His plea for her to be here waiting for him had been laden with the heartache of already having lost one woman and fearing to lose another.

But if she found more holy water and used it to keep her 1382 body alive, would she be content living in the past for the rest of her days? Or would she eventually regret making the decision? Would being with Nicholas make up for everything she would have to give up—her career, the conveniences, the security, her friends? Would she regret not finishing her search for Dr. Lionel? What about Dawson?

A slice of bitterness pricked her. Dawson hadn't cared about her for years. And if she died, maybe he'd finally regret driving her out of his life. Maybe. But probably not.

She pushed herself up and groaned at her dilemma. The decision she had to make was heavy and hard. Either way—whether she attempted to return to the present or stayed in the past—she would need holy water to have any chance of surviving. And in order to search for holy water, she had to get better at riding a horse. That had to be her first order of business for her time in the village. And the second was similar. She had to become better at using a bow and arrow, since the methods of self-defense she'd learned in modern times might not be as useful in 1382.

With another grunt, she swung her legs over. She fumbled for her boots only to find that one had disappeared under the bed. She knelt on the hard earthen floor and peered into the dark space. She was surprised to find that it was crammed full of containers and what appeared to be medicinal bottles.

She'd gathered that many monks and nuns were trained to be doctors of a sort, that often the poor would seek out medical care as charity from a local abbey rather than having to pay a physician. Was Father Fritz the doctor in this community as well as the priest?

Perhaps he'd been able to bring his medicines with him when he fled from wherever he was serving before being accused of spying. No doubt he'd shoved all the items under the bed when he'd vacated the home for Nicholas and her.

Grabbing her wayward boot, she sat up. She couldn't live in this place by herself—not without Nicholas, and not when the village was counting on Father Fritz to be available to help doctor them whenever they needed it.

Even as she slipped on the boot, she tried to ignore the empty ache at the center of her chest, the one that Nicholas had occupied and filled to overflowing. She had to stop feeling sorry for herself and make good use of the time he was gone to find holy water. If she didn't, she would surely die.

- 24 -

NICHOLAS COULDN'T SHAKE the premonition of impending doom. Not even the sight of the coast ahead eased his unrest. Normally he appreciated the magnificence of the white-chalk cliffs that rose several hundred feet above the coastal water that was as calm and clear and blue as the sky. But not today. Not after failing to locate and draw the attention of Simon's men. After two days of searching, Nicholas hadn't come across them and had finally conceded that they'd left the Weald altogether.

He'd decided to ride on to Dover and take advantage of the lull to seek out Walter to cipher the numbers from Simon's missive. Once there, word was sure to reach Simon of his whereabouts.

Breathing in the scent of seaweed and brine, Nicholas pushed his mount onward toward the town with Dover Castle rising above it. Every time he visited, more work had been done to fortify the walls to protect the people from French marauders. The presence of ships farther out in the Channel attested to the king's fleet patrolling the sea, keeping watch for French raiders who were a danger to English vessels and towns.

But as far as Nicholas could assess, everything was peaceful with no signs of peril from the enemy without.

The trouble for him this time wasn't from without. It was from within. His own brother sought to eliminate him just as he had every other Worth man. Although Simon would never take responsibility for the death of their brother as well as cousins, all had perished in accidents he'd orchestrated. And now Nicholas was the last remaining relative who posed a threat to Simon's progeny.

Simon needed to be held accountable for his crimes. At the very least, Nicholas couldn't let him obtain the victory this time. Simon very well might have if Sybil hadn't set him free. She'd given him a second chance to bring about justice for himself, his family, and all those Simon had hurt, and Nicholas couldn't squander it.

Earlier, when he'd passed through Folkestone and visited his goldsmith friend, he'd learned Simon had sent couriers all throughout Kent to spread the news that Nicholas had escaped from prison and was wanted for treason. If that wasn't cruel enough, Simon was offering a sizeable reward for bringing him in alive.

The friend had urged Nicholas to remain in hiding, not to show his face in Folkestone or Dover. But Nicholas couldn't trust anyone but himself to deliver the numbers to Walter. He just prayed the numbers really were a code. If not, he'd be back at the starting point with finding evidence that Simon was the one working for the French and not him.

The road widened and grew busier with those coming and going to Dover's market as well as to the city's harbor. As one of five coastal Cinque Ports, the town abounded with travelers and merchants.

Nicholas slowed his horse and pulled the hood of his cloak farther over his face. Though it was late in the afternoon, he didn't have the option of waiting until the cover of darkness to venture into town since the gates would be closed. No, he needed to enter now while the traffic was heavy so he wouldn't draw attention from the guards in the gatehouses or on the town walls.

He slid from his mount and began to lead it, attempting to blend in with the crowds. Biggin, the northern gate, would also be busy since it was where the road from London and Canterbury entered town. Such a thoroughfare was heavily traversed, used by royalty as well as church dignitaries. As a nobleman, he'd be less noticed there.

At least he could rest in the assurance that Devil's Bend was safe. Perhaps on the way out of Dover on the morrow, he'd drop a hint that he was continuing along the coast, drawing Simon's men even farther from the Weald.

He would do anything to keep the people there from harm. Even more, he needed Sybil to be secure.

"My wife," he whispered, as sharp need mingled with sharp pleasure at just the mention of her.

All throughout the past two days of being apart, his thoughts had gone back to her continually—his first visions of her when he'd been in the dungeon, her aid in escaping from Reider Castle, her bravery in leaping from the castle into the moat, her strength and stamina in keeping up with him as they ran through the Kent countryside to get away. He'd recounted their wedding and the feasting afterward, the night holding her in his arms, two blissful days of spending every waking moment with her, every look and word they'd exchanged.

Then there were the kisses. Even as he imagined the feel of her lips against his, he ached for another opportunity to kiss her. A part of him was relieved he'd stayed strong and hadn't pressured her into more. But another part wished he'd taken the chance to be with her as man and wife while he could . . .

Always at the back of his mind was the nagging worry that maybe she wouldn't be there when he returned. She hadn't been able to give him the reassurance he'd sought. What if while he was away, she was called back to the time and place from whence she'd come?

As he passed through the gate, the heavy odor of salted and drying fish permeated the air, along with the ever-present tang of the sea.

The bustling entrance rang with the calls of a town crier as well as a group of boys with sooty faces who were approaching important-looking men, calling out offers to direct them to an inn and to care for their horses.

Merchants mingled about, selling wares from their shops. Their narrow townhouses rose three or four stories in height, allowing them to conduct business on the ground level with living quarters above. The bottom half of each large shop window was lowered, providing a counter to display goods, and the top half was hinged up to allow for a shelter.

All around were signs of the destruction from the earthquake a fortnight ago—crumbling walls and piles of rubble, although he'd heard that Canterbury had suffered the worst and that outlying towns like Dover hadn't been affected as significantly.

At the first alley, Nicholas ducked out of the traffic with his mount. He hastened his steps into a jog, dodging piles of refuse and animal droppings. The stench of excrement was strong, and he breathed through his mouth.

As he passed by one of the stables he'd used previously, he left his horse before continuing on to a quieter and more respectable business area where the buildings were constructed of stone with glazed windows and tiled roofs.

When he reached the scrivener's door bearing a sign of a quill and inkpot, he glanced both ways. From what he could tell, he'd made it through the town without anyone taking notice of him. Now he prayed he would find refuge and a warm meal with Walter this night.

He slipped into the workshop to find his friend seated on a stool and bent over an angled table with a parchment laid over it. In the process of dipping his quill into ink, he paused, letting his pen rest above the pot before shifting his attention. His eyes widened at the sight of Nicholas standing just inside the door.

"Sir Nicholas." Walter rose hastily, nearly tipping one of several inkpots spread out around him. "What brings you to my humble abode?" A simple cap hugged his head, leaving only a few strands of his brown hair visible. He wore a dark tunic— one that mostly hid the inkblots that had accumulated there over the years.

Nicholas took in every detail of the room in a sweeping glance. The other two scriveners—both older men—had already left for the day, exactly what he'd been hoping for. Their angular writing tables were empty of parchment and their quills at rest. The weighted sheets of the stiff paper were hanging from lines along the sides of the room, the ink in various stages of drying. The men had been busy writing out legal documents, deeds, wills, and anything else required of them, mostly from the merchant class who lacked the ability to read and write for themselves.

Walter lived alone in the room above the shop, which meant they would be undisturbed. Even so, Nicholas had to proceed with caution before bringing up the code-breaking.

"I have need of your skills. I should like you to draw up a marriage license." He paused. "For me."

At the news, Walter's legs gave way, and he dropped onto his stool, clasping the writing table with his ink-stained fingers to steady himself. Walter stared with an open mouth before allowing a smile to blossom.

The license was just an excuse to visit Walter, since Nicholas didn't care one way or another if he had an official document. Even if he hadn't been a hunted criminal, he still wouldn't have done things properly by having the banns posted for three Sundays. He would have obtained their license from the bishop to avoid the three-week delay. But as he was now married, Walter's document would serve more as a record of the event than official permission.

"I did not think I would ever behold this day, sire," Walter spoke reverently. "I am verily astounded and joyful."

Walter had been like a father to Jane and Eric after their own had passed away when they'd been children. The kind-hearted man had provided for their mother for many years, never once asking anything of her in return even though he'd loved her.

After the attack against Rye by the French, Walter, like Eric, had never been able to return to the scene of so much heartache and loss. For the past five years Walter had been living in Dover, continuing his work as a scrivener in a shop with several other men of his guild.

Unlike Eric, Walter hadn't wanted Nicholas to grieve over Jane forever, had encouraged him to be open to loving another maiden. Always Nicholas had objected, had insisted that he never would care for anyone the way he had for Jane.

But now that he'd met Sybil, he knew how foolish his declaration had been.

"Sire, this is the best news. Truly." Walter had a soft-spoken voice, one that Nicholas had never heard raised in anger. "May I ask when the blessed occasion is to occur?"

"It already has."

Walter's mouth dropped open again.

"I did not expect to marry so quickly." Nicholas still wasn't sure what had prompted him to make such an impetuous decision. But now that it was done, he was relieved Sybil was his and that he need not worry about another man claiming her. "She is unlike anyone I have ever known."

Walter's eyes crinkled at the corners as he studied Nicholas's face. "I can see it in your eyes. You love her."

At his wedding, he'd denied such feelings when Beatrice had declared the same thing. But now, with the strength of the emotion that had been churning through him since leaving her behind, he could almost believe Walter was right.

"I feel for her deeply," he admitted. "'Tis different than what I shared with Jane."

"You and Jane were both young. Your lives had yet to experience seasoning."

"But I was with Jane for three years. Surely that would allow for *seasoning*."

"Seasoning happens best through fire and heat."

"Fire and heat?"

"God uses trials and hardships to mature us in ways that nothing else can."

Had his trials and hardships helped to season and mature him so that now, after all he'd gone through, he was able to love others more fully and completely? Had Sybil's difficulties done the same for her?

Though the tragedies he'd experienced were terrible, somehow through them he had grown in sympathy, the need to fight injustice, and the longing to help the helpless. Would he have had the burning desire to take up the causes of the people in the Weald if he hadn't experienced his own pain? In fact, if not for Eric's crime and subsequent need to seek refuge, Nicholas might not have sought out Devil's Bend for Eric, might not have met the people of the Weald at all.

For so many years, he'd been blaming God for the difficulties, had even given up respecting God. But what if, all along, God had been using the fire and heat to make him better, stronger?

He had always appreciated that he could be honest about his struggles with Walter, who responded with such wisdom and patience. "I confess that I fear the depth of my attraction to my wife. I fear such desire will turn me into a man commanded by his lusts and selfish needs the way Simon is."

Walter watched him with his fullest attention, his eyes as kind as always. "If you make it your goal to always put her needs above your own, then you do not need to be afraid of anything."

Was that what Walter had done? Put Jane's mother's needs above his own? If only Jane's mother had set aside her grief for her husband and allowed herself to see past Walter's plain appearance to love him in return.

"The lusts of our flesh can control us powerfully." Walter offered one of his warm smiles. "But sacrificial love, when given freely, has the greatest power of all."

Nicholas nodded, taking in the counsel he hadn't realized he'd so desperately needed. He wanted to be different for Sybil. Maybe there was hope after all that he could learn to love her the right way.

Walter stood once more from his stool, retrieved a clean piece of parchment, and placed it on one of the other writing tables. "I am guessing you have come to me for more than marriage advice and a marriage certificate. But I shall create one for you before closing shop. Then we will share a meal in my quarters, and you will tell me everything."

Nicholas glanced at the door and then took a step closer to Walter. "I cannot deny that I am in peril."

"Simon has a bounty on your head."

A stone settled in Nicholas's stomach. "Then everyone in Dover is aware?"

"Simon's riders have come through now twice." Walter situated his ink and pen before sitting down in front of the blank sheet.

Nicholas's muscles tensed. How long before someone sent word to Simon's men that he was here at Walter's? "I should go. My presence here will only cause you harm."

"We have time." Walter dipped the quill into the pot, tapped it to release the extra blots, then lifted it and made several quick marks. "You must leave when the town gates open at dawn and go north by way of the sea. I know of a fisherman who will take you as far as Ramsgate."

Walter was right. Simon's men would likely be lying in wait near the gates, expecting him to travel north by horse. By the time they realized he'd left by sea, it would be too late for them to predict where he'd gone.

"Unless you need a ship to take you directly to London." Walter didn't glance up as his pen scratched against the parchment, words taking shape, but it was clear the man knew exactly why Nicholas had come to visit him.

• ● •

"I have it now." Walter sat at the table in his upstairs room, bent over a sheet filled with mathematical equations. The light of the candle still glowed even though the stub had burned down to a puddle of tallow.

Nicholas stood next to the thick-paned window where he'd been keeping watch for most of the long night as Walter went through the meticulous steps of deciphering which letters each number represented. In French.

Walter's history was complicated, and he preferred to keep it private. From the little Nicholas had gleaned, he knew

Walter's grandfather had been a tutor to royalty. He'd been cast aside for a reason Walter had never explained, and at some point joined a guild of scriveners.

Thus, Walter had gained a better education than even Nicholas had received during his years fostered out for his knight training. Alas, Walter didn't share his knowledge with most people. Only a few trusted men knew about his code-breaking skills, and Nicholas was amongst them—had stumbled upon the information by accident when he'd once barged into Walter's home in Rye and discovered him scribbling out math problems.

Nicholas surveyed the street, still deserted save for a cat scurrying about and nightmen emptying latrines. He didn't want anyone barging in on Walter now, not when he was so close to breaking the code.

"'Tis a reverse alphabet with *A* equaling twenty-five minus twelve." Walter continued to write rapidly on the parchment.

Nicholas didn't know what any of Walter's comments meant. But his muscles loosened, and he allowed himself to take his first deep breath in hours.

Walter had discarded his cap long ago while they'd shared a simple fare of fish and bread washed down with ale. Now his hair stood on end from running his fingers through it so oft. "I knew they would not make the code overly difficult, not if they expected Simon's scribe to translate it."

From the way the darkness was slowly dissipating, dawn was not far off. And then would begin another harrowing day of traveling and praying he could keep Simon's men on his trail while also holding them at bay.

Hopefully, the furious scratching of Walter's quill meant the days of running and hiding would soon be over. "Thank you, my friend. You have been a godsend."

"I am pleased to do it, sire. I would like to see you free of Simon's wiles—" Walter drew in a sharp breath and stared at a line of letters spelling out something in French. Although Nicholas was able to speak French proficiently, his skills in reading it were lacking.

Walter glanced up, his forehead creased with more lines than usual. "The news is urgent, sire." His gaze darted to the window, then to the closed door that led to the shop below. "The French are organizing an attack on Saint Medard's Day."

Nicholas's blood turned to ice. He quickly counted the days remaining until then. Three, if he didn't include the day of the attack. "Does it say where?"

Walter read the message again. "They plan to land at Ramsgate and march to Canterbury in the night. They want Simon to find a way to unlock Newingate."

Curses upon Simon. Would he betray his own country this way?

Nicholas paced to the door, then back to the window, his mind spinning with the gravity of the situation. It was, indeed, urgent and needed to be relayed to the king with all haste. This was no longer about proving his innocence of treachery. This was about saving their beloved city from marauders.

He didn't expect the French planned to occupy Canterbury but believed they would instead wreak their destruction, possibly destroy the sacred pilgrimage site at the cathedral, as well as burn, loot, and kill—the same way they had at Rye.

"Why?" Nicholas whispered the question, unable to keep his anguish from lacing it.

Walter's face had turned pale. He was likely thinking about Rye too. He'd lived through the attack, the burn scars covering most of his backside a constant reminder of all that had happened.

"What does Simon have to gain?" Walter asked.

Nicholas shook his head in frustration but then stopped as one possibility barreled into him. "The wellspring."

"What wellspring?"

"The wellspring at St. Sepulchre. 'Tis believed to contain holy water that can cure any disease."

Walter was silent a moment. "Perhaps 'tis true, sire. I have heard rumors of healings taking place in Canterbury."

Nicholas didn't question the power of the holy water. He'd witnessed its healing at work, but he didn't have time now for detailed explanations. "Simon recently failed to wrest control of the wellspring away from Lord Durham of Chesterfield Park. Now he is utilizing this invasion of the French into Canterbury as a means of securing it." Would he request that the French attack St. Sepulchre specifically and murder everyone inside the premises?

The very idea of Simon abetting the French's attack for so selfish a gain made Nicholas's stomach roil. "How does he think he will get away with such treachery?"

"Have you considered why Simon is so eager to have you as his prisoner?"

Nicholas brought the spinning in his head to a standstill, calming the turmoil so that he could analyze the situation rationally.

He'd believed Simon had beaten him to gain information to give to the French, and he expected Simon to put him to death once he had what he wanted. But what if all along Simon had intended to keep Nicholas alive but weak, taking him to Canterbury on the night of the French attack and making it appear that he'd unlocked Newingate? With his reputation as a skilled archer, he would be an easy scapegoat. Simon would have no trouble making the night guards' deaths look like they'd been overcome by someone like Nicholas. And if his dead body was found at daybreak with the keys to the gate, no one would be the wiser for Simon's involvement with the French.

Simon needed him, especially after naming him as a spy for the French. The attack was drawing too nigh for Simon to find someone else to blame for the crime, at least not without drawing suspicion upon himself.

Nicholas squared his shoulders. All the more reason to evade Simon. If he didn't, he would inadvertently aid Simon in destroying Canterbury.

Walter used his knife to slice off the bottom of the parchment where the numbers and the transcription were written. He held it out to Nicholas. "I will pray for you to stay out of Simon's clutches so you can take this warning to the king."

Nicholas folded the parchment into a small square before he slipped it into an empty sheath in his boot. "If you hear of my capture, will you please warn the king yourself?"

Walter hesitated but a moment before he nodded.

"And if anything should happen to me, find a way to tell

Sybil I have loved her." Without waiting for reassurances that would offer him little hope, Nicholas opened the door and hurried down the steps.

'Twas time to put an end to Simon's plans, even if it cost Nicholas his life to do so.

~ 25 ~

SYBIL SIGHTED THE TARGET, then released the bow, the soft *twang* having grown familiar after practicing for hours. Her fingers were covered in blisters beneath her gloves, but Beatrice had been slathering them with the healing salve from the tin Nicholas had left behind. Much to Sybil's amazement, the salve had taken away the sting and begun the healing process as easily as if she'd put on a topical ointment from a pharmacy.

She stood back and stretched. If only the salve could remove the other aches and pains in her body. She'd expected to have an easier time sleeping on the hard pallet on the floor of Beatrice and Ralph's cottage, but she'd awoken every morning, including a short while ago, with sore muscles she hadn't known existed.

From her periphery she could see Eric readying to leave for market, all the while observing her. He'd gone hunting again the past couple of days, and she'd been spared his angst. But after returning last night, he'd seemed to linger near her, watching her as though he knew she was different but couldn't figure out how.

A young boy raced around gathering her arrows. Most were hitting the inner rings of the target now. She was getting stronger, and with a little more practice, she'd be able to use her bow and arrow well enough if there was need.

She'd asked Ralph to teach her how to shoot and ride simultaneously, but he'd told her to focus on her horsemanship first. And he was right. He'd been a strict but good teacher, helping her learn how to saddle and bridle a horse and taking her out every day into the surrounding woodland and meadows to continue her horse-riding lessons.

He only issued instructions as necessary, which meant mostly they rode in silence. But she didn't mind, had learned to work with all sorts of men over the years, and his reticence didn't frighten her. Rather, she'd relished the opportunity to explore the Weald, imagining the terrain in modern times. Most of the landmarks were unfamiliar, but upon crossing certain rivers or creeks the closer they drew to Canterbury, she'd catch her bearing and picture the primary school or supermarket or library.

"Want to shoot another round?" The boy came bounding toward her across the butts.

She glanced in the direction of the well where Ralph was yet helping to fix the waterwheel, which had become stuck that morning while some of the men had been drawing water for the livestock. He appeared busy and would call her over when he was ready to go.

He didn't seem to mind being pulled away from his duties in order to teach her. And always on their return ride to the village, he'd shoot game to bring back with them, usually a hare or a bird like a grouse, partridge, or snipe.

She reached for the arrows, but at the sight of Eric crossing toward her, she halted. Something serious in his expression told her he intended to have a word with her whether or not she wanted to have one with him.

His attention flicked over her hair and then over the length of her. Nothing in his gaze held interest the way Nicholas's had. Instead, his contained only suspicion.

She folded her arms and spread her feet—although the long tunic prevented him from seeing her defensive stance. With every passing day, she was tripping less over the long, cumbersome material always tangling in her legs. Still, she loathed having to wear the gown. It was hot and itchy and dirty. She'd worn it every day, and it was in sore need of a washing. She'd done her best to spot clean it. And she'd hand laundered her socks, underpants, and bra. But after several days at it, she'd begun to understand why the other women went without undergarments unless they were having their monthly cycle.

She'd still resisted wearing the wimple over her hair as the other women did, and Beatrice had stopped trying to pin it in place every morning after brushing and plaiting her hair. "Mark my word," Beatrice had scolded, "your hair will be needing a washing or lice-picking soon if you're not more careful."

If only she had her baseball cap . . . and a warm shower, clean clothes, and her own toothbrush. Beatrice had a small toothbrush of sorts that she'd shared with Sybil, a short wooden stick with bristles on the end along with a fine powder made of crushed cloves and salt that actually seemed to clean her teeth. But Sybil was considering creating her own toothbrush from a hazel twig after watching several women chew the end of the twigs until they turned into softened and moistened bristles.

Even though she missed some of the basics of easy hygiene, she'd found herself adjusting well to the food since it was all fresh and organic the way she preferred. She loved the clean air and being outside. And she loved the stress-free rhythm in the village, the tasks all revolving around what was necessary for survival.

She'd offered to assist in any way she could. Even though she couldn't ever picture herself enjoying the domestic chores the other women did for long hours without complaint, she'd wanted to do something to repay the villagers for sheltering and feeding her while Nicholas was away.

But every time she'd tried to join in their work, Beatrice had shooed her away. Sybil had finally sat with the fletcher in the shade outside his cottage, and he'd allowed her to smooth split wood with sandstone or glue feathers into the notches with a pasty mixture of animal fat. When Beatrice had tried to draw her away from the task, Ralph had stepped in to her defense. Ever since, Sybil had spent her free time making arrows and listening to the fletcher tell stories of the battles he'd fought over in France.

Now, she ran her fingers over the goose feathers at the end of an arrow in her quiver. It wasn't one she'd helped to create, but it was strange to realize that everything in the village had value because of the intensive labor involved. Nothing was wasted. Everything was reused.

"You're not who you say you are." Eric stopped only a

meter from her and looped his fingers through the belt that cinched his tunic.

Though his statement took her off guard, she kept her expression from revealing any emotion. "And who do I say I am?"

"A friend of the Worth family." His words came out an accusation. "'Twas not difficult to ask around and learn the Worths have had no guests staying with them recently."

"I am a friend of Nicholas."

Eric studied her face more closely. "He's never mentioned you before and then comes back here and marries you? That makes no sense. Not after how devoted he's been to my sister these many years."

A number of unfriendly comebacks raced to the tip of her tongue, but she sensed a dangerous—maybe even lethal—anger in Eric. She'd witnessed such resentment and rage cause people to act irrationally, even carelessly. And she didn't want to trigger more strife with him when he already seemed set against her.

"Nicholas told me how much he loved your sister."

"Loves." Eric narrowed his eyes. "He still loves her and always will. You'll never be what he needs."

What could she say to that? Perhaps it was true. Perhaps Nicholas would never be able to give his whole heart to her the way he had to Jane. Would she be alright with that?

"You don't belong here."

Eric's instincts were keen. She had no way to defend herself, hadn't considered fabricating a tale to explain her presence in the past, hadn't needed to yet beyond the simple tale Nicholas had devised.

"Where are you from?"

She had to say something—couldn't remain mute, or he would judge her even more. "My country is one you haven't heard of."

His jaw flexed. And his penetrating gaze radiated with mistrust.

"Eric!" Ralph called across the butts.

Eric didn't budge except to fist his hands.

Would she need to fight this man, here and now? She wasn't sure how well she'd be able to execute her kicks with the skirt getting in her way, but she could still punch.

"Come take over fixing the waterwheel for me," Ralph ordered, drawing nearer.

"If you're working for the French, I'll see you hanged," Eric ground out.

"I'm not. I know nothing about the French." She held herself motionless, hoping he could read the truth in at least this one thing.

"Eric! Now!" Ralph's command turned threatening.

Eric took a step back. "I don't know where you really came from or what you're really doing here, but I suggest you return to wherever it is you belong."

She didn't flinch. She'd learned never to let a man intimidate her. But this time, his statement rattled her.

With a final glare, Eric spun, retrieved a sack, then strode toward the woodland. Within seconds, he disappeared into the thick depths.

Ralph halted halfway across the butts and stared after the

spot as though contemplating summoning the young man back.

Sybil remained where she was, stiff and uncertain. Maybe Eric hadn't exactly figured out she wasn't from 1382. But he sensed something. If he could so easily recognize she wasn't who she claimed to be, how many others would wonder the same? Or perhaps already had?

"How do you fare?" Ralph shifted to assess her.

"I'm fine."

Was Eric also right that Nicholas would never be able to love another woman besides Jane? Would he always have his former love at the back of his mind when they were together, comparing her and finding her lacking?

Over the past few days of his absence, she'd done little else but think about him, so that her longings for him had only increased to almost unbearable proportions. It was worst when she had nothing to do or when she was lying on her pallet at night.

She missed him and replayed the time she'd had with him, reviewing each detail about him, every nuance, every word. In doing so, she'd only fallen more in love with him. And now she lived for his return, hoping he'd charge through the thick brush, ride right up to her, dismount, then grab her into another one of his kisses that upended her world.

But maybe it was time to push aside her desire for him. Maybe Eric was right, that she wouldn't be any good for Nicholas. Those thoughts already lingered—that Nicholas would be better off without her. If she left him now, she'd spare him the heartache that would come later if she didn't live through the entanglement in two eras.

She'd been putting off searching for the holy water as if that could put off the inevitable decision of whether to stay in the past or return to the present. She'd delayed long enough.

"You sure you're faring well?" Ralph's gaze turned sharp.

She started toward the livestock pen. "If you can spare the time, I'd like to ride to Canterbury today."

He hesitated. "It's best if we stay clear of busy places."

"I understand." She didn't break her stride. "If you feel safer waiting outside the city, I'll go in by myself."

"No, you won't."

She stopped and fisted a hand to her hip, biting back a retort. What did she expect she could accomplish in Canterbury? She couldn't just walk up to the doors of St. Sepulchre and demand they give her holy water. She'd likely need to sneak in. But the truth was, if Simon hadn't been able to wrest control of the well with armed knights at his disposal, how would she be able to succeed by herself?

Would she need to make her presence in the past known to Arthur Creighton and his daughter Marian? Although she hadn't met Arthur, she'd worked briefly with Marian. Harrison and Ellen had insisted Arthur and Marian had gone in the past. But the newlywed couple hadn't known Arthur's fate. Maybe he was dead.

Although Sybil hadn't wanted to entangle her time in the past with either Arthur or Marian, what if she had no choice? Especially since Harrison had mentioned their ties to the wellspring at St. Sepulchre. Was it possible, once they knew of her circumstances, they would allow her to retrieve the holy water she needed to return to the present?

There was only one way to find out.

"If not Canterbury," she said to Ralph, "then I'd like to ride to Chesterfield Park."

He rubbed at his beard, then released a sigh. "We'll have to stay off the main trails and roads."

"I'll follow you."

• ● •

The ride took them nearer to Canterbury than she'd been on any other day. And the closer she drew, the stranger she felt—light-headed, dizzy, even tired.

As she clung to the reins and nudged her mount up a short hill, a wave of nausea hit her. She swayed, and the jarring of the horse threw her to one side so that she almost toppled off.

"Hold up," she called to Ralph, who was several lengths ahead of her. The nausea swelled with a pressure that told her she would be sick to her stomach at any second.

She reined in and scrambled to dismount. She'd been getting better at climbing down from the horse, but this time her haste made her clumsy. Thankfully her feet made it to the ground before she threw up.

When finished, she braced her hands on her thighs, drawing in deep breaths. But the dizziness swirled around her so she would have fallen if not for Ralph already at her side, steadying her.

"You need to sit down and rest." He spoke as firmly as always, as if she were one of the archers under his command.

She was too faint to resist, letting him lead her to a grassy spot in the shade of an oak where she lowered herself and reclined against the trunk.

He hovered above her, his expression stern but his eyes radiating with worry. "What ails you?"

Had she eaten something that had given her food poisoning? Or had she caught an illness? After all, her body wasn't used to the food and diseases of the era. Was it possible her body in the present was dying, causing her body in 1382 to deteriorate?

"Speak to me, my lady." Ralph's tone took on an urgency. "Have you need of a physician?"

"I don't know." Without modern medicine and technology, what could a physician in the Middle Ages do to help her?

Ralph straightened and rubbed at the back of his neck. "Do you think you might be in the family way?"

She shook her head. Her arrangement with Nicholas was nobody else's business, but she couldn't let Ralph think she was pregnant. "It's a little too soon for that." It was the best answer she could come up with under the circumstances.

"We should head back and have Father Fritz examine you."

"If I rest for a few minutes, I'll be fine." At least, she hoped so. Because at the moment, she couldn't imagine having the energy or stamina to stand and climb back on the horse.

Ralph peered around as though to determine if they were safe. So far on their journey, they hadn't seen anyone else. The ability to go for miles without sight of another human was another difference between modern Kent and this one, where urban sprawl hadn't taken over the countryside.

As another wave of nausea started to rise, she laid her head back and closed her eyes. Drawing in deep breaths, she tried to calm her racing pulse and quell the queasiness. But as before, the pressure built until she vomited again.

She was sick off and on and lost track of the time, finally dozing in her misery. She wasn't sure how long she slept, but voices roused her.

"Sorry. Her organs are failing." It was an unfamiliar male voice. Had someone new joined Ralph? Maybe he'd gone after a physician after all? "With both renal and heart failure, I don't think she'll make it much longer."

Renal and heart failure? That couldn't be right. She tried to pry her eyes open, but her lids were heavy, her body lethargic, and her mouth dry. It had to be food poisoning. She'd had it a few years ago after eating fried chicken takeout and had been miserable for several hours.

A deep sigh came from above her along with a squeeze to her hand.

Suddenly she was conscious of a whirring and beeping, like the sounds of hospital equipment. She inhaled only to find that plastic covered her mouth and nose. Elastic straps pressed against her cheeks and wrapped around her head. From the soft bellow of the air flow, she guessed she was on a ventilator.

Her heart picked up its pace. Had she returned to the present?

"Isn't there anything we can do for her?" came a question from above her, from a voice that sounded terribly like Dawson's.

"We've done all we can, and the MRI, CT, bloodwork, and all the other tests we've run aren't showing any underlying causes." The medical terms were most definitely modern, which meant Isaac—or somebody—had located her body in the closet under the stairs at Reider Castle and had taken her to the hospital.

She quickly calculated the passage of time. If she was doing the math right, then she'd been unconscious in the present for eight days.

With all the energy she could muster, she attempted to push herself up. But she was too exhausted . . . or perhaps she was still in a coma and could hear what was going on around her but was unable to communicate back. She'd heard that sometimes happened to comatose people—they were conscious of voices and other sensory details.

"C'mon, Baxter. We have to do something more." The voice was hard with anger—an anger she recognized well. Dawson. He was at her bedside. Was he the one holding her hand?

"I've done all I can." The doctor gentled his tone. "In fact, I've already done more than I'm allowed."

Baxter was another one of Dawson's war buddies and had been instrumental in trying to help Dawson since the accident. He'd relocated to Canterbury to be close to Dawson and Acey.

"I'm sorry, Dawson," Baxter said again. "If only we'd found her sooner."

So she'd been in the closet awhile, possibly several days if her organs were failing.

"I can't lose her too." Dawson's whisper came out anguished.

At his heartfelt declaration, Sybil's pulse seemed to stop beating. Yet according to the steady, unperturbed beeping of the vital signs monitor, nothing had changed in the rhythm.

Dawson couldn't be sad she was in a coma, could he? After everything he'd said to her about wishing she was the one who'd disappeared . . .

"You should get some rest. Maybe a shower." This voice came from across the room and belonged to Acey. "I'll drive you home."

"No." The one word was as testy as usual. "I'm not going anywhere."

He really was there for her. He'd gotten out of bed. He was at the hospital. And he was refusing to leave her side. Did that mean he still cared about her after all?

The voices lapsed to silence. Her mind whirled with the information she'd gleaned. She was dying. That was abundantly clear. And she didn't have long to live.

No one had thought to contact Harrison about her being in a coma. And why would they? None of them knew the details of Harrison and Ellen lapsing into comas after taking holy water, since she'd kept the information as private as possible.

If Isaac had discovered the empty glass bottle in the closet with her, he wouldn't have understood its significance. Although, as a good investigator, he'd likely had it tested to see if the remnants were related to her unconsciousness. Even then, he wouldn't have discovered anything in the molecular structure other than the components of regular water.

Harrison had studied the holy water and conjectured that it

wasn't of this world, that its origins had to come from God Himself. Of course, he subscribed to Arthur Creighton's theory that the holy water was somehow related to the Tree of Life that had existed in the Garden of Eden, that somehow the special properties of the original tree had added longevity to lives by rejuvenating the body and healing it from illness.

Indeed, the early patriarchs of the Bible had lived to very old ages, often hundreds of years. But Sybil wasn't sure how remnants of the Tree of Life would have survived centuries or how they would have ended up in England. Harrison also had theories for all of that too. And although she'd listened to him carefully, she hadn't known how to separate fact from fiction.

Even if the theories were a bit muddled, she was clear on one thing—the healing she'd witnessed had defied all possibilities of earthly medicine and had to be otherworldly. And now that she'd experienced the effect of the holy water taking her to the past, she couldn't deny its power to do more than most people understood.

She strained her ear, waiting for Dawson to say more. She didn't think he'd ingested the holy water she'd left for him. Otherwise, the energy in the hospital room would have been more positive. One of his friends would have mentioned the healing, wouldn't they? Such a miracle was too massive to ignore. And if Dawson hadn't considered the holy water for himself, then he clearly hadn't considered giving it to her either—not that she wanted him to use it to save her. She still wanted him to drink it and experience a better life for himself.

The silence continued, more pervasive, the whirring of the medical equipment gone. Had she lapsed back into oblivion?

At the chatter of squirrels and the trill of a songbird, she stirred, digging her fingers into the cushion of grass underneath her.

Her eyes flew open, and she found herself peering up at a canopy of branches and leaves. And Ralph's anxious face. He knelt beside her, his forehead grooved and his lips pressed into a stern line.

"Praise be." His shoulders sagged. "I was starting to fear you might not awaken and that I'd have to bear wretched tidings to Nicholas."

She pushed up and fought through a wave of dizzy exhaustion. The overgrowth of the woodland told her all she needed to know. She hadn't returned to the present and was still solidly living in the Middle Ages.

Relief spilled through her in such overwhelming waves that she knew with certainty where she wanted to belong. If only she could figure out a way to stay.

~ 26 ~

"YOU GAVE ME QUITE THE SCARE." Ralph finally spoke over his shoulder to her after the nearly silent ride back to Devil's Bend.

The tiredness that had clung to Sybil for most of the return journey was starting to abate. "I'm feeling better now."

Twilight was settling around them, and the shadows lengthened. Although Ralph had been right to make the decision to head back to Devil's Bend, she was disappointed anyway. She was no closer to finding holy water than she had been from day one in the past. In fact, she might even be farther from it now that she'd scared Ralph with her . . . episode.

She wasn't sure how to label what had happened. In some ways the experience felt similar to the short overlaps with Nicholas after she'd consumed the droplets of holy water. Except this time, she hadn't had any more holy water. And still she'd been with Dawson, Acey, and Baxter in the hospital room.

She'd also considered the possibility that her bodies in both eras had been in proximity to each other. Although she hadn't been able to distinguish exactly where she was in 1382 Kent, they'd been on the outskirts of Canterbury and very well could've been near the hospital. Maybe her quantum particles had somehow been drawn to one another.

Whatever the case, Baxter hadn't given her long to live. She suspected she had hours, maybe another day. Perhaps that's why she'd experienced the fatigue and illness. As her present-day body deteriorated, she would weaken and worsen until she died in both time periods.

That meant her mission to find holy water was more urgent than ever. She couldn't expect Ralph to take another day to ride with her to Chesterfield Park—or anywhere else, for that matter. She'd have to work out another way to go. Maybe sneak out while he was busy. Or perhaps early in the morning before he arose. Such a move would be difficult, especially since she would have to pass his pallet to exit the cottage.

But if she wanted to live in the past with Nicholas—which she desperately did—she needed holy water.

Ralph reined in his horse sharply, and Sybil managed to bring her horse to a halt alongside him, glad for her quick reflexes.

"Do you smell that?" Ralph lifted his nose and sniffed.

She took in a whiff but couldn't smell anything out of the ordinary. "What is it?"

"Smoke."

The medieval air always held a hint of wood-fire smoke. It was becoming a familiar scent. Perhaps given enough time, she wouldn't notice it anymore—if she had enough time. . . . But for now, between the odor of the woodsmoke along with the horse and the forest, she couldn't distinguish anything else.

Ralph stared up through the branches, but the forest was

thick and hardly allowed for a glimpse of the sky. Even so, his eyes narrowed. "There's fire."

Without another word, he slapped at his mount and kicked it into a gallop. He didn't give her time to question him, and she refrained from shouting after him. Was this a forest fire? Was the village in danger from it? Or was one of the cottages on fire?

He glanced behind to check her progression, but he needn't have, for she kept on his trail, guiding her horse as fast as she could.

She recognized some of the landmarks as they drew nearer to the village—a coppice of hazelwood with fresh sprouts, a fenced-in pigpen for the farrowing sows, a pile of hardwoods awaiting the turner's spring pole lathe.

When they reached the edge of the forest that bordered the sheep meadow, Ralph pulled up short, his horse shying back a step and snorting. His low curses filled the air.

Sybil reined in next to him.

He had his bow in position and an arrow nocked before she could follow his gaze to the village. When she did, her heart ceased beating.

The villagers huddled together on the edge of the butts, a group of knights surrounding them. Two of the men of the village were tied to the targets, their arms and legs outstretched, their bodies riddled with arrows. Lying on the ground a short distance from the targets, two other men had been tossed aside, motionless, the blood staining their clothing, evidence they'd already been tortured to death.

She wanted to curse too, but she bit back angry words. She

needed to remain calm and levelheaded and couldn't let anger cloud her judgment.

Someone had discovered the outlaw town. Who? And why were they treating these men so cruelly? What motivation could they have?

She narrowed her sights upon a dark-haired knight with a forked beard standing at the edge of the butts, longbow in hand. With broad shoulders and thick limbs, he had an air of strength and power about him.

Ralph started to draw his bow, but Sybil shot out a hand to stop him. "Not yet." Her tone was the same that she used when commanding a team hostage situation. "Your aggression might cause more bloodshed."

"I'll kill Lord Worth right now and put an end to this."

So, this was Lord Worth. Simon. Nicholas's older brother. She studied him again more carefully, noting the family resemblance in the dark hair and eyes, but that was it. Simon's face was wider and fleshier, his eyes bigger, and his body plumper, showing his age.

If Simon could beat his own brother until he was barely alive, then his cruelty toward strangers would be boundless.

Ralph started to buck her hand off his arm, but she gave him a swift and hard punch that knocked the bow from his grip.

He turned rounded eyes upon her, looking first at her balled-up fist and then at her face.

"If you shoot, you risk his knights turning on the others." She spoke gravely, having been a part of a tense hostage situation only six months ago in which a disgruntled postman locked himself and his coworker into the post office for twelve hours.

Without waiting for Ralph's response, she slipped from her horse, surveying the village. Several cottages were burned to the ground, the fire still smoldering. Livestock lay dead. Furniture and belongings were strewn in the grass, smashed and broken.

From what she could tell, most of the men and women had been herded to the butts. The women were weeping quietly, and the men's faces were drawn with fear.

"Where are the children?" None were in sight, and she prayed they'd had time to run away before Simon could corral them. She only hoped Simon had a shred of decency and hadn't locked them in the cottages before burning them down. He certainly fit the profile of a man who'd do something like that.

"There." Ralph pointed toward the southern side of the village and to the woods beyond. There in the shadows of one of the hedge fences, Father Fritz was crouched and waving at them.

She led her horse back a dozen paces, tied the lead line around a low branch, and then picked her way as silently as possible through the shrubs. Ralph crept behind her, not as proficient in stealth as she was. Nevertheless, they reached the southern-hedge fence undetected. Once they were behind it, she breathed out a sigh of relief at the sight of the half dozen children.

Keeping her head and body low, she raced along the back of the fence toward Father Fritz with Ralph on her trail. The tangle of the skirt in her legs prevented her from running as fast as she normally did, and she wished now, more than ever, for her jeans and T-shirt.

The children were crowded together, tears streaking their cheeks, their wide eyes regarding her warily. As she neared, Father Fritz started toward her, bending his broad frame and attempting to imitate her crouched run. However, he loped along like a clumsy ape, going only several paces before stopping and patting his perspiring forehead.

Upon reaching him, Sybil dropped to one knee, and Ralph did the same beside her. "Simon is seeking information about Nicholas?" she asked pointedly, forgoing a greeting.

Father Fritz nodded vigorously, his jowls shaking and his eyes overflowing with a deluge of tears. "I've tried to get the children to leg it, that I did. But they be too fearful to get on."

If she'd been Father Fritz, she wouldn't have given the children a choice, would have led them far away from this scene of terror. But that was neither here nor there now. All she could do at the moment was work out a way to appease Simon. Or fight him. But as she mentally recalculated the number of weapons the knights were carrying, she knew that engaging in combat would only cause more deaths, especially since the men didn't have their bows.

Beside her, Ralph was breathing heavily. "How long's Lord Worth been here?"

"Arrived a few hours ago, that he did."

"And who led him here?" Ralph's eyes held a deadly gleam.

"Well now, we can't be certain. But it seems Lord Worth has eyes and ears in the Canterbury market and got word about our dear Nicholas taking himself this bab as his bride."

She exchanged a glance with Ralph. Eric had headed off to the market today. Had he said something then?

In her professional assessment of Eric, she didn't think he'd resort to outright betrayal, even in his anger and hurt. He was a deeply wounded man, but he wasn't vicious and wouldn't willingly put this village in danger, not after the outlaws had become his family.

However, it was likely he'd said something inadvertently, something that had gotten back to Simon. And this time, in pursuit of Nicholas, Simon had pushed his men onward through the Weald, not giving them a choice to retreat when faced with the thick, haunted portion of the deep forest.

"I'll need to slay Lord Worth," Ralph whispered, having picked up his bow and brought it with him. "And then take out as many of his knights as I can before they harm anyone else."

Father Fritz shook his head, the tears welling again. "If anyone attempts to fight, Simon's threatened to start using the women for target practice."

Ralph spat into the dirt, disgust etched into his face.

Sybil's mind spun with options, but none were safe. "He has to realize the people don't know where Nicholas is, or someone would have revealed it by now."

The sadness in Father Fritz's eyes flipped Sybil's heart over and flattened it at the bottom of her stomach. Suddenly she knew exactly why Simon had come to Devil's Bend . . .

Father Fritz nodded as though to confirm her conclusion. "He's not waiting on Nicholas to return. He be waiting for—"

"No," Ralph said harshly, shaking his head at Father Fritz.

"Don't say it."

"Say what? That Lord Worth's after this sweet bab?" Father Fritz patted Sybil's cheek.

Ralph muttered several more colorful curses.

He had to know even if Father Fritz hadn't revealed the truth, she was smart and had already figured out what Simon wanted.

"I'm guessing he's been here for about four hours?" Her mind went to work putting the rest of the details together.

Father Fritz nodded, opened his mouth to say more, but upon glimpsing the fury darkening Ralph's face, he clamped his lips together.

"Four hours," Sybil whispered. "Four dead men."

Again, Father Fritz nodded but pressed his mouth closed, using his hands to mime his words. But from the way he flapped his hands around and waggled his fingers, Sybil would have guessed he was talking about chickens and geese rather than people.

How much longer before he drew new men to the targets? Probably not long.

As she glanced at the children nearby, she knew what she needed to do. She had no choice. In fact, she had to act before Ralph could stop her. Because stop her he would . . . out of loyalty and devotion to Nicholas.

She gathered up her skirt so she wouldn't trip over it. Then she rose and sprinted forward, needing to get away from Ralph as well as the children before she revealed her identity.

Behind her, she could feel Ralph lunging for her. She spun and delivered a spinning hook kick to his shoulder, one with enough power that it sent him over backward, landing him and knocking the breath from him in one move.

With him disabled, she continued until she was well away from the hedge and out in the open. "I'm Sybil. Nicholas's wife. If you release these people, I'll hand myself over to you."

"No!" came Ralph's breathless call.

A glance over her shoulder told her that Ralph was already scrambling to his feet and had no intention of letting her give herself over to Simon so easily. "Take me in her stead, my lord."

Simon had lowered his bow and was staring at her with a calculation that didn't frighten her. Even so, she had to be careful. Displaying too much bravado with men like this only angered them. They needed to feel in control and thrived on seeing fear in the faces of their victims.

At the same time, she had to make sure Ralph didn't get ahold of her.

She picked up her pace and saw Simon exchange a glance with one of his knights—Potter, the older knight who had been guarding Nicholas the eve of his escape from prison, the knight whose hand Nicholas had impaled to a door.

As the knight nodded, Simon turned his gaze upon her with more interest. "Get her." His terse command rang out over the butts.

Above, the sky was painted with beautiful streaks of rose and gold as the last rays of the setting sun made its mark before darkness settled. Was that what her life here with Nicholas had been? The gloriousness of a sunset before the coming night?

Most likely if Simon took her, he'd dangle her as bait,

enticing Nicholas to hand himself over in exchange for her freedom. She couldn't let Nicholas do that.

With Simon's guards quickly surrounding her, she halted and spun to face Ralph. Several men of the village had latched on to him. His body strained against their hold, and his face was turning red with his mounting anger.

As the first of Simon's guards gripped her arms, she stifled her natural instincts to fight. She could have taken them by surprise, using her expert defensive moves before they knew what had hit them. But she was handing herself over willingly. For Nicholas. After all, she was doomed to die soon without the holy water. And now she could die in peace, knowing she'd saved Nicholas from his brother.

Across the distance, she met Ralph's tortured gaze. "Don't let my sacrifice be in vain."

"No!" His roar filled the silence, and he thrashed to free himself.

She allowed Simon's guards to bind her hands in front of her and then assist her onto a horse. As one of the men mounted behind her, she held herself stiffly, ready to defend herself if he decided to take advantage of her. A rope around her hands wouldn't stop her.

But the man remained a respectable distance from her, almost as if he was afraid of touching her for fear of reprisal from Simon.

He urged his mount through town. Potter and several others were tossing flaming pieces from smoldering rubble onto the cottages. The moment the fire hit the thatch, the sparks spread rapidly.

She cast a final glance over her shoulder at Ralph and Beatrice and the rest of the villagers standing at the edge of the butts, unable to do anything but watch the destruction of their homes. Devil's Bend would be gone in a matter of minutes—not only their homes, but their furniture, dishes, wool, blankets, and every other precious item that had cost them hours of labor to create.

Ralph cried out angrily, jerked free, and began to race after her. In the next instant, one of Simon's men let loose an arrow. Before Sybil could cry out a warning, the arrow struck Ralph in his chest, dropping him to his knees.

Guilt rose into her throat like the bile she'd felt earlier in the day. She'd done this to Ralph, to everyone. This was her fault.

She shouldn't have crossed back in time. At the very least, she shouldn't have come with Nicholas to the village. Then she would have prevented causing him and these people more heartache.

· ● ·

Darkness fell quickly, and Simon and his men rode hard without stopping. When they finally reached Reider Castle, only a few torches flared at the late hour, guiding them through the gatehouse underneath the rotting body of a guard swaying from a rope.

Sybil couldn't distinguish much, but she guessed he was the young soldier who'd been guarding Nicholas in the dungeon. No doubt Potter had cast blame upon the man for Nicholas's escape, saving himself in the process.

As they dismounted, the knight who had her in his charge led her through a side entrance. She'd become familiar with the castle layout during her investigation in the present and could picture exactly where he was taking her—to the dungeon.

With just one guard escorting her, she guessed Potter hadn't revealed her fighting abilities out of self-preservation or in saving himself the humiliation of admitting he'd been defeated by a woman. Or perhaps he wasn't worried about her trying to escape, since she was far outnumbered.

When her escort motioned her into the same cell that Nicholas had used, he waited respectfully for her to enter before he closed the door. He bowed his head toward her before walking away, his footsteps echoing in the silence.

She was struck that during the whole journey, this young guard had maintained a level of civility with her even as his prisoner. His attitude reminded her that not every antagonist was evil. Some were merely swept up into schemes that weren't of their own making.

Maybe that's how it was with Dawson too. After the overlap with him earlier, she knew he wasn't her enemy. It was even possible he hadn't wanted to hurt her, but the pain and heartache had held him captive, driving him to a dark place where she couldn't go.

If that was to be her last interaction with Dawson, she was grateful she could die knowing he'd been by her bedside, holding her hand and caring about her.

When the main oaken door closed and darkness fell over her, she gave way to the shudder that had been building inside.

Then she groped along the wall until she found the spot where Nicholas had made his bed. She slid down and felt around until her fingers connected with the blanket he'd used.

She retrieved it and wrapped it around her shoulders. With the cold and dampness of the cell, she would need to get up and move from time to time to stay warm. But for now, the heaviness of all that had happened weighed upon her, and all she wanted to do was curl into a ball.

Why was she always losing the people she cared about the most? That seemed to be the recurring theme of her life, losing her father, mother, Dawson, and now Nicholas. What was wrong with her that people left her?

With a sting of tears burning the backs of her eyes, she leaned her head against the wall and expelled a tight breath.

A wave of dizziness and nausea hit her as it had earlier in the day when riding with Ralph. She'd had nothing to eat since emptying her stomach then. And as the queasiness swelled, she rose to her knees, bent over, and heaved. Nothing but watery ale and bile came up.

When the episode passed, she wiped her mouth and closed her eyes against the light-headedness. But a few moments later, the pressure built again. She was sick to her stomach endlessly, until at last, she lay exhausted and delirious in the rotting hay, unable to move. Her heart rate was slowing, as was her breathing.

This time, she recognized what was happening. . . . Her comatose body in the present was dying. And there was nothing she could do to save herself.

~ 27 ~

DARKNESS SHROUDED NICHOLAS UPON HIS MOUNT. He'd traveled the high road from London to Canterbury more times than he could count over recent years, could traverse the route in his slumber if need be. Even so, tonight he rode with extra caution as he led the king's retinue.

At the sight of Westgate ahead, Nicholas slowed his horse, allowing Lord Clayborne to fall into step beside him. With St. Medard's but a day away, they didn't have long to institute their plans to repel the French.

When Nicholas had arrived by ship in London two days ago, he'd had to sneak through the city. Even when he reached the garrison for the king's guard, he'd done so under cover of darkness, keeping to the shadows. He approached the commanding officer, Lord Clayborne, only after everyone else had retired for the night.

At first Nicholas had been afraid he might have to fight the seasoned knight. But his old friend had given him an opportunity to explain the accusations of treason leveled against him. When he finished, Lord Clayborne had clamped him on the shoulder. "You have been a man of integrity and honor since the first day I met you. Your brother's accusations against you rang hollow, but I had no way to prove he was lying until now."

Nicholas gave Lord Clayborne the secret message and shared his speculations of Simon's plans regarding the attack of the French against Canterbury. Thankfully, the commander had taken the threat seriously and presented the information to the king.

Even though Nicholas hadn't had the physical letter to use as solid evidence against Simon, word had already reached the king and his advisors that the French were readying ships and men along their coast. They'd feared the French were preparing for a raid, but they hadn't known when or where . . . until Nicholas arrived with his news.

"The guards at the city gates," Lord Clayborne spoke gravely as he peered ahead. "What think you? Are they loyal to Simon? Has he put his own men in place already?"

"I do not believe Simon will risk putting anyone associated with him at the gates, not yet. 'Twould cause overmuch suspicion."

Torchlight burned from the walls just inside the closed and locked gate. Built only three years previously by the former archbishop, Westgate was the largest and best of the Canterbury gates. Made of Kentish ragstone, the lofty towers on either side of the bridge rose sixty feet with battlements that were strong and would aid them in repelling French forces.

The current archbishop, William Courtenay, had also poured funds into repairing and fortifying Canterbury's walls. The true test of their viability was finally at hand, and Nicholas could only pray the walls would be able to withstand the assault.

He assessed the city as best he could. Some windows were still lit, but most residences and businesses were dark, with only the faint light of the moon reflecting off tile and thatched roofs and the spires of Canterbury Cathedral rising above them all. "I suspect Simon will wait until the night of the offensive before planting his men into position within the city to unlock Newingate."

The French had picked one of the gates that would lead into the heart of the city and allow for the most destruction. It also passed near St. Sepulchre. 'Twas convenient for Simon in his efforts to take control of the wellspring.

Ahead, outside the gates, were several encampments of pilgrims who'd flocked to the cathedral and the shrine to St. Thomas Becket. There were also camps of laborers who had no home or refuge within the city. At the thudding of the horses' hooves against the road, the people around campfires began to rise and watch the approaching knights. The sight of two dozen of the king's fiercest warriors would spark fear in the breast of any man.

Lord Clayborne had already decided to meet inquiries with the tale that they were riding out to Dover on the morrow. Not only would the king's retinue circle back and lie in wait for a surprise attack against the French on the Dover Road, but word had gone out to other knights around Kent to converge upon Canterbury. It wouldn't be long ere dozens more armed men arrived to defend the city. In addition, His Royal Majesty had ordered additional naval forces to patrol the coast with the hope of staving off the French from landing altogether.

While Lord Clayborne and his men laid a trap, Nicholas

planned to ride with a few men to Reider Castle on the morrow and ambush any men Simon might send out to Canterbury to open the city gates. If he could disable Simon, then the French wouldn't be able to enter the city if they happened to make it past Lord Clayborne.

As Nicholas reached the first encampment, he nodded at the men, recognizing a few from his travels around Kent. "We'll be making camp here tonight and passing on our way to Dover on the morrow."

"Problems with the French, sire?" The light of the fire cast a glow over wary faces as they watched the rest of the knights halt nearby.

"Could be." Nicholas jangled the coins in the leather pouch at his side. "What information can you give us?"

All eyes focused on the pouch. The same fellow spoke again, this time more eagerly. "We heard rumors that Lord Worth is searching for your new bride."

The words punched Nicholas in his gut and sent panic rippling through him. "When did you hear such news?" He was surprised his question came out so calmly instead of as an anguished shout.

The laborer shrugged and stared pointedly at Nicholas's bag.

Nicholas jumped off his mount and was barreling toward the man before he could blink. This was no time to be playing games. He grabbed the man's neck and squeezed. "Reveal all you know. Now."

The poor fellow's eyes widened with fear. And as soon as Nicholas released him, he stumbled several rapid steps back.

"Earlier today, Lord Worth rode into the city and offered a reward to anyone who could lead him to your bride."

"And did anyone do his bidding?" This time his question echoed with a deadly rage.

"I don't think so. But I don't know for certain."

Nicholas gazed around at the other men who'd also retreated from the fire, ready to flee from his wrath. Yes, he was being a brute. But he didn't care. Not when Sybil's life was at stake. "Did he succeed in capturing her?"

Another of the cowering men shook his head. "We don't know of anyone who took up the offer to guide him into the Weald."

Nicholas's pulse raced with an urgency that drowned out all other thoughts. He had to get to her before Simon did. Tonight. Now.

With heavy steps, Nicholas returned to his horse and mounted. As he gathered his reins, he paused before Lord Clayborne. "I pray you will forgive me for parting ways from you this night, my lord. But I must be off to prevent my brother from harming my wife."

Lord Clayborne wrapped his reins around his gloves more firmly. "Perhaps Simon is baiting you. If you go after your wife, you will find yourself in his clutches once more."

"Be that as it may, I must ensure her safety above my own." As soon as he reached her, he would hasten her away from Devil's Bend. He'd have to ride with her to London and seclude her in the garrison or perhaps plead with the archbishop to give her sanctuary at Lambeth Palace. It didn't really matter where she resided as long as she was some place that Simon couldn't go.

"I would rally the men," Lord Clayborne said, "and go with you myself if the matter at hand here were not so serious."

"I thank you, my lord." Nicholas situated himself in his saddle. "I shall do my best to remain true to the plan and thwart Simon at Reider Castle on the morrow." He would see it done himself or beseech Ralph and some of the archers to stake out the castle.

He didn't wait for Lord Clayborne's response. Instead, he kicked his steed into a gallop, not bothering with the road but angling toward the Weald and Devil's Bend with the shortest route possible.

His heartbeat thundered with the rhythm of the pounding hooves, and silently he cursed himself for leaving Sybil behind. He'd believed the isolation and remoteness of Devil's Bend would be better than riding through the countryside with him evading Simon. But now, he wanted to thrash himself for making such a terrible mistake.

The only thing he could do was frantically pray as he raced through a league of hills and meadows before at last he reached the woodland. Once he was in the thick of the forest, he couldn't maintain the same pace and had to go more carefully. But he pushed hard, the fear in his chest propelling him.

He'd ached keenly for her over the days apart. Even when he'd been busy and occupied with the important message he'd needed to deliver, his heart hadn't felt settled, as if he'd left a part of it behind with her. He hadn't expected to feel so torn, hadn't expected his longing for her to grow almost unbearable.

But it had. Not because of his physical needs—although he

could admit those were still as strong as ever. But he wanted to be with her because he loved her companionship, her calm presence, her courage, her sense of adventure, and so much more.

Of course he loved her body and how beautiful she was. What man wouldn't be attracted to someone like her? He'd loved holding her, loved her boldness in touching him, and loved when they kissed.

Was it time to finally acknowledge what everyone else had already seen—that he loved Sybil?

Nicholas scrubbed a hand down his face, only to realize his fingers were trembling. Now that she was his, he couldn't imagine life without her. He wanted to be with her forever.

Once he had her safely within his arms, he had to convince her to stay, to put aside all thoughts of leaving. He had to make her see they belonged together, were better together, were whole together. Because, yes, he loved her—loved her more than anything or anyone he'd ever known.

As the first signs of dawn began to light the sky, he reached the last section of woodland that led to the heart of the Weald and Devil's Bend. The scent of smoke stung his nostrils the closer he rode to the village. It started a pounding in his head—one that brought back too many memories of when he'd raced through the night to Rye, to Jane.

The smoke had been thicker in the air the nearer he'd drawn, until at last he'd crested a hill and taken in the town in the distance, his heart halting altogether at the sight that met him: Rye lying in smoldering ruins, demolished and burned to the ground, with the haze of smoke wafting all around like low clouds coming off the sea.

He'd kicked his horse into a frantic gallop, the other king's archers following on his heels. No words had been needed to understand the direness. With their bows and arrows ready to fend off any remaining enemy, they'd poured down into the coastal city to find that the only structures that remained standing were those made of brick—the monastery, Rye Castle, and the Friars of the Sack.

The lucky citizens who'd had time to take refuge within those buildings had crept out to dig amongst the ruins. As Nicholas and his fellow soldiers had made their way through the devastation, they'd been forced to listen to the tales of the French attackers looting and raping before leaving and setting the town aflame.

When he'd arrived at the tenement where Jane, Eric, and their mother had resided, he hadn't found their bodies amidst the rubble, had held out hope. But when another of the citizens had discovered more dead along the shore, mostly women who'd been taken as prisoners to serve the French soldiers' lusts, Nicholas had stumbled upon Jane's battered body there, the waves ebbing around her as if to draw her out to sea.

He'd fallen to his knees in the wet sand. That's where Walter had found him, clutching Jane's lifeless body and nearly incoherent with grief. Nicholas wasn't sure what he would have done if not for Walter's calming presence. As it was, as soon as they'd buried the dead, Nicholas had gathered his archers and set out for revenge. He'd taken his fill at Dover, repaying the French and forcing them to retreat from England's shores.

He shook his head to dislodge the memory. Nothing like

that had happened to Devil's Bend. Surely not. Surely God would spare him from going through the same nightmare twice in his life.

But would God really? Hadn't Walter spoken of the hardships and difficulties shaping them into stronger and better people? Maybe he hadn't said so in those words, but that was the general idea.

Could he hold to such inspiration no matter what he found when he arrived at Devil's Bend? Could he trust that though the difficulties wouldn't ever get easier, he would learn to bear them better?

With a final kick of his heels into his horse's flank, he burst out of the woodland into the meadow. Even in the shadows of dawn, the evidence of the destruction was all around—the outline of the rubble where cottages had once stood, glowing embers in the heaps of ashes, smoke hovering throughout the barren grassland.

The truth hit Nicholas as sharply as a dozen arrows striking all at once. He was too late. Simon had already attacked Devil's Bend.

~ 28 ~

NICHOLAS CHARGED FORWARD, DREAD PUSHING HIM. At his approach, several of the men raised bows, their arrows at the ready.

"My wife?" he called as he thundered across the meadow.

As the men recognized him, they lowered their weapons, and others rose from a center firepit where they'd been sleeping. A few, pulling on their tunics, ducked from the cottages that had escaped fire.

No one answered his question. But their silence and the gravity in their faces told him all he needed to know. Simon had Sybil.

He had the sudden and overwhelming urge to rear his horse around and ride directly to Reider Castle, storm inside, and murder Simon.

But he guessed that was exactly what Simon wanted. Lord Clayborne had assessed Simon's tactics correctly. His brother hadn't been able to locate his whereabouts, even with a generous bounty. So Simon had resorted to a more barbaric tactic—holding his wife captive and demanding he hand himself over in her stead.

'Twas obvious that not only had word spread about his

marriage to Sybil, but rumors had also abounded about his affection and desire for his new wife. Clearly, Simon knew him well enough to understand they were alike in their passion for women—that such passion would drive him to do just about anything.

As he neared the village, Nicholas clenched his jaw. His fingers tightened around the reins, and his muscles turned rigid. He had to resist falling into Simon's clutches again. He wouldn't profit Sybil if he allowed himself to be captured. Then his brother would have no reason to negotiate for her release. Simon would keep and kill them both, perhaps conjuring up treasonous charges against Sybil as well.

Instead of acting rashly, Nicholas had to approach Reider Castle with a plan Simon wouldn't expect. If he could bring about his brother's demise, not only would he be able to save Sybil, but he'd also protect the country from Simon's devious scheming with the French.

Using every last vestige of self-control, Nicholas slipped from his mount and forced himself to release his reins. Simon wouldn't do anything to Sybil, not yet. Not while he still needed her.

One of the youth hurried to take his horse. He released it to the boy's care and turned to face the growing crowd of men in front of him. Though they were yet shrouded by the shadows of night, the anger and sorrow etching their faces was clear enough.

He crossed his arms to keep from grabbing the back of the tunic of the boy leading his horse away, then he swallowed his own anger and sorrow. "Tell me what happened."

* ● *

Nicholas knelt next to the fresh graves on the edge of the village, the damp soil staining his leggings. He bowed his head, whispered a prayer for the souls of the men Simon had killed, then prayed for himself and the rest of the archers who insisted on accompanying him to Reider Castle.

They were as furious as he was at Simon's brutality and the needless destruction of their homes. Although Ralph was still alive, the arrow had come dangerously close to his heart. Father Fritz and Beatrice had been doctoring him all day, but he remained unconscious.

Nicholas had spent part of the morn at Ralph's side. The remainder of the time, he'd consulted with the other archers, devising a plan of retaliation against Simon and how best to extricate Sybil without any harm befalling her.

At a commotion behind him, Nicholas finished his prayers and lifted his head. Afternoon sunlight pierced through the leaves as if to remind him of the urgency of the mission ahead and the need now to be on their way.

"I didn't do it! I swear by all that's holy."

Eric was back.

The word going around the village was that Eric was the one who'd betrayed them to Simon. Nicholas hadn't believed Eric was capable, hadn't wanted to blame his friend, had hoped there was another explanation.

Two of the archers held Eric between them. He was disheveled, his hat gone, his hair unkempt and matted with blood, his clothing torn. Worse were the bruises on his face, the welt swelling one of his eyes shut, the bent angle of his nose, the oozing gash at his neck where a knife had nicked him.

Eric was lifting his chin, almost defiantly, as though daring Nicholas to say something.

Without breaking eye contact, Nicholas crossed to the young man. With every step closer, the fear in Eric's eyes darkened, telling Nicholas what he needed to know. Eric had done it.

Nicholas came to a halt in front of Eric and didn't realize he was gripping his dagger until Eric's gaze flicked to it.

All around, the villagers ceased their work at cleaning up the destruction to stare. Eric deserved to die for what he'd done. He'd aided Simon and, in doing so, destroyed lives and homes. He'd also ensured Sybil's departure from the village. Perhaps that had been his motivation behind telling Simon about his marriage. Because he hadn't wanted anyone to disrupt the memory of his sister.

Nicholas lifted his hand to slap Eric. But at the young man's flinch, he halted. Eric had been beaten enough by Simon, no doubt in an effort to extract information. Eric had obviously tried to resist but had eventually given in and relayed to Simon the details he wanted about Sybil and the location of the village.

Regardless of the pressure exerted against him, Eric had been cowardly, disloyal, and weak. He deserved more punishment, but Nicholas wouldn't give it. Instead, he wanted to view the situation and Eric with wisdom and kindness, the way Walter would have.

After all, he'd already learned his lesson from all that had transpired at Rye. One wrong shouldn't lead to another. Doing so only brought regret.

At least it had for him. While others praised his defeat of the French at Dover, he'd always felt uncomfortable with the lauds because he knew the true nature of what had happened during the fight—how he'd made the French pay for what they'd done at Rye, had shown no mercy.

In the moment, he'd thought the retribution would bring him peace. But to this day, he lived with the guilt of his brutality.

Eric had taken out his rage too, but his had been directed against the abbot for preventing the women of the town from taking refuge inside the monastery when the attack had started. Eric might have been justified for his resentment against the abbot for adhering to the male-only rule during a time of crisis. The abbot should have been punished. Just not by Eric. And not by death.

Nicholas had set a poor example to the young man then. But today, was it possible he could redeem his actions and pave a course for Eric to follow—one that showed honor in the face of tribulation rather than revenge?

"Go to Walter in Dover." Sheathing his dagger, Nicholas took a step back. "He will give you shelter and direction for what to do next."

Eric would no longer be welcomed by the community of outlaws, not after the role he'd played in leading Simon to Devil's Bend. And Eric would always have to worry about someone linking him with the death of the abbot from Rye. But perhaps he could find a new life on the Continent.

Eric's expression was wary, as if he couldn't grasp the fact that Nicholas was setting him free.

"I wish to let my difficulties drive me to my knees before my Maker and not to my knees in despair." As the words left Nicholas's mouth, he knew them to be true with all his heart. He didn't want to be carried by his hardships aimlessly. Instead, he wanted to find a way to carry the hardships with grace and purpose.

With a final nod at the young man, Nicholas motioned toward the lad who had his horse. "Time to be on our way." And time to rescue the woman he loved.

~ 29 ~

THE CLANK OF A DOOR AND THE JANGLE of keys roused Sybil. The moldiness of the dungeon cell as well as the frigidness of the air were all the clues she needed to know she was still solidly in the past.

She tried to open her eyes, tried to move, tried to draw in a deep breath, but she could do nothing but cling to the little bit of life she had left.

Footsteps drew nearer, as did torchlight. Someone was coming for her—or at the very least was checking on her. She guessed she'd been in the cell for at least twelve hours, that it was possibly sometime the next day. But without her mobile to check the passing of time or a window to see the amount of daylight, she couldn't be sure.

"She looks dead," came a hushed male voice.

"She must have caught the plague too," whispered another.

The plague? Nicholas had spoken of the plague during one of their conversations—describing an outbreak in London and the surrounding areas.

Their footsteps clattered away, and the light went with them. When the main dungeon door closed, Sybil shivered. She tried to pull the blanket around her more securely but couldn't make her fingers work. They were too cold and her muscles too weak.

Even as fog wafted through her mind and darkness obscured her thoughts, she was aware enough to know she didn't have symptoms of the plague, which was carried by fleas on rats. The fleabites caused fevers, headaches, chills, and painful swollen lumps under the skin—none of which she was experiencing.

Nicholas had explained to her that the disease was so deadly that people could go to bed healthy at night and be gone by morning. Unfortunately, it often passed through entire households and even villages, sometimes leaving no survivors.

If Lord Worth's guards wanted to believe she'd caught the disease, then so be it. There wasn't anything they could do to help her anyway, not with her body dying in the present day. At least now they would leave her alone. Nicholas's mutilated back was vivid proof of the torture Simon Worth was capable of doling out. After witnessing Nicholas's pain, she would much rather rot in a prison cell than be subjected to the whip.

She was just surprised she hadn't passed away yet. She supposed Baxter and Dawson and Acey were still using every means possible to keep her alive. But it was only a matter of time before they would run out of options.

Her biggest regret was having to leave her husband.

"I'm sorry, Nicholas," she managed to whisper. "I never meant to hurt you." The closer she drew to death's doorway, the more she wanted to cling to this life she'd just begun with him. She wanted more time with him. Even if just a little.

"Please." She whispered her prayer through parched lips.

"Please give me a few more days."

But would she be satisfied with mere days? Would a week be enough? Or two? A year?

She wasn't sure that any amount would be long enough with Nicholas . . . unless it was for eternity.

~ *30* ~

NICHOLAS HID BEHIND THE THICK HEDGE, his gut churning. Something wasn't right. His gaze alternated between the gate and the embattlements on the outer wall, as it had for the past hour of waiting and watching.

The silence over the castle was eerie. Gone were the usual calls of the guards, the clanging of the smithy, the clatter from the kitchen, the chopping of wood, and the clop of horses. Even the dogs and chickens were strangely silent, sensing the tension of the imminent altercation.

With the coming of eve and sunset but a short time away, Simon should have sent his guards out to Canterbury. But the bridge hadn't been lowered across the moat, and the gates remained upright and locked. As far as Nicholas could tell, no one had left the castle.

Surely Simon intended to have his men positioned in Canterbury by the time darkness fell in order to open Newingate to the French, even without Nicholas to accuse. Simon would find another unsuspecting victim to plant the key upon, someone else he could blame for colluding with the French.

At the very least, Simon would be awaiting Nicholas's

arrival for Sybil by now. Were his men waiting behind the battlements, eager to lob their arrows at the first sign of Nicholas and his archers moving toward the castle?

Or was Simon expecting Nicholas to step out and announce his surrender?

"What should we do, sire?" came the whisper of one of the archers crouched beside him. "'Twill be dark erelong."

Nicholas lifted his gaze to the dusky sky. Once they disabled the contingent riding to Canterbury, his archers would need to engage in a skirmish with the remaining castle guards to provide a diversion. If Simon's men were busy fighting against his archers, hopefully they would be too distracted to pay attention to Nicholas sneaking into the castle via his usual method.

Of course, Simon might anticipate such a tactic and have guards waiting to jump out and capture him as soon as he set foot inside the castle. If so, he'd have to fight his way free.

What was taking Simon so long to send his men to Canterbury? Had he already done so? Maybe earlier in the day? 'Twas possible Simon had learned of the deciphered French message Nicholas had taken to the king. Maybe Simon had worked out other plans now with the French to attack elsewhere.

Nicholas studied the embattlements again, his gaze alighting from one guard's position to the next. Even without seeing the men, he knew exactly where each was located, which arrow slits they would use, and where the safest place was for his archers to fire their shots in return.

At a sudden clanging from the castle gatehouse, Nicholas

blew out a breath. Finally. The bridge lowered slowly above the moat until it thudded against the bank on the opposite side. The inner gate creaked as the pulley and chains lifted it too. But the outer portcullis remained firmly closed.

All along the hedge, the other archers in their gray cloaks were peeking through the shrubs now, their attention fixed upon the gatehouse. They watched as tensely as he did for the outer gate to rise and a group of riders to gallop through. That would be the signal to race to a spot down the road where they would jump out and fight the small group of Simon's men, hopefully disabling them.

With every passing moment, Nicholas's body wound as tight as if he were being stretched upon a rack. If Simon's men suspected Nicholas and his men intended to waylay them, they might be using extra caution before venturing out.

"I don't think anyone is coming, sire," said the archer closest to him.

As before, Nicholas had the strange premonition that something was amiss. Had Simon lured him here to Reider but taken Sybil elsewhere? Or were Simon's men even now surrounding them from an opposite direction to take them by surprise? After all, Simon was conniving, and perhaps Nicholas had underestimated his brother this eve.

The tension inside continued to mount until at last, Nicholas slowly began to rise from behind the hedge. He had to make the first move. They could tarry no longer.

As he showed his head above the leafy branches, he braced himself, waiting for an arrow to fly his direction. But nothing happened.

He edged a little higher. When his men started to do the same, he motioned them back down, not wanting them to take risks when he was already doing so. Within a moment, he was standing tall so that anyone upon the castle walls would be able to observe him and call out a warning.

Yet no shouts echoed in the bailey, and still no arrows zipped toward him. Only a red kite circled above a nearby meadow with its distinctive forked reddish-brown tail.

He slipped through the hedge until he stood out in the open. Maybe he was being foolish, but he had to put an end to the standoff. In a moment, Simon would also come out from behind one of the merlons into the open crenel.

But the only face that appeared anywhere was one in the gatehouse tower window. And it was distinctly feminine.

Nicholas took another step forward, then another. No one rose from the battlements to speak to him, and none of the guards shot at him.

"What if it's a trap, sire?" another archer whispered loudly from the brush.

"It very well could be," he whispered back. "But I must move forward now that I have made my presence known."

"We'll be ready to shoot."

"Good."

"Ready your bows," the archer called to the others. "Nock. Mark. Draw."

Nicholas positioned his own bow as he continued to creep across the grassy open area, making his way toward the bridge. He was halfway there when someone appeared in the gatehouse. From the long tunic and wimple, he could view a woman, possibly the same from the tower.

Sybil?

His heart gave an extra beat but then evened out at the realization that Sybil didn't wear a wimple. Besides, she wouldn't have stood back so timidly. She would have kicked and punched her way free and found a way to open the outer gate.

From what the men had told him, she'd handed herself willingly over to Simon to quell the slaughter of any more villagers. She'd sacrificed herself for people she hardly knew to keep them safe.

As the woman moved through the gatehouse, a stooped-shouldered man cowered several paces away from her.

Nicholas's pulse gave a jolt, and he paused his striding. Was his mother standing there? With her faithful old servant?

The woman held herself regally and with grace, just as his mother had always done. Had Simon instructed her to lure him in, to take him off guard before the coming confrontation?

She didn't speak or move, as though she wasn't sure of his intentions either.

Even if Simon was using her, Nicholas had come too far now to turn back. He started toward her again, and as he reached the bridge, he tensed, waiting for the gate to lift and Simon and a group of knights to come charging across the outer bailey toward him.

But strangely, all remained quiet, and he faced no opposition.

As he stepped onto the bridge, his mother held up a warning hand. "Come no farther, Nicholas."

He halted and beheld that she was unharmed. Although pale and thin, she was still a beautiful woman, even if only a shell of what she'd once been.

"What is this about, Mother?" The bailey behind her was deserted, not a soldier in sight. But he tensed anyway. He couldn't let down his defenses, kept his bow and arrow ready to shoot.

"The castle is besieged by the plague." She spoke as softly as always. But her voice contained a thread of urgency. "You and your men must go away lest you are exposed to it."

At once, the strange silence of the castle, the lack of the presence of any guards, the failure to engage in combat—it all made sense.

His mother wrung her hands together. "The first of the servants became ill more than a day ago. And now the plague has spread to almost everyone. My servant brought me news just a short while ago that even Simon is ill."

Was that why she'd made her presence known? Because she had no opposition? Clearly she'd guessed he would be coming today. Perhaps she had overheard Simon discussing the situation.

"How do you fare?" He scanned her but saw nothing amiss.

"I am untouched by the illness so far, and I am doing my best to provide relief to those who are afflicted."

His mother was a good woman. Instead of running away or sequestering herself, she was putting herself at risk to bring comfort to those who were dying.

If everyone else was ill, then he would face no opposition in freeing Sybil. He had no doubt Simon had locked her away in the dungeon. But at least there she would remain safe from the plague. "Tell your servant to lift the gate. I have come for my wife."

His mother met his gaze, and the sadness in her eyes tore at him. "I regret to inform you she succumbed to the plague earlier today."

- *31* -

THE ENTIRE WORLD AS WELL AS every function in Nicholas's body came to a halt. He could only stare at his mother, unmoving, unblinking.

"I am sorry, Nicholas." Her words, though gentle, hit against him with the force of hot tar and heavy rocks pouring from the gatehouse murder hole. He nearly buckled to his knees and had to grab the iron bars of the portcullis to hold himself upright.

"I tried to go down to visit her shortly after she arrived," his mother said, "but Simon's guards wouldn't let me pass. And this morn, they brought news to Simon that she hadn't made it through the night."

Nicholas closed his eyes against the nightmare. Once again, he'd been too late to rescue the woman he loved. And now she was dead. How could he endure this again?

The ache in his chest radiated with such force he pressed a hand to his heart, not sure how he could live without her. He couldn't . . .

This was Simon's fault. If his brother hadn't captured Sybil and exposed her to the plague, she would still be safe at Devil's Bend.

Anger pumped through Nicholas's blood. Simon was the worst of miscreants, and he deserved to die. Today. At this very moment.

Nicholas bunched his fists together and let bitterness burn through him. He would go into Simon's chamber, stand above his bed, and look him in the eyes. Then he would plunge his dagger through the man's cold, evil heart. Simon deserved it. Worse. He deserved to be hanged, drawn, and quartered. Yes, Nicholas would do that to Simon this very day while he was still alive and could feel the pain.

Even as his entire body threatened to tremble and give way to consuming grief and rage, he lifted his head, and from the corner of his eye, caught sight of his archers waiting for him at the hedge, their bows and arrows still at the ready.

Many of them had faced death and grief just yesterday with Simon's visit to Devil's Bend. Yet here they were today, willingly helping him. If they could live with such courage, then he couldn't give way to his grief . . . or to the rage.

Maybe in the short term, he would find release in torturing Simon. He would give his brother a taste of the pain he'd caused others. But once he'd made Simon suffer and die, Nicholas knew he wouldn't experience any happiness or relief. Instead, he'd have to live with the regret of lowering himself to Simon's level. His retaliation against the French had already taught him that.

Could he be different this time? Could he rise above his anger and need for revenge to walk away from Simon and allow God to judge him instead?

Pulling his shoulders back, Nicholas crossed the bridge and

peered through the iron bars at his mother a dozen paces away. "I would like to retrieve my wife's body and give her a proper burial."

His mother shook her head sadly. "You cannot touch her. You must leave her be for now."

"If you can touch those who are sick, then how can you prevent me from doing so?"

"This is different, Nicholas—"

"I cannot leave without my wife."

"And I cannot let you put yourself at risk. You are my only son."

"Please, Mother. I love her." He didn't care that his voice rang with anguish. As his mother met his gaze, he held nothing back. He let her see inside to the depths of the love he had for Sybil. Even though their marriage had been short, he'd shared with her something powerful and consuming.

His mother hesitated but then touched her pocket. Finally, she nodded to her servant still hunched in the shadows of the gatehouse. "Open the portcullis for Nicholas."

The servant bowed his head and then shuffled toward the gatehouse tower stairway.

Nicholas motioned at the archers in a silent command to stand down. The young archer who'd taken the leadership in Ralph's absence jogged toward Nicholas. While waiting for the gate to open, Nicholas filled him in on the news.

"You and all the men," Nicholas said, "must return at once to Devil's Bend and stay far from the plague."

The young archer shook his head, his expression grave. "I'm afraid it's too late for that, sire. If Lord Worth's guards already have it, then they likely passed it to us when they came the other day."

Dread twisted at Nicholas's innards. That was the way of the plague. It spread like an army advancing in the night, taking everyone unaware.

"We will have to pray that is not the case." Nicholas watched as the portcullis rose one slow inch at a time, already silently petitioning God that the poor people of Devil's Bend would be spared another tragedy amongst the many they'd already suffered. "Either way, you must depart for the village with all haste."

The young man nodded. Nicholas didn't need to spell out the reason for the haste. Everyone knew just how quickly the disease could spread, and the men deserved to say good-bye to their loved ones if the plague had indeed infected Devil's Bend.

Even so, the man hesitated.

"I shall be fine on my own here since Simon and all his men are ill and can do me no harm."

The archer nodded and started to turn away but then stopped. "I'm sorry about your wife, sire. She was a fine lady, and I could tell she made you a happy man."

Nicholas's throat clogged with emotion. He couldn't formulate a response and simply gave a nod. As the portcullis clanged to a halt, he strode into the gatehouse. He approached his mother, reached for her hand, and kissed her fingers in greeting.

She smiled at him sadly. "I am honestly sorry, Nicholas. I wish I could have met this woman who made you so happy."

He had been happy with Sybil—happier than he'd been in

a very long time. Though he'd hoped for many years of such happiness with her, he would have to cherish the few memories he had rather than sinking down into despair. The task would be difficult, but he had to do it, lest he grow into a man like Eric rather than Walter.

As he crossed through the outer bailey and into the inner courtyard, he could behold how dire the situation had become in such a short time. Doors were closed on the thatched workshops along the wall. A few fearful faces peeked out of the cracks of shutters as he passed, laborers having closed themselves off with the hope of avoiding the disease.

A lone dog nosed at a pile of scraps outside the servants' entrance, and a young boy was drawing water from the well. But otherwise, the usual chores and activities had come to a standstill. The silence hung as heavily—if not more so—than what he'd noticed from outside.

He followed his mother up the stone steps toward the main entrance, the tall center keep rising several stories above them in all its stately glory. It had been a while since he'd arrived at the castle so openly.

The inside of the castle was as deserted as the outside. The servants had either locked themselves away for self-preservation or were too sick to notice his presence.

The doorway at the top of the dungeon stairway was open, and a waft of cold, damp air greeted them. No guards stood watch anywhere. They'd abandoned their post either from illness or because they'd learned their prisoner was dead.

He made quick work of finding a torch before hastening down the steps. Upon reaching the bottom, he held the light up. At the sight of a deserted gaming table and stools, his thoughts returned to the night Sybil had helped him escape. She'd saved his life, even though she'd hardly known him, just as she'd done for the people of Devil's Bend.

She'd been an honorable and noble woman.

The ache in his throat pulsed, and tears stung the backs of his eyes.

The cell keys hung on the wall peg near the door. As he opened the thick panel and stepped inside, he was again taken back to the first vision of her, when she'd flipped him over onto his back. Her eyes had sparked with fire, and her beauty had been enchanting.

With a heaviness to his steps that matched the heaviness in his chest, he started down the row of cells, peering through each barred door until he found her lying motionless and covered by the blanket in the cell he'd occupied. At least one of the guards had the decency to allow her the blanket his mother had provided.

He latched the torch into the wall holder, then easily found the key and unlocked the door. In two steps he was at Sybil's side. Unable to prevent a groan of anguish, he dropped to his knees, gathered her in his arms, and drew her against his chest.

"Oh, my love." He kissed the top of her head, not caring that he was exposing himself to the plague. He needed this chance to touch her again one last time, even though she was cold and listless. Her arms flopped away, unable to wrap around him the way they had in the past.

The burning in his throat swelled so he wanted to roar out his grief. But his mother stood in the doorway behind him.

Instead, he bent in and pressed another kiss to Sybil's head. If he had the ability to forfeit his life so she could live, he would do it without a second thought.

"I have loved you, wife," he whispered in her ear fiercely, "as I have loved no other." It was the truth. If only he'd had time to show her how sacrificial his love could be . . . the way Walter had indicated a husband ought to love his wife.

He squeezed her tight and at the same time squeezed his eyes to hold back tears. He didn't easily give way to tears. But this moment, losing her, it was just as painful as losing Jane, if not more so.

At a soft, warm puff against his neck, he froze.

Had Sybil just released a breath?

He thrust her back and stared at her face, his heart hammering so fast he almost felt light-headed. Her head lolled lifelessly, her beautiful face was pale, and she didn't move, not even a twitch.

Had he just imagined a breath?

He pressed shaking fingers to her lips, hoping to feel more. He held them there for long seconds.

"Heaven help me," he whispered.

"Does she yet live?" his mother asked, now kneeling beside him.

"I thought I felt her breathe." Maybe if he kissed her again. He bent in and kissed her forehead as passionately as before. Once again, he was rewarded with a soft breath, this one against his chin.

He sat up with a start, a burst of energy coursing through him. "The breath of life still flows through her." His chest swelled. Saint's blood. She was on the verge of dying but was somehow still clinging to life. He had to keep her that way. But how?

His thoughts raced through every possibility, and he could think of only one way to save her. He had to find holy water. Would the closet under the stairs still contain one of the bottles he'd stowed there?

Gently, he placed Sybil back onto the straw, then he jumped up, grabbed the torch, and strode down the passageway. As he crossed to the stairway closet, he tore the square door open, nearly wrenching it from the hinges. He held the torchlight inside. The hiding place seemed undisturbed.

He crawled inside, wiggled the stone loose, and scanned it. From what he could tell, it was empty. But he stuck his hand in nevertheless and skimmed the smooth stone.

Curses upon him. The second bottle was gone too. Sybil had mentioned drinking some of the holy water to allow her to travel through time. Maybe she'd taken the second one for herself.

He backed out of the closet and stood, his heart thudding with renewed urgency. Did he have time to ride to Chesterfield Park and beg Lord Durham for holy water from his supply? After all that he'd done for Lord Durham's kin, he didn't think the lord would deny him.

Nicholas glanced to the steep stairs. Did he dare go now that he'd been exposed to the plague? He didn't want to put anyone else at risk. But maybe he could stand at a distance and voice his request. They could work out an exchange where no one had to get near him.

He shook his head, his frustration rising to strangle him. By the time he made the ride to Chesterfield Park and back, Sybil would be dead, since she was nearly so now. He didn't have time.

"What do you seek?" His mother's question cut into his silent rampage. She stood in the arched doorway watching him.

Instead of answering, he took the stairs two at a time and made his way to the curio just inside the great hall where Arthur had placed the other two bottles. Even though Nicholas had already checked there previously and hadn't found them, he threw open the wooden doors and shoved aside glass containers, crocks, and vials of every sort and size. Several rolled out and crashed to the floor. But he didn't care. He had to locate the bottles. Surely they were still here, just pushed farther back.

Unable to keep in a growl of frustration, he swept his arm over the shelf, dumping more items to the floor. Once again, his mother had followed and stood silently observing him. She likely thought he was demented. But he didn't have the time to explain what he sought. Not when Sybil might possibly be taking her final breath.

"Are you searching for this?" Something in her tone halted him. He turned around, his sights locking in on a green glass bottle that she'd pulled from her pocket and now cradled in her palm.

From the color and shape, he recognized it as one of the bottles Arthur had placed in the cabinet. "How did you come upon it?"

"I keep an extra supply of my daily tonic in the cabinet.

301

And the morn of the second earthquake, I discovered two new bottles there, including this one."

"And where is the other?" The question came out harsher than he intended.

She shrank back almost fearfully. "I do not know. I only took the one, and when next I looked, 'twas gone. I swear it, Nicholas."

He held out his hand for the bottle.

She hesitated. "With all the talk of holy water, I suspected 'twas what it contained, and I knew God had given it to me to keep you safe from Simon. I planned to revive you when he left you for dead."

Her intentions were certainly noble and done out of love for him. Regardless, he needed it for Sybil. "I am safe from Simon, and now I must have it for my wife."

"But with the plague . . ." Her eyes pleaded with him. "You need to take the holy water with you to save you from dying."

Suddenly he understood why she'd allowed him to come inside the castle. She believed that if he fell ill with the plague, he could drink the holy water and be saved. The truth was, he was very likely to catch the plague. Most people exposed to it did, and he was surprised his mother hadn't yet come down with symptoms.

"You have no thought of using the holy water for yourself?" he asked.

"I have lived long enough. The only thing that matters to me is that you survive."

What good would it do to save himself at the expense of the people he loved? How could he live knowing he'd chosen life but had allowed others to die in the process? Surely his mother knew him well enough to understand he could never do something so selfish.

However, he had no time to argue with her about his philosophies. The only thing that mattered was saving Sybil. This was what he'd just prayed for, the chance to give up his life for hers. As Walter had said, he needed to love Sybil sacrificially if he wanted to demonstrate that he truly loved her.

"I must prove that I am different than my father and Simon in my marriage by how I treat my wife. Let me give Sybil the holy water so I can do what they never could."

Mother's hand shook, and he feared she might drop the bottle. He wanted to snatch it from her by force and race down to Sybil. But he held himself back and prayed she would understand.

After another second of hesitation, she held it out. "I also want you to be different than your father and Simon. But I do not want to lose you."

"Does Holy Scripture not say that the man who loses his life for Christ's sake will find it?" Was that, then, the true secret to life? In the sacrificing and dying to oneself, a person could find a deeper sense of purpose and joy?

With tears welling in her eyes, she thrust the bottle into his hands.

He bowed his head to her. "Thank you, Mother." Then without another word, he sprinted back to the dungeon. As he fell to his knees beside Sybil, his breathing was labored and his pulse pounded.

He reached for her, but as before, he could behold no

visible signs that she was alive. Was he too late?

"Stay with me, Sybil." His demand was harsh, borne of need for just a few days more with her. If that's all he could get before the plague caught up with him, he would take that instead of naught.

Gently, he slipped his hand behind her neck and lifted her head. He'd already removed the cork, and now he tipped the bottle up, careful to touch it to her lips. From what he'd assessed, she didn't seem to have the plague. He could see none of the usual symptoms. It was almost as if she'd simply fallen asleep but couldn't wake up.

"You must awaken for me," he whispered, dribbling the liquid inside her mouth. There wasn't much, which had to mean every drop was powerful and important. He couldn't let even the tiniest amount go to waste.

As soon as he'd made sure the liquid went down her throat, he tapped the bottle again. When nothing was left, he lowered her. Then he sat back on his heels and watched her face for a sign the holy water was working its miracle.

Silently he prayed, knowing he wasn't worthy of this beautiful, smart, and courageous woman. But he would do all he could to ensure that she had a good life ahead of her. He would leave her everything he'd saved over the years of working for the king. It wasn't a huge amount, but it would be enough to sustain her whether she wanted to live in the Weald with the outlaws or maybe even with Walter in Dover. Beatrice could continue to be her maidservant wherever she resided.

"Please, Sybil." He brushed his fingers down her cheek. "Do not give up the will to live."

She remained motionless. Too silent. Too still.

Despair seized him. Had he been too late? His body tensed with every passing second. Finally, with a cry of frustration, he drew her up, grasping her as he had before, willing his own life to flow into her.

He kissed her forehead, then her cheek. He didn't know how he could ever make himself let go of her. He couldn't leave her. Couldn't accept she was gone.

An agony more intense than any he'd ever felt before cleaved his chest, taking his breath away. Heaven help him. He wanted to die beside her.

Another cry pressed for release, but he swallowed it and buried his face into her hair. He would be stronger, and he would do better this time.

Even so, he allowed himself a long last hold, relishing the softness of her hair against his cheeks and the warmth of her breath against his neck.

Warmth of her breath?

He sat up so quickly he almost dropped her. He could hardly get his fingers to her lips fast enough, but when he did, the gentle and steady flow of air in and out brought swift tears to his eyes—tears that, this time, he couldn't hold back.

She was alive.

His shoulders sagged, his chest aching with gratitude.

At a motion in the doorway, he glanced up to find his mother standing just inside the cell, tears streaming down her cheeks. "You have shown yourself to be different than your father and Simon already in many ways, and now in this, having such great love that you are willing to lay down your own life for your wife."

He lifted Sybil's hand to his lips and kissed it, feeling warmth in the flesh that had been cold and clammy only moments ago.

"I shall pray that God in His mercy will spare you," his mother continued softly, "so that you might share a lifetime of love with your wife."

But even as Nicholas nodded his thanks, he suspected they would need another miracle for that to happen. And one miracle—having Sybil brought back from the brink of death— was enough for him.

~ 32 ~

SYBIL AWOKE TO SWAYING AND WARMTH. Her body felt light and drowsy, but somehow invigorated, as though she'd slept soundly for several days.

She stretched, her muscles relaxed and her body in a state of calm and peace she'd rarely experienced before.

Arms tightened about her—strong arms with thickly corded biceps. Her face rested against a hard, muscled chest. Her head was tucked into the crook of a man's neck. And she was sitting on his lap, on the back of a horse.

The scent of earth and woodsmoke emanated from him as strongly as his power and intensity.

Her heart pumped faster. "Nicholas?" Her voice came out but a whisper.

He pressed a hard kiss against her temple, one filled with a possessiveness and determination that sent flutters throughout her.

She wasn't dreaming, was she? She was with Nicholas. But how?

Her thoughts flew back to the last thing she remembered— lying on the floor of a dungeon cell in Reider Castle. She had died. She was sure of it. At least in the present time. A strange part of her had been aware of her body going numb, her organs shutting down, her vitals halting.

She'd almost felt as though she was floating above herself, but she hadn't seen anything or anyone. And then everything had faded to nothing. Until this moment . . .

What had happened? Was she still alive in the past?

"Nicholas?" This time his name was stronger on her lips, and she pushed against him to sit up.

He drew sharply on the reins, and in the same motion, he pulled back from her, likely to observe her.

She struggled to open her eyes, and as she did, she found his handsome face hovering above hers. Nothing and no one had ever looked better than he did. Framed by thick lashes and dark brows, his brown eyes were as shadowed as a woodland at night. The scruff on his jaw and chin was darker and thicker than usual. Wavy strands of his hair blew across his forehead, which was wrinkled.

"How do you fare?" he asked as he caressed her hair back from her cheek.

"I'm alive." She tried to raise her hand so she could stroke his face in return, wanting to assure herself that she was really with him. But she was weaker than she realized and could hardly move.

He nodded, his throat moving up and down in a hard swallow. He glanced away from her, as though overwhelmed with emotion and needing to gather a measure of control.

She used the moment to gain her bearings, taking in the sky through the branches overhead. The blue was light with hints of pink. Was it time for a sunrise or a sunset?

From the thickness of the vegetation, she guessed they were already deep into the Weald, that he was riding back to Devil's Bend. She didn't know how she'd managed to stay alive. Even more, she was surprised that he'd been able to sneak into Reider Castle and extricate her.

"How?" She managed to croak the one word.

Nicholas swallowed hard again. Then he glanced around. "Let us take a break here, and we shall eat of the fare my mother packed for us."

"Your mother?"

Nicholas nodded again but didn't answer as he dismounted and carefully settled her on a blanket in the tall grass. Even though he encouraged her to recline and continue to rest, with every passing moment, she seemed to be regaining more strength so that she could sit up easily.

Only as she situated her skirt around her legs was she aware that she was wearing a different gown, this one more luxurious and feminine, a velvety emerald green with fancy embroidery at the neckline of the bodice and at the sleeves. It was beautiful, even if it felt like it belonged on a queen and not a simple woman like herself.

From the strange barrenness underneath the gown, she could tell her bra and panties were gone and that she was wearing only a thin chemise. Although the thought made her a little sad, she guessed she should have known the longer she was in the past, the more likely she'd have to give them up eventually.

Nicholas's vest stretched tightly across his shoulders and back as he untied a pack from the saddle.

What if he'd been the one to undress her? The very thought sent a burst of heat through her—a burst that wasn't filled with embarrassment but laced with crackling anticipation.

She glanced away from him, not wanting him to see such blatant desire. She focused her attention instead on a cluster of pale-purple flowers. She didn't know the names of many wildflowers, but it was a kind she'd never seen before in modern Kent, where certain vegetation and wildlife had become extinct over the centuries.

As Nicholas crossed to her with the pack and knelt beside her, she wanted to wrap her arms around him, drag him down on the blanket, and assure herself he was real, that this wasn't some kind of dream she was having as she floated through a place between two worlds.

But she held herself back as he pulled out a cloth bundle, untied it, and spread out an assortment of dried fish, bread, and cheese beside her.

Her stomach gurgled with the need for sustenance. How long had it been since she'd eaten?

When he lifted a wedge of cheese to her mouth, she reached for it, knowing she was awake enough now to feed herself. Her fingers brushed against his, and she lingered, letting the solid feel of his hand ground her in the reality of his presence. She was here with him. They were together again.

At her caress, he grew motionless, and she could feel him examining her. When she lifted her gaze to his, the dark wanting in his eyes enveloped her. And the warmth inside her only expanded. She was hungrier for him than she was for food. Could he see that in her eyes? She wanted him to, not caring how wanton that made her.

His gaze dropped to her mouth.

Kiss me, her whole body seemed to shout. And suddenly nothing else mattered. She didn't need to know how he'd saved her and gotten her away from Simon. She didn't need to know about the dress and whether he'd put it on her. She didn't even need to know what time of day it was.

All she needed was him—desperately.

Her breath got lost somewhere deep inside and so did any words. She slid her hand around his, pried loose the cheese, and let it fall into the grass. Without breaking gazes, she drew his hand toward her, placing it on the bare spot of her chest just above the embroidered edge of the bodice. Since it was lowcut and exposed a slight swell, she let him draw his own conclusions but hoped he understood her offering. That she welcomed his touch.

The muscles in his jaw rippled. He didn't move except to let his thumb drop and caress her chest, brushing against her bodice.

Tight desire unfurled within her.

Maybe it was still too soon. But she couldn't push aside this need to be with him, to show him how much she loved him while they still had time. If there was one thing she'd learned over the past week, it was that love could come quickly and be torn away just as fast. Now that she was with Nicholas, she wanted to make the most of the time before something threatened to split them apart again.

He leaned in a fraction.

She lifted her head, her lips already parted. She'd been dreaming of kissing him since that morning he'd kissed her good-bye and ridden off. No doubt her need was etched into every fiber of her being and on display for him to see.

He bent in farther, then released a soft huff before standing and striding to the horse. He grabbed the reins and wound them around his hands. Then he leaned in and pressed his forehead against the mount's neck.

She didn't realize she was trembling until she pressed her hand to her chest. Something was wrong. He was acting strange, almost afraid. And if she'd been more alert, more herself, she would have seen it right away. She had a feeling that their escape and his fear were related.

She drew in a breath to still the erratic beating of her heart caused by his nearness and his effect upon her. "What's amiss, Nicholas?"

His shoulders were stiff and his fists taut against the reins. "I have sacrificed already to give you life, and I must sacrifice again to keep you alive."

She glanced around, searching for clues that could help her understand his bold declaration. Normally she could deduce evidence, find obscure details, come to conclusions, but today her mind was sluggish.

"Maybe you had better start at the beginning." She guessed the story wasn't necessarily one she'd like.

"The plague has spread throughout Reider Castle. I have been exposed to it. And if I am already sick, I would not willingly pass it along to you."

"I've been around the guards and have been exposed to the

plague just as you have."

"The holy water has healed you of the plague—or whatever was ailing you—and now that you are healthy, I would do my best to keep you that way."

The holy water had healed her? What did that mean?

As if sensing her questions, he finally turned to face her and made short work of explaining all that had transpired while he'd been gone in Dover and London and then what he'd discovered when he'd returned to Devil's Bend and ridden to Reider Castle.

"Two bottles of the holy water were in the curio. My mother took one that she intended to save for me. Someone else must have discovered the other one."

Sybil's mind flashed back to the intense search she'd conducted after recovering Ellen from Lionel's lab. She'd scoured the castle—or nearly so and had located a bottle in the ancient cabinet. She hadn't known how it had gotten there, only that Harrison and Ellen had needed it.

Never would she have imagined that the second bottle from the same cabinet would end up saving her life in the Middle Ages. It was strange how events and time were so intricately related.

"She wanted to preserve the holy water for me," Nicholas continued, "but I convinced her to relinquish it to me so that I could save you."

Sybil clutched her hands together, feeling the pulsing of her blood and the vitality of life flowing through her. Although she was alive in the past, she could feel that her connection to the present was now completely severed. She would never be able to return to the world she'd always known and the life she'd always lived. It would be a loss, and she would miss many things. But maybe eventually, she would adjust . . . if she survived.

The fact was, she still needed a second dose of the holy water to successfully transition out of a time crossing.

How long did she have before she needed that second dose? Days? A week? Did she have enough time to ride to Chesterfield Park as she'd originally planned and beg Marian for the holy water that could keep her alive?

As before, she didn't think she'd suffered from the Black Plague, but maybe it had affected her body differently. With having modern immunizations and being a part of genetic changes over time, her body could react differently to the ancient diseases, and it was possible she might not experience the same symptoms.

Even so, Nicholas was wise to be careful. She didn't want to pass anything along to him either. If the plague could be transmitted via air particles, then in riding together in such close quarters, they'd likely already exposed each other. All the more reason to go to Chesterfield Park for holy water. If Nicholas fell ill with the plague, she needed to have a way to save him.

She smoothed the velvety material of the gown. There was only one person who could have given it to her. "I'm surprised your mother gave me this gown."

"She is a generous woman."

She had been generous, indeed, in giving Nicholas the treasured holy water. Why had she done it? "After taking her holy water, I would have expected her to send me away in rags."

Nicholas still hadn't freed himself from the reins tied around his hands. "You are my wife. And she will respect you."

"Simon. Will he live through the illness?"

"My mother went in to tend to him. He was delirious with fever and did not recognize her."

"Then not only is she generous, but she is kinder than I am. After seeing the torture Simon inflicted upon you as well as the people of Devil's Bend, I would have let him die alone."

Nicholas was silent for several heartbeats. "I also."

If she'd thought her relationship with Dawson was rocky, it was nothing compared to what Nicholas had experienced with Simon.

She wanted to stand up, walk over to Nicholas, and comfort him. What he'd experienced during the last day had to have been horrifying.

Yet, with the risk of the plague, the situation was already precarious enough, and she couldn't make it worse. Her relief at seeing Nicholas again, her growing love for him, the aching attraction, the undeniable chemistry—she had to contain it. For now. It was best for them both if she did.

~ *33* ~

Nicholas brought his horse to a gradual halt, trying to ignore the faint pounding of a headache. He didn't want to awaken Sybil, but they'd reached the outskirts of Devil's Bend, and he needed to dismount and put some distance between them. He would do better at resisting temptation if she wasn't pressed up against him, her entire beautiful body just begging him to explore it.

Thankfully, she'd slept for almost the entire rest of the ride. And though he'd wanted to bend in and kiss her regardless of the consequences, the memory of her nearly dead on the dungeon floor had stopped him. He needed to minimize how much he touched her. He wasn't naïve about the spread of the disease. People could catch it even without physical contact. But kissing her was out of the question. As was all the other intimacy he wanted.

During their break from riding a couple of hours ago, he'd almost lost all his reserves. Saint's blood, he'd been undone when she'd placed his hand on her chest and seemed to give him leave to take his pleasure with her.

Even now, just thinking about the moment made his body heat with need. He was, after all, only a man. She was his wife.

And she'd never looked more enticing than she did in the emerald gown that matched her eyes. A part of him wanted to throw all caution aside, carry her to their cottage, and spend the day in bed with her.

"No." He admonished himself harshly, even as she began to stir. If he survived the plague, he would remain strong and wait for the right moment when he knew he wasn't being selfish. Only then would he tell her of his love and show his devotion to her body.

As he slipped down, he lifted her with him.

Her eyes flitted open, the green clear and calm and rested. "Are we stopping again so soon?"

"We are here."

At his pronouncement, she strained to free herself from his hold, as though she was embarrassed to be seen in his arms by the villagers.

She needn't have worried. No one was paying them any heed. Usually busy at midmorning, the village appeared deserted, except for the livestock. The sheep grazed on the new thick grass. The oxen and the cows and goats were penned up and seemed content enough.

Wisps of smoke rose from the holes in the thatched roofs of the remaining cottages. The rubble from the homes that had burned to the ground had been separated. Anything salvageable sat in one pile—including ashes for soap making. The rest had been pushed into heaps waiting to be carted off or buried.

The silence and stillness did not bode well.

Sybil struggled against him again, giving him no choice but to lower her to her feet. She wobbled as she gained her bearing.

He steadied her and was tempted to gather her into his arms once more. But she straightened herself and studied the barren town just as he had, her keen eyes not missing a detail. "The plague is here, isn't it?"

"'Twould appear so."

"What should we do?"

"You must stay here on the outskirts of the village away from the sickness."

"And will you do the same?"

"I shall assist those too ill to care for themselves." He'd contemplated heading on to Canterbury to observe firsthand how the city fared. In fact, when he hadn't been thinking of Sybil, his thoughts had centered on the battle that had been waged in the dark hours of the night. Had Lord Clayborne's army prevailed? Or had the French launched an attack against Canterbury?

However, as much as he wanted to ride out and assist Lord Clayborne, the king's men, and all the other knights who had rallied to defend their land, to do so would only risk spreading the plague. For now, he had to stay here and do his best to aid those already languishing.

"If you intend to care for the ill, then I do too." She lifted her chin and flashed defiant eyes at him, giving him a look that only made him want to claim her mouth and ravage it.

He forced himself to avert his gaze. "There is yet a chance of saving you."

"And there's still a chance of saving you." She tugged free of his hold and leveled a glare at him.

"Lord in heaven above be praised," came Father Fritz's call.

The priest had stepped out of his house and was carrying a vial of medicine in each hand. He was staring at Sybil as if she'd been resurrected from the dead. "The men said yer wife was dead and gone. But blimey. I've never seen a woman more alive than she."

Though weariness hung over Father Fritz, causing his shoulders to droop, he beamed at them. "She be a fitting sight of the bride described in Song of Songs: 'How fair and how pleasant art thou, O love, for delights! This thy stature is like to a palm tree, and thy breasts—'"

"Father Fritz!" Nicholas hastened to silence the priest's commentary. He didn't even want to think about why the priest had a section of Song of Songs committed to memory.

Sybil had covered her mouth and was coughing. Or was she trying not to laugh?

"No need to be embarrassed by marital love, my dear son," Father Fritz continued without a blink of an eye. "Now that yer back, I'll be giving ye the house again so that ye can—"

"We shall make camp here in the woodland."

"I insist. Ye cannot deprive me of the great honor of having the fruit of yer loins conceived in my bed."

Great honor?

Sybil's eyes had rounded even more at Father Fritz's brazenness.

At the sparkle in her eyes, Nicholas fought back his own mirth and cleared his throat so his voice wouldn't contain any laughter. "We intend to help you tend those with the plague."

"Oh no ye don't." The priest shook his head almost furiously, the morning sun glistening on the bald spot at the top. "Either ye'll leave the village with the rest of those who haven't been afflicted, that ye will, or ye'll stay in my humble abode and keep away from those who be sick."

Nicholas breathed out a sigh to know that some of the villagers hadn't yet been struck by the plague and had left. Hopefully they would remain safe.

"How is Ralph?" Sybil asked. "And Beatrice?"

"Ralph still lives, praise be. And Beatrice be resting, praise be." The priest touched the wooden cross hanging around his neck from a long chain. Even as he did, he closed his eyes, his head lolling while a snore slipped out.

"Father?" Nicholas called.

Father Fritz startled, and his eyes flew open. "Yes, I'll weed the garden, Yer Grace." He glanced around, his face reddening. "What I meant to say is that I'll be on my way to *feed* the sick from the garden." Without waiting for a response, Father Fritz scurried toward the closest door and disappeared inside.

"He's exhausted." Sybil's delicate brows drew together in concern.

A wave of weariness hit Nicholas, and he fought to stave it off. He hadn't slept well or oft in days. What he wouldn't give to fall upon a bed—for a few hours to ease the ache in his head.

The throbbing had multiplied since he'd dismounted, and now it was radiating against his temples, so much so that a chill slithered up his backbone.

Sybil's fingers closed in around his arm. "When's the last time you slept?"

After giving Sybil the holy water last night, he'd moved her to a guest chamber, and his mother had offered to bathe and change her. He'd allowed himself an hour of sleep then. But it hadn't been enough.

He swayed.

Sybil grabbed on to him. "You need to rest, Nicholas."

As she steered him toward the priest's cottage, he hesitated. "The horse . . ." The poor creature needed food and water.

"I'll tend to it after I put you to bed." She didn't allow him to stop.

He stumbled along, his muscles aching, his body suddenly as cold as if a winter frost had settled over him. All he wanted to do was lie down.

When they entered Father Fritz's cottage, the pungent odor of a dozen herbal remedies clouded the air. The priest's table was littered with bottles—some open, others toppled. Several pestles and mortars were filled with crushed dried herbs that spilled out of scattered leather pouches. The hearth fire at the center of the cottage had a low flame, and several pots bubbled with what appeared to be additional tonics.

Nicholas wasn't sure how well Father Fritz could doctor. The kindly man never seemed to know exactly what he was doing any time he attempted to assist with the ailments around the village. From the looks of things this morn, he appeared to be trying everything and anything to bring relief to those who were suffering. Although Nicholas guessed the priest's efforts would fall short as always, 'twas better than doing nothing at all.

Sybil guided him to the bed, but he needed no prodding, not with the pounding in his head. When he reached the edge, he flopped down, heedless of his garments or boots. As his head connected with the pillow and his eyes closed, he had one final thought ere sleep claimed him.

He had the plague.

~ 34 ~

SYBIL UNLACED NICHOLAS'S BOOTS and slipped them off. He'd been more tired than he'd let on.

She reached for the weapons belt at his waist to divest him of the bulky item, but as her fingers brushed against his hips, she drew back, suddenly all too aware of his body.

The smallest touches awakened desires in her that needed to remain dormant. At least for now.

She took a step away from the bed.

Even though she'd slept off and on during the journey, she was still tired and guessed her body was giving her the message that she needed to have that second dose of holy water to live.

While Nicholas slumbered, maybe she'd ride to Chesterfield Park. Could she make it there and back without trouble? And without any roads or signs to lead the way?

Mentally, she tried to calculate the distance. When riding with Ralph, she'd decided Devil's Bend was near modern-day Elham. She didn't know for sure, but she guessed she had about ten or twelve miles to reach Chesterfield Park near Canterbury. She might be able to span the distance in three hours. In total, she'd be gone six to eight hours.

She had to at least give it a go, had nothing to lose if she went but everything to lose if she didn't.

She changed back into her jeans and jacket and donned a cloak to hide her hair and face, hoping that if anyone saw her, they'd assume she was a man and not a woman out riding alone. She wished for paper and pen to leave Nicholas a note so he wouldn't fret about her when he awoke.

Instead, she found Father Fritz in one of the cottages, asleep on a stool amidst the sick resting on pallets. She woke him and explained her plans and was thankful when he didn't offer any resistance. She did her best to tend to the horse, then she hoisted herself into the saddle and started off, riding as hard as she could through the woodland.

As she made her way into the outskirts of Canterbury and the landmarks became more familiar, she kept off the main roads. Although part of her missed the ease of having a car to quickly reach her destination, another part of her relished riding out in the open where she could see firsthand the beauty and wildness of the land yet untouched by modern development.

When the sun reached its height and the warmth of the summer day made her want to shed the cloak, she finally arrived at the gates of Chesterfield Park. Even though the manor was smaller than the one that belonged to Harrison, it had the same three-story center structure with the high tower on the east. The addition of the outbuildings and gardens made the surrounding area look like a small village.

The biggest difference was the outer stone wall. It was larger and built to defend the estate from an attack. The front gate, too, was imposing and impenetrable... and well-guarded, for as soon as she guided her horse toward the gate, an arrow ripped through the air and hit the ground directly in front of her.

"Don't come any closer." A soldier on the battlement had his bow and an arrow aimed at her. "Or the next arrow won't miss the mark."

"I need to speak with Marian Durham." She didn't attempt to disguise her voice, guessing Marian would be more likely to admit her if she knew the truth about who she was. Marian would surely remember her from just a year ago, wouldn't she?

"No one's allowed in."

"Tell her Sybil Huxham is here. If she knows, she'll want to see me."

"Lord Durham's orders." The man's voice was unyielding, as was his bow. She had the feeling if she nudged her horse any closer, he'd carry through on his threat to shoot her.

"I'll stay out here and speak to her from a distance. I won't get anywhere near her."

"That's right. You won't be getting near because you'll be leaving now."

She tensed. The guard was only doing his duty, but she couldn't let this be a failed mission. She had to speak with Marian. Or Arthur. "Tell Arthur he has a visitor. A friend of Harrison Burlington."

The guard let loose his arrow, and Sybil had no choice but to spur her horse away. She rode into the woodland until she was out of sight and safe from danger. Then she halted and turned back around.

Lord Durham was clearly worried about the plague and was

taking every precaution to protect his household. Regardless, she had to find a different way to speak with Marian or Arthur.

Maybe if she waited in the woods until one of them came outside, then she could reveal herself and shout out to them. If only they knew she was here in the past, they'd definitely want to speak with her and discover what had happened.

Staying out of sight, Sybil circled the estate as best she could. But other than a few servants going about their daily work, she saw no one who resembled Marian or Arthur. As the afternoon began to pass into evening, her body sagged with fatigue, as though someone had cracked open a valve, giving her a slow leak that was draining the life from her body.

Finally, she guided the horse back the way she'd come and started toward the Weald. She couldn't delay any longer, had to ride while it was still light and while she still had the energy to stay in the saddle. But she resolved that she would venture into Canterbury the next morning and beg for holy water at the gates of St. Sepulchre.

Night had fallen by the time she reached Devil's Bend. The village was silent and dark, as if everyone had either left or died. Even Father Fritz's cottage was unlit. Hopefully the priest had given Nicholas the message regarding her plans so he hadn't needlessly worried.

As it was, she waited for him to duck out of the cottage and stride toward her, anger in each step and etched into his face— anger that she'd left when he'd been helpless to stop her, anger that she'd put herself in danger, anger that she'd taken so long.

But when he didn't appear, unease niggled at her. He'd gone somewhere, probably searching for her.

As she slid down from the mount, her legs could hardly bear her weight, and she grasped onto the saddle to keep herself from tumbling to her knees. Maybe she would have to tell Nicholas the truth about needing another dose of holy water and ask him to ride to St. Sepulchre for her. Or to Chesterfield Park. Perhaps he'd have more luck in swaying the guards to allow him to speak with Marian or Arthur.

After caring for the horse, she shuffled into the cottage. A few embers in the center hearth glowed, but it was clear no one had added fuel, perhaps even since she'd left.

At a groan and movement from the bed, her heartbeat came to an abrupt halt. Through the darkness, she could see Nicholas's outline in the bed. In an instant she knew why he hadn't stalked out to greet her . . .

There was only one thing that could keep him down—the plague.

She'd known his catching it was a possibility, but she hadn't really expected it, had believed he was too strong, too determined, too healthy to be affected the way other people were. But now he was suffering and would possibly die within a day, maybe even during the night.

Nicholas dead?

She took a step back and bumped into the doorframe. She'd lost too many people she loved already. How could she bear to lose another?

Closing her eyes, she clutched the rough wooden beam. Everything within her pulsed with the need to run. Run. She would run somewhere, lie down, and die. Then she wouldn't have to face the pain of losing Nicholas.

Isaac's words from one of their last visits together in the lab clamored at the back of her mind: *"You and Dawson are more alike than you realize. After losing your mum, you're both running scared."*

Had she been running scared? Running from pain? And running from people who could end up leaving her and hurting her again?

Maybe that's why she'd left Isaac. That's certainly why she'd wanted to leave Dawson. And now . . . she was afraid of losing Nicholas.

She didn't want to watch him die. But how could she do anything but stay with him during his last moments and try to bring him as much comfort as possible? Even though she wanted to protect herself from another loss, she had to remain by his side until the end, even if in doing so she lost her soul.

She pushed away from the door and crossed to the fire. She grabbed a handful of kindling and added it to the embers, stoking the coals until several of the twigs flared, providing more light.

Then she crossed to the bed, sat on the edge, and took stock of Nicholas. His skin was hot, and yet he was trembling. His dark hair had come loose from his hair tie, likely from all the thrashing, and now his hair stuck to the perspiration on his forehead and neck.

For a heartbeat, panic reared up inside her. Before it could claim her, she stood and forced herself to gather supplies to treat Nicholas. First, a rag and a basin of cold water. She bathed his face to cool him before she laid the rag across his forehead. Then she raised his head and gave him sips of ale so he wouldn't get dehydrated. As she lowered him, her fingers brushed against a swollen lymph node near his armpit—a tennis-ball size lump.

Hardly able to breathe past the fear constricting her airway, she lit a rushlight and sought out Father Fritz, hoping he would have instructions on which herbal remedies and tonics would be the most helpful.

She found him in the same cottage where she'd left him earlier in the day. But this time, he was lying on the floor, delirious and shaking from chills. From what she could tell, everyone who remained in the village was either sick or already dead. Even Beatrice had taken to her pallet beside Ralph.

As she returned to Nicholas and took in his still form, she tried to keep at bay the voices in her head telling her the situation was hopeless.

"I have to do something." Her whisper came out harsh, even angry. But in the next instant, helplessness washed over her. The only thing she could do was pray and provide relief.

She'd start with Nicholas, then move her way through the remaining cottages. She wasn't sure how much time she had left for herself, but she'd tend to the sick and dying until she no longer could.

She knelt beside the hearth and stirred the sticky paste in one pot and the watery substance in the next. She didn't know what either was used for, but she guessed one was for a poultice and the other some kind of tonic.

For long hours, she went from one patient to the next, giving sips of ale and the tonic, wiping foreheads with cool cloths, and plastering swollen spots with poultice. By the time the night had passed, she could barely think straight past her weariness.

At the first tinges of dawn, she perched on the bedframe beside Nicholas, clutching his hand, praying he would awaken. But he tossed his head from side to side and mumbled in agitation. He wasn't getting any better. And neither was she.

A small part of herself once again taunted her, told her that she wasn't worthy, that the people in her life left her because they didn't love her enough.

"No." She let her voice echo in the quiet of the cottage. She couldn't give up. Giving up was equivalent to running away.

She pushed to her feet and returned to the table and the assortment of medicines Father Fritz had abandoned and left in disarray in his haste. She skimmed her fingers over the scattered herbs and the open bottles. She didn't know what herbs went together to make specific medicines the same way that Marian and Arthur might. They were intelligent scientists and would be able to test and discover remedies. But surely she could find something to help Nicholas and the others.

Several wooden boxes from underneath the bed now sat beside the table, still filled partially with a hodgepodge of canisters, crocks, and bottles. She knelt to examine them, hoping to locate one of the small bulbous bottles that she'd found in the closet under the steps, or even one of the green glass bottles similar to what had been put in the cabinet at Reider Castle. But finding something like that in this makeshift medieval medicine cabinet was a pipe dream.

She stifled a yawn and let her fingers graze a tall brown vial shaped like a thin flower vase. As she traced a raised pattern of a large *W*, something tugged at her memory. She'd fingered a raised *W* like this before. But where?

She took the bottle out from among the others and shook it. A small amount of liquid inside sloshed against the sides. Her fingers brushed against a second engraving on the opposite side of the vial. It was a simple flower. She traced each raised petal and then returned to the *W*.

A distant part of her brain scrambled to uncover the clue, but her mind was growing fuzzier with each passing moment. Her energy was waning. And she knew from what had happened to her body in the dungeon that she was fading. She didn't have long before she would be incoherent.

"For pity's sake. Think, Sybil." With the tip of her knife, she pried out the cork that stoppered the bottle. It crumbled, telling her the vial hadn't been used in ages, maybe even for centuries. At the very least, Father Fritz had never opened it.

Once the mouth of the bottle was free, she swished the liquid again and then sniffed.

It was odorless.

She sat back on her heels. "Walsingham." Her mind spun to remember all the details Harrison had told her. A shrine had existed there—the Shrine of Our Lady. It had been a popular pilgrimage spot, much like Canterbury Cathedral . . . because of the miracles that happened there.

Harrison's antiquarian had searched Walsingham for ampullae containing the holy water and had found just one. And it'd had the *W* on one side for *Walsingham* and the flower on the other representing new life. When Harrison had ingested the holy water, it had helped him travel back in time.

Of course, at the time, she'd been skeptical of the ability of the water to instigate the time crossings. But now, she knew better. Much better.

What if the liquid in the brown vial was more of the holy water that had once come from Walsingham?

She swished it again. If she had to estimate, she'd say it held a cup of liquid.

A thrill wound through her. If this was truly holy water, then she'd discovered a treasure of the greatest sort.

A flash of blinding pain pierced her head and nausea rose swiftly. She pressed a hand against her head and drew in a deep breath. She was losing time and couldn't waste another second.

The holy water always seemed to take some time to run its course through a person's system and work its miracle. That meant she had to give a dose to Nicholas before she took a sip. If she didn't provide him a drink first, he might not be alive when she awoke—if she awoke.

Crawling on her hands and knees, she inched toward the bed, carrying a spoon and the bottle as carefully as she would a crown jewel. When she reached the edge, she pulled herself up until she was sitting beside Nicholas. But the effort only caused the pain in her head to radiate, becoming unbearable so that she had no choice but to bend over and retch into the chamber pot.

As she straightened, she fought the dizziness that threatened to plunge her into oblivion. Then, drawing in a deep breath, she measured out a tablespoon and used the last of her strength to lift Nicholas's head. She tipped the spoon to his mouth and dribbled in the liquid.

With the room spinning around her, she poured out another spoonful. She situated the bottle safely on the floor. Then she placed the spoon in her mouth and let the liquid slide down her throat. In the next instant she fell against Nicholas, and the world went black.

~ 35 ~

WARMTH FLOWED THROUGH NICHOLAS and surrounded him, almost as if he were soaking in a hot spring.

What had happened to him? Had he died and gone to paradise?

The last thing he remembered was that he'd been suffering from the plague. He'd made it into the cottage ere collapsing into bed. He'd been feverish during the few times he'd awoken and been lucid. He'd called for a drink, but no one had come, neither Sybil nor Father Fritz.

He'd tried to get up a time or two, but the swelling under his arm had been so painful that the efforts hadn't been worth it. After what had felt like an eternity, his fever had escalated so that he'd fallen in and out of slumber, not caring what became of the world around him. He'd known he was dying, and whenever he could, he'd prayed for Sybil, that she'd stay healthy and wouldn't catch the plague from him.

He stretched one leg, and the thin straw mattress beneath him shifted . . . and a leg tangled with his.

He tried to lift an arm, but it was pinned down by a body—a very soft, warm, curvy body.

Full consciousness coursed through him, awakening every

nerve, every limb, every inch of him . . . to the reality that a woman was lying on top of him.

His eyes flew open to the glow of morning light. While not bright, it was enough for him to know that Sybil was with him and boldly spread out over him, her body covering his, her face tucked into the crook of his neck.

Helpless frustration wound around his gut, replacing all the warmth from moments ago. She shouldn't be lying with him in the bed, not when he was dying of the plague. She needed to stay far away from him.

He'd get out of bed, would lie on the floor if need be.

Carefully he shifted, reaching for her hips to lift her off. As his fingers connected with her waist, they brushed against her bare flesh. From what he could ascertain, she'd changed into her old clothing, including the tight leggings and the short, close-fitting shift. Apparently, during her sleep, the short shift had crept up, leaving an inch at her waist uncovered. And now his fingers rested in that spot—that soft, alluring spot.

He brushed his thumb over her skin and began to trace a line to her hip. But with a silent curse, he forced himself to stop.

What was he doing? He was sick, and he needed to get away from Sybil. No doubt she had already caught the disease, but just in case she hadn't, he had to take this precaution.

He started to lift her, but she slipped her arms around him and nuzzled her nose against his neck. If that wasn't enough, she released a contented sigh, as if she was exactly where she wanted to be.

"Stay with me, Nicholas," she mumbled before pressing a

kiss into his neck. Her lips lingered, and in fact lifted to his jaw. She kissed the scruff where his jaw ended, right near his ear.

Heat began to thrum through him . . . life and energy and desire. How could that be when he was dying?

He wiggled his fingers, flexed an arm, and partially lifted one of his legs. None of the pain under his arm, the tiredness, or the fever remained. How could that be? Maybe he was in heaven with Sybil. Or dreaming.

Even as he blinked to wake himself up, he turned his head slightly to see the hearth fire, the assortment of Father Fritz's medicines strewn over the table, one of his plain cloaks hanging from the peg on the back of the door.

The scent of the smoke, the tickle of Sybil's hair, the rumble of hunger in his gut . . . he was most assuredly alive. From what he could tell, the plague was gone from his body.

What had happened to bring him back from the brink of death and cure him?

Sybil's lips found his ear, and when she gave a soft nip of his earlobe, desire flared deep inside. And in the next instant, ere he could react, she whispered again, "I love you more than I've ever loved any other man."

A keen, sweet longing swelled in his chest. He was alive. And his wife loved him.

What more could he ask for?

"I love you," she whispered again, sliding one hand over his cheek, letting her fingers glide languidly over his stubble. "And I want a lifetime to show you."

He held his breath. He suspected her boldness came

because she believed he was unconscious and dying.

At another breathy kiss against his ear, he groaned. Aloud. With pleasure.

She jerked back, her eyes rounding.

Heaven help him, but he had to kiss her now. He shifted her so that she was more squarely on top of him, and in the same movement he took possession of her mouth. One of his hands slid up her back and dug into her hair, maneuvering her for the perfect kiss.

She opened to him willingly, eagerly, until they were both feasting like two starving prisoners who'd just been set free. She didn't hold back, wasn't timid, was as strong in her passion as she was in everything else.

But as he slipped his hand underneath her shift, he stalled, closed his eyes, and broke the kiss. He pressed his mouth instead against her temple, kissing her hard, bringing himself under control. This wasn't the right time to take more from her, not when he reeked of illness and death.

No, when he next kissed her and shared the bed, he would make sure he could love her properly, taking his time and showing her both tenderness and pleasure.

He was learning more every day. One sacrifice at a time was making him stronger and turning him into the kind of husband who would be able to love her unreservedly.

"You're healed." Her whisper held awe and joy.

He'd never felt better. It was almost as if someone had given him holy water.

With a start, he sat up, bringing her with him. She'd done it, had saved him. "Where did you get the holy water?" He rubbed both hands up her arms to her shoulders and then to her cheeks—as if at any minute she might somehow disappear and he'd find that he was in the afterlife far away from her.

She broke free of his embrace, bent over the side of the bed, then straightened with a brown bottle in hand. "I found it among Father Fritz's medicines. I recognized the flower and the *W* on the bottle and suspected the holy water came from the Shrine of Our Lady in Walsingham."

He took the bottle and examined the pattern on both sides. He'd never seen it before, wouldn't have guessed it was from Walsingham. "The shrine has healing waters too?" He'd heard of miracles happening there during bygone years but hadn't realized they'd occurred because of the holy water the same way they had in Canterbury.

"With Father Fritz serving in a priory in Walsingham, it makes sense that he'd have a bottle of holy water from the spring of Our Lady in his possession."

"'Tis likely he did not realize he had it."

"Probably not."

"And you? You are free from being ill with the plague too?" She appeared vibrant and full of life, with no signs of sickness.

"I admit, I had to take another dose. It's a long story, and one I'll share with you soon. But first . . ." She glanced toward the shutters and door before pushing up to her knees. "We might still have time to save some of the others."

He knew what she wanted to do. She was offering to use the remaining holy water to heal everyone else in Devil's Bend. It didn't matter who they were or what they'd done. She wanted to help them with no thought to saving the holy water for a better occasion, for worthier people, or for those who could pay handsomely.

He couldn't help himself. An overwhelming love drove him, so that he caught her against him, seizing her mouth once more in a kiss that contained his past, present, and future. It was unreservedly hers for the taking. Just her. That was all he would ever need to be content.

She responded as eagerly and intensely as always, giving him a kiss that contained her past, present, and future.

Although he wanted to keep on exploring, he pulled back and let his labored breathing mingle with hers.

"I may have once believed I'd found love," he whispered. "But I did not know what love truly was until I met you."

Her eyes, filling with wonder, never left his.

"You are my destiny." Somehow the Almighty and His miracles had brought and kept them together. And he would forever be thankful for so boundless a gift.

"And you are mine," she whispered passionately.

He leaned in, needing to kiss her again.

But she scrambled off the bed before he could stop her. She stood at the edge, her eyes bright, the bottle clutched tightly. She held out a hand. "Let's go give the miracle to as many people as we can."

He took her offering, and as he stood, he knew he'd been given the greatest miracle of all. The chance to love a woman as amazing as her.

~ 36 ~

A MONTH IN THE PAST. She'd lived an entire month in the year 1382.

Sybil reined in her mount on the drawbridge of Reider Castle and waited as the outer gate lifted. The stone walls spread out on either side of the bridge in a perfect symmetry of workmanship. The gatehouse towers stood tall above her, flags flapping in the breeze. The afternoon sunlight glistened on the moat.

Was it possible that a mere four weeks ago she'd been in the castle as an investigator, searching the abandoned fortress that had lain in disarray and ruins? And now here she was with it fully alive and whole and retaining all its magnificent glory.

She breathed in and let her sights wander to the tufts of grass growing along the wall and the bright whites and yellows of wildflowers. The scents of horseflesh and hay mingled with the smokiness that still filled her awareness.

Somehow she'd survived the dangerous but permanent transition to the past, and now her life was more real and alive than it had ever been, as if she'd been living in a black-and-white world that had suddenly turned to color. In fact, the longer she was in the past, the more the memories of her other life turned duller. Eventually, maybe they'd become so distant they'd feel like a dream.

Yes, there were still adjustments. She plucked at the skirt of her gown, another elegant creation that Lady Theresa had given her, this one a deep crimson Nicholas claimed suited her. She was still irritated that someone had destroyed her jeans, T-shirt, and leather jacket, although she still had her combat boots.

But she was becoming more proficient at managing the flowing skirts and maneuvering in the tight bodices. She'd decided the inconvenience was worth it to see the flare of desire in Nicholas's eyes whenever she allowed the servants to turn her into a proper lady. He'd look at her with a smolder that would only grow hotter, until at last he'd make up an excuse to get alone with her.

She couldn't hold back a smile at the memory of only last night at supper, how she'd caressed his hand under the table until he'd commanded her sharply to accompany him to the kitchen so they could discuss the need for more seasoning. His footsteps had slapped almost angrily as he'd pulled her along, down the passageway toward the kitchen. He'd stopped abruptly at one of the storeroom doors, kicked it open, and started to kiss her before managing to pull her inside and close the door behind them.

On the mount beside her, his leg brushed against hers.

She bit back her smile and met his dark eyes, as rich and unfathomable as always.

"Have I told you yet today that I love you?" His question was low, meant for her ears alone and not the archers who'd ridden with them.

"Not yet." He might not have spoken the words, but he'd shown it in a dozen different ways.

"I love you with all of my being." His eyes held hers, and this time he trailed the length of her arm with his gloved hand.

The contact brought a quick shudder of pleasure and an eagerness to be alone with him. How long would she have to wait? Would they have time to retire to their room? Or would they have too many matters needing their attention before the evening meal?

They'd spent the day riding the perimeter of the land in the Weald that now belonged to them, a gift from the king to Nicholas for his courage and his role in protecting England and Canterbury from a French attack. The majority of French ships hadn't been able to make it past the extra English patrols in the Channel. The contingent that had landed and started on their way toward Canterbury had been ambushed by the king's forces, led by Lord Clayborne. They'd been forced to retreat— chased to the coast, where most had been captured or killed.

While Simon had been lying abed with the plague, Nicholas's mother, Lady Theresa, had searched for and gathered the various French missives Simon had hidden throughout his solar. She'd sent her old servant to find Nicholas, bearing the package of communications with the French that had effectively sealed Simon's fate and officially exonerated Nicholas from any guilt.

The king's men hadn't needed to come and arrest Simon. He'd died in his bed.

By the time the plague had run its course, at least a third of the people at Reider Castle had perished. Those who'd survived were left with the task of mourning those they'd lost and burying the dead. Thankfully, Lady Teresa and her old servant had remained untouched by illness.

While Simon's oldest son was next in line to inherit Reider Castle and the other Worth holdings, the king had granted the inheritance to Nicholas instead, making him the new lord.

At first, Nicholas hadn't been sure if he wanted to rule his brother's people and land. Sybil knew how much Nicholas feared becoming like his father and brother, but she had urged him to use his leadership for good, especially for the outlaws who'd lost their homes in Devil's Bend. If he remained in charge, he could provide refuge and new opportunities for many more people to come.

Although hesitant at first, Nicholas had begun to embrace his new position. Sybil was relieved he'd allowed her to be a part of helping him. They'd spent countless hours talking and planning. And riding out to their new land.

Nicholas leaned in and brushed a kiss against her neck. Then he pressed his mouth to her ear. "I would show you my adoration, if you would permit me."

Another shiver of pleasure coursed through her. She wanted to press in and touch her lips to his. Instead, she nudged her horse onward, casting him a look she knew contained her desire. "I'll think about it, my lord."

She could hear him clattering behind her, his gaze searing into her and setting her afire. Her skin flushed and her stomach clenched with need. She was surprised at how much she loved being with him and sharing the marriage bed. It was all the sweeter because of how sensitive he'd been, waiting until after his healing from the plague for another week to give them more time to spend together, getting to know each other better.

As she rode through the gatehouse and through the bailey into the inner courtyard, she couldn't imagine being anywhere else but here with him. Even though at times she thought about Dawson and how her death might have affected him, she was at peace in knowing she'd done all she could for her brother. Now it was time for him to find his own way without her.

Once in a while, she also regretted that she hadn't been able to bring Dr. Lionel to justice. But she knew that even if she'd gone back to the present, there was the very real chance she might never have been able to catch him.

"There be the blissful couple!" Father Fritz shouted as he stood at the base of the steps leading up into the keep, his long robes swirling around him. Although he'd been breathing his last when she and Nicholas had arrived in the cottage where he'd fallen ill, thankfully, the sip of holy water had revived him, and now he was back to being his eccentric self.

With a wide smile, he beamed at a couple standing beside him. "Ye best be speaking yer business to the lord and his bride before they be sneaking away to their bed. Then ye'll not be seeing them for a long spell."

The archers riding behind Nicholas and her guffawed but then rapidly became silent as Ralph stepped out of the garrison and leveled a glare upon them. The older man had nearly died of his arrow wound, but she and Nicholas had given him the holy water in time too, along with Beatrice. The older woman was delighted now that she was serving in the castle as Sybil's main maidservant.

They'd used up most of the holy water. All but a scant few tablespoons remained at the bottom of the bottle from Walsingham. Nicholas had corked the vial and placed it in their bedroom in a secret compartment in the wall. He'd wanted to keep the remainder, just in case they ever needed it.

They both still battled old fears and maybe always would. But they were getting better at facing the things that held them back.

As Nicholas took in the visitors, his handsome face creased with both irritation and anger. "Who allowed in strangers? With the plague still ravaging the countryside, we can ill afford more exposure."

"Stop the aggin', my dear son." Father Fritz leveled a stern, fatherly look upon Nicholas. "He be a good friend of mine, and never in a rain of pig's pudding would he bring ye harm."

Nicholas didn't dismount. "Who are you and what do you want?" His question was blunt and unfriendly. But Sybil had learned to trust him, that in all his interactions he only had the best interest of the people he loved at heart.

The taller visitor removed his wide hood first, revealing the distinguished face of a middle-aged man. "I am Lord Wilkin of Barsham in Norfolk." With the streaks of silver in his dark hair and trim beard, he had the bearing of a man of means. He regarded Nicholas with keen eyes, although Sybil sensed no malice in him.

"Lord Wilkin." Nicholas's grip upon the hilt of his sword relaxed. "I have heard of your valor at Beauce with the Black Prince."

Lord Wilkin bowed his head. "And I have heard of your valor as well."

His wife had turned now. With her hood shadowing her face, Sybil couldn't distinguish any features, but she had a sudden strange feeling she knew the woman.

"Lord Wilkin." Nicholas's tone grew more congenial. "This is my new bride. Lady Sybil."

Lord Wilkin bowed to Sybil before waving a hand at his wife. "May I introduce my wife as well. This is Lady Cecilia."

A shiver worked its way up Sybil's backbone. Cecilia. That was her mum's name. What were the odds?

The woman nodded, then slowly lifted her hood away from her head, letting it fall to her back. As she shifted, Sybil found herself gazing into green eyes the same color as hers and into a face she hadn't seen in four years.

Her breath stuck in her lungs.

The woman's eyes brimmed with tears, and her lips trembled. "Hi, Sybil." Though the woman's hair was covered with a veil, the dark brown was unmistakable.

"Mum?" Sybil couldn't dismount fast enough. She was on the ground before Nicholas could assist her down.

In the next instant, she found herself being swept into the arms of the one person she'd never thought she'd see again.

How had this happened?

Her mum squeezed her hard, and Sybil returned the embrace, never wanting to let go.

When her mum finally pulled back, she stroked Sybil's hair, even as tears continued to flow.

"How did you know I was here?" Sybil wiped at the

wetness on her own cheeks.

"When I heard of an Arthur Creighton arriving in Canterbury, I came just as soon as I could. I knew of his name in conjunction with Mercer Pharmaceuticals and was aware he'd been working on what he called the 'ultimate cure.' I had to see for myself if it was really him."

Sybil nodded. She had so much to tell her mum. And clearly her mum had a story of her own. Had she lived for the last four years in the past? Her language and mannerisms were more formal and certainly attested to it.

"We arrived in Canterbury yesterday, and just this morn I learned Nicholas Worth had recently taken a wife by the name of Sybil Huxham. I came here straightaway to see if it was you."

"It's me."

Her mum's eyes welled with fresh tears. "I never meant for this to happen to you. Never. I am so sorry. So, so sorry."

The guilt rounding her mum's eyes was strange. For some reason her mum thought she was responsible for Sybil crossing to the past. "You're not to blame, Mum. Not at all."

"But the Hamin. I'm the reason they captured you—"

"No one captured me." Sybil glanced sideways, relieved to find Nicholas had also dismounted and was talking with Lord Wilkin and Father Fritz again, that no one was listening to them.

"Then the Hamin didn't force you to cross into the past for them too?"

Sybil shook her head. The Hamin Sahaba was one of many Middle Eastern terrorist groups who had cells within the UK.

She'd considered the possibility that they were linked to Dr. Lionel, but she hadn't found proof of it and now never would. "Too? Does this mean they forced you to be their courier in the past for holy water?"

"Yes. My captors threatened to harm you and Dawson if I didn't deliver for them."

Sybil's mind spun back to all the times she'd felt as though she was being watched or followed. Had it been the Hamin all along? Once they discovered she'd fallen into a coma and deduced that she'd gone into the past, what would they do to Dawson?

She shuddered. At the slight movement, Nicholas stepped up beside her and wrapped his arm around her shoulder, drawing her into the crook of his body. His brows rose in a silent question.

She laid her hand over his in response. She would have much to explain to her mum about how she'd come to be in the past. But at the moment, only one thing needed to be said: "I chose to come here. I chose to remain. And I intend to stay with Nicholas, the man I love, so long as I have life."

For many years she'd felt lost, that she didn't know who she was. But here, now, with him, she was finally home.

Author's Note

Hi, friends!

I hope you enjoyed this new installment in the Waters of Time series. After receiving so much feedback from readers to write a third book, especially a story for Sybil and Nicholas, I decided I had to give it a try. And I'm sure glad I did!

They were an intense couple and so full of passion that the heat was fairly scorching the pages at times! Not every couple is quite like that, but these two were both strong, direct, and practical people that it made sense for them to feel things more deeply.

As always with my time crossing stories, I tried to weave in true history so that you get a blend of fact and fantasy. In this particular story, I chose to make the Black Plague more of the focus. The first and biggest plague began in 1348. At that time, chroniclers note that there were hardly enough living to care for the sick and bury the dead.

In 1382, England experienced another significant outbreak of the plague, but its scope and devastation weren't nearly as deadly. It spread from London into the countryside more slowly than I portrayed in this story. But the fear and the devastation left in its wake were very real, especially because at the time they still didn't know what caused the painful plague, and they had no way to cure it. People literally went to bed at night well and were dead by morning. That's how lethal it was.

In the midst of dealing with another outbreak of the plague, the English were still at war with the French in what has become known as the Hundred Years' War. The coastal town of Rye really was brutally attacked and devastated in 1377. Such assaults forced the English to take more care in fortifying their towns, not only along the coast but also in towns like Canterbury (although the threat specifically to Canterbury in 1382 was fictional).

Spies were also a troublesome problem for both the French and the English, and the English prisons were filled with people who had been accused of being spies for the French, including priests.

And the archery! Don't you just love the Robin Hood vibe of this band of outlaws living in the Weald? Yes, archery really was important for every Englishman to learn. Archery Laws were in place that made archery practice mandatory. And, of course, I had to give Sybil a chance to learn to wield a bow and arrow, although most women at the time didn't learn the skill.

So, as we close this story on Sybil and Nicholas, you might be wondering, will there be a fourth book in this series? A story to discover more about Sybil's mum and brother? Well, you'll be happy to know Dawson does indeed get his own happily ever after, and you'll get to find out more about Cecelia and her adventures too.

To stay up to date on all my book news, please visit my website at jodyhedlund.com or check out my Facebook Reader Room, where I chat with readers and post news about my books.

Until next time, farewell!

Jody Hedlund (www.jodyhedlund.com) is the bestselling author of over 40 historical novels and is the winner of numerous awards, including the Christy, Carol, and Christian Book Awards. Jody lives in Michigan with her husband, busy family, and five spoiled cats. She loves to imagine that she can really visit the past, although she's yet to accomplish the feat, except via the many books she reads.

BOOK 1 of the

Waters of Time Series

Come Back to Me

Scientist Marian Creighton was skeptical of her father's lifelong research of ancient holy water—until she ingests some of it and finds herself transported back to the Middle Ages. With the help of an emotionally wounded nobleman, can she make her way back home? Or will she be trapped in the past forever?

BOOK 2 of the

Waters of Time Series

Never Leave Me

Ellen Creighton's outlook on life is bleak as she comes to grips with the final stages of an inherited genetic disease that also took her mother's life. When her longtime friend, Harrison Burlington, locates two flasks of holy water that he believes will heal her disease, can he convince her to take it—especially when she believes the holy water led to her father's and sister's deaths? When dangerous criminals enter the equation, Ellen soon learns they will go to any length to get the powerful drug—including sending her back into the past to find it for them.

Connect with
JODY

Find Jody online at

JodyHedlund.com

to sign up for her newsletter and keep up
to date on book releases and events.

Follow Jody on social media at
Twitter: @JodyHedlund
Facebook: AuthorJodyHedlund
Instagram: jodyhedlund
TikTok: @authorjodyhedlund

CPSIA information can be obtained
at www.ICGtesting.com
Printed in the USA
LVHW040409120123
736863LV00002B/149